A NEW LIFE

They donned the protective gear and stepped through the ropes onto the mat. The moment Ash straightened, Barney attacked, his fists flying at her face and body. It was all she could do to block his punches. All she wanted to do was hide her head in her arms and roll into the familiar fetal position, but she was never going to do that again. Instead, she waited for her opening—and when it came, she kneed the older man in the groin.

This wasn't at all what she'd thought boxing would be like.

Barney jumped back, but not quickly enough and his face showed his distress. At once, she dropped her guard and stepped toward him to help, overwhelmed with guilt.

Without hesitating, Barney stepped forward and slammed a padded fist into her gut.

The breath whooshed out of her and she dropped as if felled.

When air finally started trickling back into her lungs, she opened her eyes to find Barney standing over her, shaking his head.

"How many times do I have to tell you, girl? If you're fighting for your life, you don't stop until the other guy is dead or unconscious. You drop him and run." He scowled at her, worried. He'd only known her for a couple of weeks, but that was long enough to sense that something was very wrong in the girl's life, something she needed to be able to protect herself against. She'd never be able to do that if she didn't get past this need to be nice.

BOOKS BY THE AUTHOR

Mendenhall Mysteries series:
The Shoeless Kid
The Tuxedoed Man
The Weeping Woman
The Untethered Woman
The Forsaken Man
The Wronged Woman

A'lle Chronicles series:
The A'lle Murders
The A'lle Mutation

Standalone books:
A Little Strangeness (collection)
Ghosts of Morocco
Identity Withheld
Jilimar
Kirwan's Son
Obeah
On Her Trail
Shelter

SHELTER

by
Marcelle Dubé

FALCON
RIDGE
PUBLISHING

SHELTER

For Kris and Dean, with thanks

CHAPTER 1

The hundred-year-old farmhouse on Hawk Street stood aloof from its neighbors, dominating the crest of the knoll, at the end of a street that had still been farmland ten years ago. Streetlights were coming on, illuminating a series of wide, shallow steps that were cut into the grassy, well-tended hill. They led to a wide walkway that in turn led to a set of wooden steps and a porch running the length of the house. A recently-painted white railing contrasted with the dark gray fieldstones on the front.

A stone farmhouse, thought Ash. Not something she was used to. No other home on the street was made of stone. They were all much newer.

The posts supporting the narrow roof over the porch were squared off, and wider at the bottom than at the top. Two dormers jutted from the green metal roof, their windows dark with the fading day. The front door was a slab of wood, light-colored, with an ornate brass knocker beneath the thick, beveled glass insert. The doorknob matched the knocker.

A sign planted in the middle of the lawn proclaimed that the house was for rent via Albans Realty.

Ash took it all in while the realtor, Maddie Bowen, waited patiently on the walkway by the porch steps.

Other houses ranged the street, set apart from the one on the hill as if shying away. Each had its own style; some were bigger but most were smaller, and all were under ten years old. Cars filled the driveways and lights gleamed from windows. Dinnertime smells floated on the cool wind that blew red and yellow leaves around the lawns and sidewalks.

Would neighbors be able to hear screaming from the house on the hill? Would they call for help?

"Pretty grand, isn't it?" said Maddie. The realtor was a middle-aged woman in black pants, sensible brown leather flats, and a heavy, red plaid car coat over a white turtleneck. "Come on," she said cheerfully. "Let's get out of the wind." With a determined step, she turned to lead the way up the steps.

Ash nodded, even though the realtor had turned her back, and followed more slowly, adjusting her small leather backpack. Inside were all her important papers: birth certificate, change of name papers, health care card, driver's license, passport—and her important numbers: safety deposit box number, bank account numbers, her lawyer's phone number, and the pre-paid cell phone. The backpack came with her wherever she went.

Just before climbing the steps, she glanced up at the roof. From those dormer windows, she would see anyone coming up the road. Her battered Volvo would stand out in this settled, affluent neighborhood of new Nissans and Hondas, but maybe she could park it around the back.

She would stand out, too, a young woman alone on a street full of families.

At the top of the steps, she turned to follow Maddie Bowen's gaze. It wasn't quite dark yet, but the sun had set a while ago and all the lights in Albans proper spread through the long, shallow trench of the Ottawa River Valley. A smile flitted across her face at the sight.

Pretty.

Most of the people on this street probably worked in Ottawa, commuting the hour there and back by train. During the day, most of these houses would be empty.

Next to her, Maddie suddenly shivered as the wind picked up. Without a word, they both turned toward the dark house. It surprised Ash that Maddie hadn't made sure the lights were on to greet them. Wasn't that Realty 101?

Maddie unlocked the door, silently cursing Dave, her partner. He could at least have turned on the porch light for her. She was always the one to show this house to prospective renters. Dave didn't like setting foot in it. She had no idea why.

The house had beautiful lines and a great location. It had been completely renovated when the owner decided to use it as a rental property instead of living in it.

She couldn't figure out why it was so hard to keep it rented.

"Sorry about the darkness," she said, speaking over her shoulder at the girl. "I sent someone by to turn everything on earlier today, but clearly they forgot."

Maddie got the door open and stepped inside. She flipped the porch light on and the girl—Ash Gantry—blinked in the sudden brightness.

"Come on in," said Maddie, taking her by the arm and leading her through the doorway. The girl was skin and bones, for Pete's sake. She looked like a waif. And she was underdressed for an Ontario fall in that light windbreaker. Maddie found the second light switch and warm light flooded the wide entrance. She stood aside, watching the girl take it all in.

To Ash's right was an open room with a stone fireplace and chimney, and a tall ceiling. A tufted black leather couch faced the fireplace, while mismatched club chairs huddled closer to the fireplace, facing each other across an oval glass coffee table resting on a rug patterned in blue and silver. Paintings hung on the wall, but it was hard to tell what they depicted since the entrance light didn't reach that far into the room.

Nice, thought Ash. She liked the wide hallway and the wide-planked pine floor with its dings and nicks. Maybe it was the original floor. She took a deep breath. The place smelled… sterile. As if someone came in once a month to dust but otherwise, no one had lived here for a long time.

"This way," said Maddie, leading her toward the back of the house.

On the left, across from the living room, Ash glimpsed another room, closed off with French doors. It looked like it might contain a desk. Halfway to the kitchen, they passed a wide stairway with black wooden steps and white risers. Maddie flicked on the lights as she passed but swept right through into the dining room and kitchen.

"Gas range, quartz counter tops, glass-tiled backsplash, counter and stools, big table," Maddie rattled off as she strode through the dining room to another pair of French doors beyond the table. She opened the doors and stepped out onto a large deck. "Come on out," she invited. "I don't want to turn on the lights until you see this."

Ash obediently stepped out next to her and a small gasp escaped her.

"Yes, indeed," said Maddie with satisfaction.

The view of the valley Ash had glimpsed at the front of the house was in full glory here. A swath of darkness immediately below her gave way to an expanse of lights, mirrored above by the stars just beginning to emerge in the night sky.

"You can't see it now," Maddie continued, "but just below your house, at the bottom of the hill, is the river."

Ash noted her judicious use of "your" but let it go. She hadn't even seen all of it, but she liked the house. Still, it wasn't as if she was planning to buy it. She just wanted to rent it for a few months while she figured out her next move. Albans seemed like a good place to stop. It was big enough to hide in but still had a small-town feel.

She took a deep breath of the cold air, inhaling the scents

of cooking and wet leaves and, faintly, sawdust. For a moment, her throat closed up as tears threatened. It smelled like home, the home she used to have when Mom and Dad were still alive.

"Let's go upstairs," said Maddie, oblivious to Ash's reaction. They headed back inside, through the kitchen, past a small powder room, and up the stairs. Upstairs were four bedrooms, three of them smaller and sharing a bathroom, and the fourth slightly bigger, with a small ensuite. The bigger room faced the backyard. All the rooms had moldings, deep window seats, and mullioned windows.

All of the rooms—the entire house—seemed to be fully furnished.

"Of course," said Maddie once they returned to the house's entrance, "you would need to see the house in daylight, but when you mentioned you were looking for a house to rent, I immediately thought of this one." Her voice held an odd note.

Ash saw the look in the realtor's eyes and looked away. She knew that she looked younger than twenty-four. Sometimes that was an advantage, but mostly, it led people to discount her, or worse, patronize her.

Maddie kept the smile plastered on her face, but she was beginning to suspect that the girl was wasting her time. She looked eighteen, for crying out loud. She couldn't afford this place, even at the rock bottom monthly rental it was going for.

"Why is the rent so low?" Ash looked directly at Maddie. "What's wrong with it?"

Maddie shook her head. She hadn't expected the question. Most people didn't ask. "Absolutely nothing," she said firmly. "The rental market is a little depressed right now, and this is a big house, bigger than most people need."

Ash looked around one last time, taking in the pine floors, the cream walls with warm wood trim, the faint smell of cedar and mothballs.

"How long has it been empty?" she asked.

For the first time, Maddie hesitated. "Seven months," she admitted.

Ash looked at the realtor. Seven months was a long time.

As Maddie reached inside for the door handle, Ash gave the interior a last look. Maddie had turned off the light in the kitchen and hallway, but in the light spilling inside from the porch, just before Maddie pulled the door closed, she thought she glimpsed a woman standing at the foot of the stairs.

CHAPTER 2

The next day dawned clear and cold. The grass crunched underfoot as Ash cut across the tiny lawn of the Starlight Motel on her way to the parking lot. There was a restaurant in the motel, but it only opened at six-thirty. Besides, she wanted a workout before she ate.

The motel, clearly left over from the fifties, was tucked between a Subaru dealership and a long, low office building with a sign in front that proudly stated "COCOJAMS: Over 5 Million Satisfied Customers." She had no idea what a cocojam was.

A highway ran by the motel—she'd been on that highway three weeks ago, on her way north, when she realized she was too tired to keep going. The motel was the first one she'd come across that was open that late at night. To her surprise, despite its outmoded design, it was clean and freshly painted, and the bed was firm and new. In the weeks she'd spent in that tiny room, the noise level from the highway hadn't abated. Not once. It was oddly comforting.

She unlocked the Volvo and tossed her gym bag in the back seat. Yellow leaves from the poplar trees in front of the motel had accumulated next to the sidewalk but most were still on the trees. Glancing around, she tried to spot any unusual activity, any cars parked and running, anybody watching her covertly. Nothing.

She slipped in behind the wheel and started the car, sitting in it for a minute to let the engine warm up. Almost six months she'd been driving the old Volvo and it hadn't let her down once. She'd bought it from a guy in Calgary who was selling his grandfather's car. She had assumed it was because the grandfather was dead, but it turned out the old man's eyes were just too bad for driving.

That was back in March. It had taken her a week to get from Vancouver to Calgary. She had taken a train, busses, even hitch-hiked, backtracking often. No one asked to see identification. And she stayed in places where cash was more important than formal ID.

The defroster finally cleared the windshield enough for her to see. As soon as she left the highway behind, the streets became a mix of residential and small businesses. Fifteen minutes later, she was at the gym.

Like the motel, Barney's Gym had seen better days but it suited her just fine. And it opened at six in the morning. The gym took up half a block, what with the parking lot at the back. Barney's old Renault was the only other car in the lot. As soon as she walked in through the back door, the smell of sweat and old socks hit her. She toed off her street runners and pushed them onto the mat by the door. Hers were the only ones there.

"Watch out for the bucket, girl," called Barney as she walked into the gym proper. He was wiping down the ropes encircling the small boxing ring he'd set up in the middle of the gym.

Ash glanced down. Sure enough, a red plastic bucket sat on the cement floor, collecting the steady drip of water that plopped down from the ceiling.

"Did it rain?" She hadn't noticed any puddles on her way to the gym.

Barney slipped between two ropes and climbed down from the ring. He passed a hand over his face and looked up at the ceiling.

"Three days ago," he said mournfully. "That's how long it took for the water to work its way through."

Ash nodded in sympathy, though she had to fight a smile. Barney Strumgen had the wrinkles of a basset hound, which made it hard for her to take him seriously. He felt about his gym the way most men felt about their cars. Any little scratch or dent was like a blow to his own body.

"Anyway," he said. "Go warm up. I'll put the coffee on and then we can spar."

Ash nodded again and walked over to the back wall, where the punching bag hung from the ceiling. She dropped her backpack against the wall and stripped her heavy sweatshirt off. It was starting to get too cold for the few clothes she'd managed to bring with her. She was going to have to do some shopping, and soon.

Maybe today, after she took another look at the house.

She changed into her indoor training shoes and sat down on a mat to start with long, slow stretches. In the first week she'd arrived in Albans, she tried every gym she could find. Barney's was the third on a list of eight. She liked it right away, but checked out all the others anyway.

She hadn't planned to stay in Albans, not for more than a month, anyway. She was tired of running and needed a short rest. Albans seemed like a good place.

But the longer she stayed, the more she liked the town. With nearly sixty thousand people, it was nowhere as big as Vancouver, but it sat by the St. George River and there was always a breeze. A three-mile treed walkway followed the river's edge, with room for walkers, cyclists, and even wheelchairs. Small parks dotted the town, including an old-fashioned center square left over from when the town was incorporated in 1852.

In the Old Town, century homes with stone foundations sat on enormous lawns. Most of them had been converted into art galleries, or apartments, or businesses, but the town's historical society required the owners to keep the look and feel of the original homes.

And while most people minded their own business, they were friendly.

Like Barney. When she decided to extend her stay, she returned to his gym, partly because she'd liked him, but also for the boxing ring. If there was a boxing ring, maybe there were boxing lessons.

She started working out every morning and every afternoon. Whenever someone was in the ring, she'd stop and watch what they were doing. Finally, she asked Barney how she would go about getting lessons.

He had eyed the over-six-feet tall men in the ring, then scanned her five-feet-two, one-hundred-pound form dubiously.

No way was he going to let that little slip of a girl in the ring with one of these guys. It was bad enough that she was pretty, with all that dark hair and those big green eyes. He'd seen more than one of the fellas looking her over. She never seemed to notice. If he let her spar with those bozos, they might accidentally hurt her when they were trying to impress her, or worse, they might go easy on her and not teach her what she needed to learn.

"How about I give you private lessons for a while?" he had suggested. "But you have to expect some bruises."

Ash had nodded at once. She wasn't worried about getting hurt. She knew just how much she could take.

"All right, girl," called Barney, coming out of his office. He carried two sets of padded boxing gloves and the face protection. "Coffee's on and I'm ready."

Ash jumped up and ran over to him. They donned the protective gear and stepped through the ropes onto the mat. The moment she straightened, Barney attacked, his fists flying at her face and body. It was all she could do to block his punches. All she wanted to do was hide her head in her arms and roll into the familiar fetal position, but she was never going to do that again. Instead, she waited for her opening—and when it came, she kneed the older man in the groin.

This wasn't at all what she'd thought boxing would be like.

Barney jumped back, but not quickly enough and his face

showed his distress. At once, she dropped her guard and stepped toward him to help, overwhelmed with guilt.

Without hesitating, Barney stepped forward and slammed a padded fist into her gut.

The breath whooshed out of her and she dropped as if felled.

When air finally started trickling back into her lungs, she opened her eyes to find Barney standing over her, shaking his head.

"How many times do I have to tell you, girl? If you're fighting for your life, you don't stop until the other guy is dead or unconscious. You drop him and run." He scowled at her, worried. He'd only known her for a couple of weeks, but that was long enough to sense that something was very wrong in the girl's life, something she needed to be able to protect herself against. She'd never be able to do that if she didn't get past this need to be nice.

Ash nodded and climbed back to her feet, and they started again.

◇◇◇

Two hours later, after a shower and a breakfast of a bagel and coffee at Tim Hortons, she stood on the porch of the house on Hawk Street and looked around. She was supposed to meet Maddie Bowen back here at nine o'clock, but she had come early to drive around and check out the area. All the streets in this neighborhood were named after raptors: Hawk, Owl, Eagle, Falcon, Harrier... She found herself wondering if there was another neighborhood nearby named for prey.

The pavement and sidewalk ended just past the house, at a blue metal overlapping gate that allowed pedestrians and bicycles through, but nothing bigger. Beyond the gate was a park, or a forest. There seemed to be a trail leading into the woods that sloped downward.

The sky was that hard, pale blue that only came in the fall. In the distance she could see the roofs of houses marching down to the river's edge. The closer to the water, the fewer homes and more businesses, but there were no buildings taller than four stories. The city continued beyond the river only to be succeeded by a forest of dark green pine and spruce and bright pops of yellow-leafed oak trees that rose to a low hill, and beyond that, into taller hills.

She took in the view for a few minutes, breathing deeply of the cool, clean air, her mind empty of everything but the moment of peace. What would it be like to be able to fly away, disappear into that wilderness, never to return?

Finally, her gaze dropped down to her street. As she had suspected, most of the driveways were empty. It was Tuesday. Work day. School day. She saw small bicycles leaning against some houses. There would be lots of kids here, playing after school, skateboarding, setting up hockey nets in the middle of the street to play shinny. Laughing.

Her hand strayed to her belly as her eyes prickled with tears of self-pity. Not for her a house full of children.

Enough, she told herself firmly. You've done that grieving. Time to move on.

She shook her head, trying to shake the grief out, but it was lodged in her heart. With a sigh, she turned to the door of the house. Maddie was late. She leaned into the window and cupped her hands around her eyes to peer past the reflection of the sky and her own small figure.

Barely six inches away, a woman stared back at her from the other side of the glass.

Ash jerked back, her heart lurching. Somebody was in the house.

Just then, Maddie Bowen pulled up in her bright red Ford Escape and honked. Ash glanced at her but immediately turned back to the door to peer through the window again.

There was no one there.

CHAPTER 3

A re you sure you saw someone?" asked Maddie, leading the way into the house. Dammitall. It was always this way with this bloody house. Just when she had someone seriously interested, something happened to spook them. Of course, this girl didn't seem spooked. She seemed mad.

"Yes," said Ash, brushing past the realtor. She glanced through the sitting room—good light coming through the window—then opened the French doors on the left. She'd been right last night. It was a small study, with a desk and dark bookshelves lining the walls. She strode in and pulled open the heavy green velvet curtains and glanced around. No one here.

The kitchen was empty, as was the powder room, and the door leading to the back deck was bolted.

Maddie was already on the steps leading upstairs and Ash ran to join her. They checked out the rooms, under the beds, and even the large linen closet at the end of the hallway. Nothing.

"Is there a basement?" asked Ash.

Maddie nodded. "A half basement. A cellar, really. Not living space. For the furnace, the hot water heater. That kind of thing." She'd toured that basement years ago when they first took on the job. It was dark and low-ceilinged, but it was dry. Someone could hide there, if they didn't mind spiders. And mice, probably.

"How is it accessed?" asked Ash when they got back downstairs. Her heart was finally beating normally again. But her anger hadn't abated. She'd seen someone, and she was going to find that someone.

"Through the laundry room," said Maddie, heading toward the back of the house.

The laundry room? Ash felt a little stupid for not asking about it. Then she felt irritated. Why hadn't Maddie shown her the laundry room before?

The laundry room was off the kitchen, past the pantry. Maddie opened the door and flicked on the light, revealing a small room with black and white linoleum tiles, a dryer and a top-loading washing machine on one wall and a set of shelves above them, and a long, narrow table on the opposite wall. A wicker laundry basket hung off a hook above the table. Nothing fancy. Certainly not as nice as the rest of the house. There were hooks on the wall by a door at the far end. That would be the side door.

"There," said Maddie pointing at the floor.

Ash hadn't noticed at first glance, but now she could clearly see the faint outline of a square opening in the floor, and the indented circular metal handle.

"I don't have a flashlight," said Maddie doubtfully. "And the cord for the lightbulb is pretty much in the center of the room."

Ash smiled tightly and shrugged the backpack off her shoulder. She set it on the washing machine and opened the main zipper. In a moment, her hand emerged with a flashlight.

Maddie's eyebrows rose but she didn't say anything. Instead she crouched to pull on the metal ring in the floor and, with an unladylike grunt, hauled the trap door open, letting it lean against the washing machine.

"I think this room was added on at some point," she said. "The cellar access would have been outside in the old days."

The opening gaped and both women stood staring down at

the steep, rickety ladder disappearing into the darkness. A musty smell of damp earth and desiccated apples wafted into the laundry room.

Ash swallowed, suddenly awash in longing. There'd been a cellar in Grandma's farm outside of Saskatoon. She and Grandpa would store their preserves and their potatoes and apple cider in there. Grandma would send her down to pick some apples from the big bushels so they could make apple pies. She stepped toward the opening.

"Oh no," said Maddie, placing a firm hand on Ash's arm. She plucked the flashlight from Ash's hand. "There is no way I let you go down there. Insurance. Wait here."

Ash wanted to argue that she was younger, fitter, and probably had faster reflexes than the older woman, but she didn't. The house didn't belong to her, after all.

Maddie shrugged out of her car coat and plunked it down on the washing machine next to Ash's backpack. She set her purse down, too, then turned toward the opening. Without a word, she clambered down the ladder, hanging on to the edge of the floor for as long as she could. The flashlight clicked on, revealing a packed earth floor barely six feet from the top of the ladder.

Then the light moved away from the opening as Maddie moved farther in. A moment later, weak light flooded the cellar.

"I don't see anything," Maddie's voice floated out through the opening.

Ash followed the realtor down the ladder into the cellar. Something in the realtor's voice told Ash she would welcome the company. At the bottom, Ash turned toward the lightbulb hanging from a wire and immediately got a face full of cobwebs.

"Yuck!"

Maddie laughed. "The cellar isn't part of the cleaning lady's routine," she said good-humoredly. "The place is full of cobwebs."

Ash wiped her face and headed toward the realtor. The cellar was bigger than she had expected, maybe half the surface area of the floor above. In the dim light of the dusty lightbulb, she could make out rafters with insulation stuffed between them, and strapping to keep the insulation from falling out. A behemoth of a furnace squatted in the far corner. It looked as old as the house. Next to the furnace was a hot water heater. It, at least, looked new. A shiny insulation blanket was wrapped around it.

Ducts traveled from the furnace through the ceiling. At five feet two inches, she had no worries, but Maddie had to crouch a little to keep from banging her head.

Without a word, Ash took the flashlight from Maddie's hand and shone it into the corners. Old wooden shelving stood against the far wall, empty. It was probably right around where the kitchen met the wall by the staircase, essentially as far away from the outer walls as possible. Another set of shelves stood by the outside wall, for stuff that could freeze without a problem. It was cool in the cellar—ideal for food storage. Any kind of storage, really. Not that she had anything to store.

"See?" said Maddie. "Nothing here."

Well, Ash couldn't argue. Except for the furnace and the hot water heater, and the empty shelves, there was nothing here. She shone the flashlight behind the appliances, just to be sure, and along the stone walls—clearly an original feature of the farmhouse—but she saw no openings, no doors, nothing that would provide a hiding spot for anyone.

Without a word, she turned and headed back to the ladder where she paused while Maddie turned the light off, then both women made their way back to the laundry room. Once the trap door was closed, Ash looked at the realtor.

"How many keys are there to this place?"

Maddie stopped brushing at her sweater and looked at Ash. It was a good question. The house had been empty for most of seven years. As far as she knew, the locks had never been changed but she didn't know for sure.

She shrugged. "I have no idea. I can ask the owner. But we

looked everywhere and didn't see any evidence of anyone being in here. Is it possible what you saw was your reflection?" Maddie didn't want to offend the girl—who probably wasn't going to rent the place anyway—but she was covered in dust and who knew what else, and was a touch cranky.

If the girl noticed, however, she didn't let on.

"No," Ash said, placing the flashlight in her backpack and zipping it up. "It wasn't my reflection." She looked at Maddie. "You should change the locks."

CHAPTER 4

Jake Slater pulled up in front of the Boudreaux place, wishing the damned house would just burn down. But even if it did, his guilt wouldn't go up in flames with it.

He gritted his teeth, grabbed his cap from the passenger seat, made sure his radio was on and securely clipped to his web belt, and got out of the patrol car he had appropriated for this familiar visit.

Standing beside the Albans Police Department patrol car, he took his time placing his cap on his head and zipping up his windbreaker jacket with the prominent "POLICE" stenciled on the back. His name tag was on the left front and the city's crest was on the right. With his rank plastered on either shoulder, he felt like a walking billboard.

Maddie Bowen's car was in the driveway. With a sigh, he rounded the navy and white patrol car and walked up the steps to the porch. Before he could knock, however, he saw Maddie coming toward him through the window in the door.

She had that red plaid coat of hers on over a pair of black slacks and a white sweater. Her hair was swept up in what he had come to think of as her "realtor bun" and she wore dangly gold earrings that caught the light as she walked. She was getting a little thicker in the middle and in the hips, but she still cut a fine figure and her spun gold hair and bright blue eyes hadn't changed much from when she was a kid. She had a few more wrinkles, of course, but didn't they all?

They'd known each other since grade four, when Jake's family moved to Albans. They'd been friends, then dated in high school, briefly, and now were comfortable with each other.

Knowing how he felt about the house, she came out to join him on the porch.

"Hi, Jake. Thanks for coming."

They automatically hugged, then Jake stepped back. "What's going on?"

Maddie sighed. She was heartily sick of this house, too, but Frank Boudreaux paid Albans Realty a tidy little retainer to manage it and until she and Dave decided they no longer wanted that nice check every month, they were bloody well going to manage the damned place.

Or, at least, she was, seeing as Dave couldn't bring himself to come near it.

"I was showing the place this morning, and my prospective client saw someone in the house."

The wind picked up, swirling the leaves on the lawn and sneaking up the back of Jake's jacket. He controlled a shiver.

"Did you see anyone?"

He didn't realize until he followed Maddie's gaze that his hand had strayed to his holster.

Maddie's eyebrow rose. "No. I was just getting here and my client was already on the porch, looking in through the window." She nodded toward the door behind her. "We searched the house—even the cellar—but didn't find anything."

It was Jake's turn to raise his eyebrows. "You searched the place?" Jesus. "Maddie, what if there'd been someone in there? Why didn't you call me right away?"

She shrugged. "I'm sure it was just a trick of the light. She probably just saw a reflection of herself and panicked. She's pretty young."

Jake's gaze strayed past Maddie to the window in the door. He could see the sky reflected in it, and clouds moving past, and the tops of the trees in the front yard. He had seen pictures of the place from when it had been a real farmhouse, on a real farm. It still had the same bones, and the porch could have been plucked straight out of the picture, but just about everything else had been modernized.

He wondered how many people had lived in this place over the decades. He knew for a fact that in the last seven years, at least a dozen people had tried living there, only to leave within weeks.

"All right," he said at last. "I'd better check it out."

Maddie placed a hand on his arm. "I've already walked through it," she said gently. "There's no one there."

Jake nodded. "Yeah. Wait outside." He wouldn't find anything. He never did. But Maddie was obligated to call, and he was obligated to search.

Maddie smiled sympathetically and moved aside. He opened the door and stepped in, taking a deep breath. The place smelled faintly of Maddie's perfume, something flowery and citrusy at the same time. He closed the door behind him and turned into the sitting room, trying to ignore the sudden feeling of oppression that came over him. It was always this way in this house. As if he was entering a prison.

He moved quickly through the main floor, making sure the French doors in the dining room were locked, then upstairs, making sure to check under the beds and in the closets. Nothing.

When he came back downstairs, he headed for the kitchen again, remembering the cellar. Only once he pulled the trap door up and got hit in the face with the musty, earthy smell did he remember that he'd left his flashlight in the car.

Crap.

He stared down at the dark hole, his mind completely blank. He didn't do so well in small dark places. Then he sighed and climbed down to the packed earth floor. He had to duck his head to keep from hitting the rafters, but he worried more about the ducts. He'd been down here before and knew roughly where the lightbulb was, but not often enough to have memorized the location of the ducts.

He moved away from the light spilling from the laundry room and stretched his hand out before him and a little above, sweeping it back and forth to catch the string hanging from the lightbulb.

A breath of movement and something cool caressed his cheek. He yelped and jumped, and something brushed his hair. He batted the air above his head and suddenly his hand hit the string.

The light bulb. Thank God. He swept the air, trying to find it again, and encountered nothing but cobwebs.

Then the trap door fell with a loud thump, trapping him in complete darkness.

Something brushed his cheek again and he reached up, grabbed the string, and pulled. Weak light flooded the cellar. He looked around. No one.

He hated this house.

CHAPTER 5

Maddie turned as Jake opened the front door and smiled at him.

"Very funny, Maddie."

"What's funny?" she asked.

He looked half mad, half amused. There was dust on the shoulders of his jacket and she brushed it off for him.

"Closing the trap door on me."

She gave him the "look," the same look his wife gave him whenever he said something particularly foolish.

"I'd never do that, Jake," she said quietly. How could he even think that? "You must not have propped it open well enough."

Jake just looked at her.

"Why doesn't Frank just sell the damned place?" he said finally.

Maddie shrugged. "Maybe he's hoping Odette will come back." Her lips pursed in distaste. She doubted Odette Boudreaux would ever come back to Frank. She had turned her back on her husband, and on Albans, seven years ago and she was never coming back.

Jake's eyebrow rose in disbelief. He was still lean and muscled, even twenty years out of high school and past his jock years. His hair was still full, with only a sprinkling of gray in the dark, and his gray eyes were still his best feature, the way they crinkled up whenever he smiled.

"Sure," he said, replacing his cap on his head. "That's why he's living with another woman." He and Maddie had known Boudreaux since high school. Jake had even hung out with him for a while in grade ten, but he eventually drifted away from Boudreaux. He just didn't like the guy.

Maddie was a better judge of character. She had always avoided Boudreaux and his posse.

Which was why Jake had been surprised when she accepted a contract to manage the Boudreaux house. Business was business, he guessed.

Jake pecked Maddie on the cheek and went down the steps to the walk. "Change the locks, if you want to be sure no one gets in."

With a final wave, he got in the squad car and drove off.

Maddie stared at the dissipating exhaust he left in his wake and sighed. She was going to have to talk to Frank Boudreaux.

Ash spent the rest of the morning shopping for clothes. It had been so long since she'd bought herself any that she was surprised to find her normal size four was now too big. Standing in the dressing room of Albans Sports, she stared at herself in the full-length mirror.

Her plain tan bra wrinkled where her always small breasts no longer filled the stretchy cups. Her white cotton bikini underpants looked more grey than white, and the only things keeping them up were the hip bones jutting out beneath the skin. Just standing there, she could count all her ribs in the mirror. Even her chest bones protruded unattractively below her prominent collarbones.

She took a deep breath and kept tallying.

Her cheekbones were much too sharp in her face, making

her green eyes look unnaturally large. She had always thought her mouth was her best feature, but now, instead of the full, generous, well-defined lips she had grown into, her lips pressed tightly against each other, as if to keep her from talking.

Or screaming.

At least her hair was still good. Thick, dark brown, and luxuriant, it fell to her waist when undone. She kept it in a French braid to keep it out of her way. Barney had pointed out several times that, in a fight, her hair would be a liability. An attacker could control her just by grabbing her hair.

She pulled the braid over her shoulder, took off the elastic, and released her hair. It spread over her shoulders, dull and brittle.

So much for luxuriant.

Under the jaundiced light of the dressing room, she looked at the scars that covered her thighs, chest, and abdomen. Old scars where Calum had punched her, ring out, or where he'd "accidentally" burned her with his cigarette. A pale white scar on her shoulder had faded over the years from where he had deliberately applied the iron to her when she'd left a wrinkle in his dress shirt.

The other injuries had healed. The broken tibia from where he had kicked her. The broken toes from where he had stomped on her feet. The cracked skull from where he had backhanded her and knocked her into the corner of the wall.

She felt under her right breast and found the hard knot where a rib had healed poorly, then ran her hands—nails short, but no longer bitten—over her arms and ribs and stopped with her fingers splayed over her taut abdomen. Those bruises had all healed too.

She had escaped him, finally, thanks to Grandma, who had reached out from the grave to rescue her.

Tears prickled and she breathed through the need to weep at all she had lost in the past four years. She studied the pale, haggard creature in the mirror. This wasn't what Grandma had saved her for.

CHAPTER 6

T he oil tank is full," said the real estate agent, "and I've arranged for a cord of wood to be delivered this week."

Ash nodded but she was barely listening. They had met at the house at nine o'clock to sign the lease and for Maddie Bowen to hand over the keys. New keys, to go with the new locks on the front and side doors. Ash had arrived early to prowl the grounds and peer into the window of the front door, but no strange woman had appeared on the other side. The backyard sloped down to the woods. Beyond the forest was the St. George River and beyond that, downtown Albans, across the bridge. With the pop of yellow and crimson leaves against the evergreens, it looked like a picture postcard and filled her with a peace she had thought lost forever.

Now she sat at the rectangular pine table in the dining room, pen in hand, scanning the lease agreement the agent had placed before her.

"Just sign on the line at the bottom," instructed Maddie. She was busy removing the cellophane from the flowers she had brought as a housewarming gift. Huge gerberas in an assortment of bright colors nestled in some kind of greenery with long narrow leaves. Pretty.

Ash finished reading through the lease agreement. It was everything they had agreed to, including the reduced rent she had negotiated and staying in the house free for the first few weeks, as it was already past the middle of the month.

She wanted to open a window and let fresh air blow through the house. She wanted to dance in the kitchen and run up the stairs. She wanted to light a fire in the fireplace and snuggle up on the couch. She wanted Maddie Bowen out of her house.

She signed both copies and turned in the chair to find Maddie looking at her, a worried frown between her blue eyes. Ash had trouble with telling age, but she guessed the woman wasn't yet forty. That wasn't really middle age, was it? She was pretty enough, with more laugh lines than frown lines, and there was very little gray in her blonde hair. She obviously favored turtlenecks and was wearing a red one today, with the sleeves pushed up her forearms, and a pair of gray slacks.

"Are you sure?" asked Maddie softly, looking intently at her. "This is a big place for one person. I could help you find another property..."

Ash shook her head. "I like it here."

She liked it here. In spite of feeling like the house hid its true face from her. She wanted to coax it out, like a feral cat, until it accepted her. This place felt right.

Maddie sighed and filled the tall glass vase with water, then placed the flowers in it. She set the vase in the middle of the granite countertop. The flowers looked lovely against the backdrop of gray. She pulled a business card out of her pocket and set it next to the vase.

The girl had signed a six-month lease. When Maddie had wanted her social insurance number to run a financial check, Ash Gantry had silently pulled out a bank draft for the full amount of the six months' rent instead. Maddie would have insisted—should have insisted—but kept quiet. This girl was clearly running from something, or someone. Maddie wouldn't push.

But now she found herself reluctant to leave, as if... she didn't

know what. But the girl called up all of Maddie's protective instincts. Maternal instincts.

Lord help her. She had her own kid to worry about.

"All right, then," she said briskly. "My card is on the counter.
Call me if there's anything. Day or night," she added impulsively,
then regretted it. What if Ash Gantry turned into a whiner like the
last tenants?

"I'll be fine," said Ash, standing up. She led the way out of the
dining room toward the front door, knowing she was being rude,
but she wanted to be alone.

Maddie nodded at the girl's back. All right, then. At the door,
she turned back to her latest tenant. "Will you be looking for a job?"

Ash blinked up at the real estate agent. She didn't need a job.
At least, not right away. But if she was going to be here for a while,
she had to find some way of filling her days.

"Yes," she said. "Part time. Do you know of any?"

Maddie smiled. "What kind of experience do you have?"

Ash looked away. None, really. She'd been at first year university when Mom and Dad died and never finished, thanks to dealing
with all the estate stuff. Grandma had helped, but she had been
trapped in a wheelchair. Still, just having her there had been a
blessing, until she went back to her own home in Saskatoon.

But Calum had stayed with her.

She sighed.

"Not much," she admitted.

Maddie swallowed a sigh. Right then. "Not to worry," she said.
"I'll call you when I find something."

She shook Ash's hand, once again surprised at the strength
and smallness of it, and left. Maddie knew better than to ask for a
resume. This would be one of those "who you know" arrangements.
It might be a challenge, but the girl was smart enough to negoti-
ate an excellent lease agreement for herself. The right job was out
there for her, and Maddie was going to find it.

Not that she knew why she was doing it.

◇◇◇

Ash's last stop before returning home—home!—was at the same sporting goods store she'd been in yesterday. There she picked out four maple baseball bats. The teenage boy at the till grinned when he saw them.

"Starting your own baseball team?"

Ash tried to smile, but her face was too stiff. "Something like that."

The bats were for the front and side doors, the glass doors to the deck, and her bedroom. She wasn't comfortable with hand guns and wouldn't know how to go about getting one, anyway, but a bat she could handle. And with all the working out she was doing, she would even have some power behind her swing.

She had to drive through downtown Albans to get back home and, impulsively, she stopped at a small place called Soup 'n Such on Main Street, only a few blocks from the river. She was hungry, and a bowl of soup would be nutritious and warming. She needed to regain some weight.

After she ate, maybe she'd walk around downtown and look for help wanted signs. Maybe the restaurant would have a paper she could look at.

The place was tiny, only half a dozen square tables and four stools at the counter. All the tables were occupied by office workers or maybe shop clerks, judging by their clothing. All but one of the stools were filled and she headed for it. The noise level was amazing for such a tiny place.

An older woman standing at a till behind the counter was busy taking cash and handing over brown paper bags with orders for takeout. She looked over her shoulder at Ash and nodded.

"I'll be right with you, dear."

She had a faint Newfoundland accent that put a smile on Ash's face. A big clock on the wall behind the counter read twelve thirty.

As she sat down at the far end of the counter, next to a woman dressed in a dark suit and high heels, an older man backed through the swinging door that led to the kitchen carrying a small tray with a steaming bowl of something, a bun on a round plate, and butter in a small ceramic pot. A wonderful smell of onions and chicken escaped from the kitchen.

"Chili for table two," he said to the back of the woman's head. He wore a striped red and white apron that hooked over his head and tied behind his back. His face was round and ruddy, probably from the heat in the kitchen. The woman at the till nodded and finished handing change to a guy in Carhartts and carrying a hard hat. Holding up one finger to the people in the line-up, she picked up the tray, slipped through the opening between the till and the wall, and handed the chili over to a man sitting alone at a table in the corner.

Dizzied by the pace, Ash wondered if she should leave, but there was something almost… not comforting, really. More… home-like about this place. She felt like she had stumbled into the home kitchen of a huge family.

She had seen a number of plastic-wrapped sandwiches and small salads inside the glass counter over which the woman pre-sided, but Ash wasn't interested in those. On the back wall, behind the woman, a blackboard listed the day's specials:

CHICKEN SOUP
VEGETARIAN CHILI
IRISH BEEF STEW

"What can I get for you," asked the woman, stopping in front of her. She had pretty blue eyes and dark hair in a loose bun that was liberally sprinkled with gray. She wore a blue and white striped apron similar to the one the man in the kitchen wore and an old-fashioned cotton dress printed with blue and yellow flowers. It was something Ash's mom would have worn.

"I'd like a bowl of chicken soup, please," said Ash.

"Good choice," the woman said. "I'll be right back."

Ash nodded and felt with her right foot for her backpack. Still wedged into the corner under the counter.

The woman returned moments later with the soup, a warm bun, a small pot of butter, and a glass of water.

"Anything else you'd like?" she asked. "Coffee? Milk?"

Ash shook her head and the woman hurried back to the till. As soon as she had her back turned, Ash glanced up at the blackboard and its beverages. No pop.

The soup was fragrant and hot, with big chunks of roasted chicken and carrots, onions, potatoes, and herbs. Ash ate it all and sopped up the remaining liquid with her bun, which had clearly just come out of the oven.

"No one's enjoyed my cooking that much in quite a while."

Startled, Ash looked up to find the cook smiling down at her, his blue eyes almost lost in a sea of wrinkles.

"It was very good," said Ash. Heat crawled up her face as she stared down at the empty bowl. She had attacked the food like a starving dog. Mom was probably rolling over in her grave.

The older woman came to stand next to the man. She was grinning. "We like to see a hearty appetite," she said. "How about a slice of pie?" she suggested. "On the house, seeing as you're a new customer."

Ash glanced around the tiny restaurant, surprised to find it almost empty. How had that happened without her noticing?

"Blueberry?" continued the woman. Now that they were standing side by side, Ash could clearly see the family resemblance. Brother and sister, more than likely.

"Did I see lemon meringue?" she asked hopefully.

"Coming right up," said the woman. The man disappeared into the kitchen, only to return a moment later with a bowl of the chicken soup. He set it down at the place next to Ash and came around the counter to sit next to her.

"That's very good soup," said Ash tentatively. He nodded his thanks, but kept eating. "Did I taste ginger?"

He looked up from his soup. "It's the secret ingredient," he said conspiratorially.

Ash nodded solemnly. "Your secret is safe with me," she assured him. Then, "Ginger always makes everything better."

"I could tell she was a kindred spirit the moment she walked in," said the woman, setting a dessert plate with a huge wedge of lemon meringue pie down in front of Ash. She handed Ash a fork.

"Thank you." Ash took a bite of the fluffy confection. The chime on the door rang out as the last customer left, calling goodbye. The pie was tart and sweet, and smooth and lemony—perfection on a plate.

"Oh, my," she finally breathed after she swallowed the last bite. "That was so good."

The woman beamed. "Thank you."

"Charlotte does the baking and the front of room stuff," said the older man, sopping up the last of the soup with his bun. "I make the soups, salads, and sandwiches. Name's Max, by the way. Max Strelzow. Charlotte's my sister."

"How do you do," said Ash automatically. "My name is Ash Gantry." She stuck her hand out and shook Charlotte's hand first, then Max's. "Is it always this busy?"

Charlotte swept the wispy hairs escaping from her bun back with both hands, a gesture that looked automatic. She glanced around the small room, at the detritus left by diners.

"Yes," she said. "Most days there's a line-up."

Ash stayed silent, but her dismay must have shown on her face. Charlotte laughed.

"We usually have a part-time waitress, but our last one went back to university a couple of weeks ago and we haven't found anyone to fill her spot yet."

The words leapt out of Ash's mouth as though they'd been waiting for their chance.

"I used to be a waitress."

Brother and sister gave each other a look Ash couldn't interpret. She blushed, realizing she had overstepped.

"I'm not suggesting—" she began hurriedly.

"Are you offer—" began Max.

Charlotte burst out laughing.

"Oh, the look on your faces!" she said.

Ash grinned sheepishly. "Sorry," she said. "I didn't mean to put you in an awkward position. I just moved here and I'm looking for a part-time job." She shrugged. "Forget I said anything. If it didn't work out, I'd hate to have to avoid this place."

One of Charlotte's eyebrows rose quizzically. She glanced at her brother, who must have signaled her somehow.

"What kind of experience do you have?"

Ash suddenly found herself incredibly nervous. She placed both hands in her lap and took a deep breath.

"I waitressed every summer from the time I was fifteen. Family restaurants, mostly. Then at university, I worked part-time at the French restaurant near the university."

She had liked waitressing, despite being on her feet all the time. She liked the people. But Calum hadn't wanted her to keep working.

"You got a resume?" asked Charlotte. "References?"

The smile stayed on Ash's face, but she could feel it freezing in place. She had a resume. And references. She couldn't use any of them. Calum would find out and track her down.

She swiveled on her seat and slid down to the floor, reaching down to haul up her backpack.

"That was a great meal," she said sincerely, without looking at either of them. She pulled out some loose bills from her jeans pocket and peeled off two five-dollar bills. "Thank you."

She was at the door by the time Charlotte caught up with her. The older woman placed a hand on her forearm to stop her.

"How about we try it for a couple of days," she said. "Ten o'clock to two. We close at three, but there's hardly ever anyone here by then. If it doesn't work out, no hard feelings."

Ash stood by the glass door, staring out at the passersby on the sidewalk without seeing them. She could say no, of course. She didn't need the job, and really, it was only part-time—how much would it bring her, anyway?

But she breathed in the wonderful, lingering smells from the kitchen, felt the comforting hand on her arm, and realized that for the last hour, she hadn't given Calum a thought, not until Charlotte asked for her references.

She'd been happy.

Ash took a deep breath and turned to face brother and sister.

"How about I start by clearing off these tables?"

When she got home later that afternoon, Ash made a big pot of spaghetti sauce. She froze most of it and made herself a plateful of spaghetti for dinner, with a liberal heaping of parmesan cheese. Maybe tomorrow she'd buy a bottle of wine. It had been a long, long time since she'd had wine.

By then the day had caught up to her. She washed the dishes and left them to air dry in the dish rack, then drew a hot bath and soaked in it until it got uncomfortably cool. She pulled on her sleeping tee-shirt, opened the window a crack, and crawled into bed in the master bedroom. It faced the backyard and the forest, and the wind through the trees at the bottom of the yard sounded like sighing. She snuggled under the clean sheets and the heavy blankets. Before turning the bedside lamp off, she made sure the baseball bat was next to her, on top of the comforter.

Maybe tomorrow, she'd find a library and stock up on something to read. For now, it wasn't an issue. She wouldn't have read more than a couple of lines before falling asleep anyway.

Fresh air flowed through the open window, bringing with it the smell of composting leaves and wood smoke. A car door slammed in the distance and a dog barked.

As sleep stole over her, images from the day ran through her mind. Barney showing her a hip check. The boy at the till smiling at her. Charlotte and Max looking at her with eyes the exact same shade of blue.

A noise startled her awake. Out of long habit, she lay unmoving, eyes closed, trying to identify what it was. At first she thought she was in her old house, with Calum. For four years, she had been attuned to his comings and goings, her ears being her first line of defense. It took a moment for her to remember that this wasn't the old house.

Breathing shallowly, she strained to hear if someone was in her house. But she didn't know the noises of the house yet. Was that the sound of someone stealthily climbing the stairs? Or was it just the house settling for the night?

Finally, she cracked an eye open and glanced at the clock. It was three forty-three.

Heart hammering in her chest, she slid her legs over the side of the bed and slowly straightened, dragging the baseball bat through the bedding until she finally stood with it clutched in both hands in front of her.

She crept to the half-open door of her bedroom and stood behind it, listening. Was that breathing? Was someone standing on the other side of the door, listening to her?

Where was the damned light switch?

Slowly, she uncurled one ice-cold hand from around the bat and reached for the inside wall by the door. There was a switch. She was sure there was. Then her fumbling fingers found the plastic light switch and she paused. Should she turn the lights on? Or should she call the police?

And tell them what? I'm scared—come save me?

Gritting her teeth, she flicked the switch on. The room and hallway beyond flooded with light. Without giving herself a chance to think, she leapt into the hallway, screaming, "Ha!" and swinging the bat around her in short, vicious arcs.

When nothing happened, she pivoted slowly. There was

nothing in the hallway.

Reaction began to set in, making her arms and legs tremble. And she was cold, just in her tee-shirt.

She did a sweep of the house, just to make sure. By the time she returned to her room, it was almost four o'clock and she lay in bed staring up at the ceiling, unable to get warm.

She had imagined it. Clearly. But as she lay under the covers, icy cold and wide awake, her mind kept replaying the sound of a woman softly crying.

CHAPTER 7

On Monday morning, five days after moving in, Ash dragged herself to Barney's Gym just as it was getting light out and parked in the back lot, next to his old Renault. There were no other cars in the lot.

Temperatures had dropped overnight, coming close to freezing, and she was glad she had invested in a wool-lined jacket with a hood. It was a nondescript brown and green and would blend into most backgrounds. She hauled her gym bag out of the back seat. Maybe she should have eaten something before leaving the house. The bag felt heavy even though it contained nothing but her usual gym clothes and a bottle of water. And the backpack she had stuffed inside.

It wasn't hunger. It was exhaustion. Every night she'd been awakened at three forty-three. Every night she got up to investigate. Then she lay awake the rest of the night, trying to figure out what the sound was.

She had tried closing the window, closing the bedroom door, searching the house before going to bed... She'd even searched for a hidden microphone. Nothing.

Then last night...

Last night she'd actually woken up at three thirty. She lay in bed listening to the sound of the wind in the eaves, the cracking of the wood casements as the temperature fell, the rattling of tree branches outside her window.

She was wide awake when, thirteen minutes later, a woman's soft sobs sounded in the bedroom. All the little hairs on Ash's body stood on end. She lay perfectly still in the bed, lips pressed tightly together, trying to convince herself that she wasn't hearing a woman crying by the dresser.

Then the sound changed to a small gasp and Ash's mouth went dry. She knew that sound. It was fear. Suddenly the blankets felt like they were trapping her. Just as she was about to kick them off, a terrible noise sounded in the hallway. Someone had fallen down the stairs.

In two seconds, Ash was on her feet and in the hallway, baseball bat in hand, but like every other night, there was nothing to see.

She spent the rest of the night wrapped in a comforter in the back seat of the Volvo.

Now, as she walked toward the back door to Barney's Gym, she wondered if she was going crazy. Hearing things. Maybe Calum was right, and she was a nut case.

She turned the doorknob and pushed the heavy metal door open with her shoulder. If she was crazy, why would she pick a hallucination that involved a woman crying at three forty-three in the morning?

The locker smell of the gym hit her as she entered, but to her surprise, the little entrance was dark. Barney must have forgotten to turn the light on. She felt for the industrial light switch on the wall by the outside door, but when she flicked it on, nothing happened. The bulb was out.

Still, she'd been here often enough to know her way in the dark. The inner door to the gym proper was only five feet away, straight ahead. She allowed the outside door to close with a heavy thunk behind her and shuffled toward the inner door, hand outstretched. Her fingers found the metal door, then trailed down to the knob. She turned it and the door swung open.

But the main lights were out in the gym, too. Only the emergency lights shone from the corners. She peered into the gloom. "Bar—"

A hard hand clamped over her mouth, startling her into dropping the gym bag. Before she could turn to face her attacker, an arm wrapped around her, trapping her arms and pulling her tightly into a big male body.

Calum! He'd found her!

She froze, waiting for the pain, knowing that this time he would kill her.

The lights came on and the hands released her. She stumbled into her gym bag and would have fallen if not for the hand that grabbed her upper arm to steady her.

She turned to look at the man who had first attacked her, then helped her. He was close to six feet tall, with dark hair cut short and receding in a dramatic widow's peak. His brown eyes smiled down apologetically at her. Only then did she recognize him as another patron of the gym. She'd seen him a couple of times.

"What do you want?" she asked in a voice made low by fear.

"It was his idea," said the man, nodding at someone behind her.

She whirled to find Barney standing by the fuse box, arms crossed over his barrel chest, looking at her with worry in his eyes.

"I asked Paul to do it," he said grimly. "You're getting too comfortable. You need to be aware of your surroundings all the time." He shook his head. "You didn't even try to fight back, girl."

Shame flooded Ash and she couldn't look at the old man, let alone the man who had attacked her. Barney was right. Absolutely right. She had been attacked and she had automatically reverted to the scared girl who didn't know how to defend herself.

Barney came close enough to touch her and lifted her chin with a knuckle. "That's why I asked Paul to jump you. Until you've experienced it, you don't know how you'll react. Now you know, and we can work on that."

Ash smiled and nodded, but what she wanted to do was find a corner and curl up in it. She *had* experienced it. She did know how she reacted. That was why she had started working out and training with Barney. So that no one could ever hurt her again.

"I know a little about self-defense," said Paul gently, coming to stand by Barney. "I can teach you a few moves, if you like."

Ash glanced from him to Barney.

"Why?"

Paul shrugged and glanced at Barney, too.

"I'm good with boxing," said Barney, spreading his hands. "But not so good with all that martial stuff. Paul here was an instructor for the Canadian army. He can teach you how to protect yourself."

Ash swallowed hard, but the lump that had formed in her throat didn't go away.

"Why would you do that?" she asked Paul.

He shrugged again. "I taught my wife and my two teenage girls. I'm thinking of offering classes here once a week. You can be my guinea pig."

Ash smiled. He wasn't fooling her one bit. Barney had put him up to this.

"Thank you," she said, looking him in the eye. "But I'll be paying you the going rate for private lessons."

He grinned at her. "Sure. We can start right now, if you like."

As Ash nodded her agreement, she wondered what use all this training would be if Calum came after her with a gun.

Maddie looked up from her computer screen at Olivia's knock. "Someone here to see you."

Maddie nodded and Olivia returned to the front. Maddie and Olivia didn't like each other, but in the five years they had worked together, they'd developed a grudging respect for one another. Especially after Olivia agreed to cover up the worst of the tattoos. As far as Maddie was concerned, a forty-year-old woman should know better than to have a tattoo of a band logo covering her belly button... and then wear a cropped top to reveal it.

To her surprise, Ash Gantry walked into her office. She was dressed in jeans—that was all she seemed to wear—but at least she had a heavier coat on. The olive green in the pattern brought out the green in the girl's eyes. Suddenly alert, Maddie looked closer at her. Her eyes were bloodshot and puffy.

Crap.

Put your game face on, she warned herself. She stood up and smiled her best professional smile.

"Hello, Ash, nice to see you." She gestured to the chairs in front of her glass-topped desk. "Have a seat."

Ash silently sat down in one chair and set her backpack on the empty one. Maddie sat down, too, and leaned forward, resting her elbows on the desk and her chin on her laced fingers.

"Are you still interested in a job?" she began. "Because I know a place—"

"I have a job," Ash interrupted.

Maddie blinked in surprise. "Well, that didn't take long. Where are you working?"

"Soup 'n Such, on Main Street." Ash didn't really want to discuss her job—although Charlotte and Max were wonderful and she was enjoying the job a lot. "I came to ask you about the house."

Maddie braced herself. She'd had tenants in that house for as little as three days and as long as two weeks, but never longer. Usually they showed up at her office and—some tentatively, some aggressively—asked to be let out of the lease. The reasons were all different, everything from getting a job in another province to a sick mother who needed care, but they all wanted out of the lease.

She sighed.

"There's a clause in the lease agreement that will let you out with a month's penalty," she said. She'd convinced Frank Boudreaux to put the clause into the lease agreement after the third tenant skipped out without leaving a forwarding address. At least if they knew they could buy their way out with only one month's rent, they were less likely to skip.

Ash stared at the realtor, who didn't look surprised so much as resigned, as if this wasn't the first time she'd had a tenant come to her, unhappy with the house.

She glanced around Maddie's office. Albans Realty took up part of the main floor of a four-story building on George Street, which bordered the river. Maddie's office was in the front and had a great view of the running track across the street and, beyond it, the river, which looked deceptively calm today.

The walls were a pale yellow and there were lots of plants—on the corner of the glass desk, on the filing cabinet, on the bookshelf at the back of the office. They all looked very healthy. A big architectural drawing was framed on one wall and a picture of a glass and marble house was displayed in another frame on the opposite wall. There were no personal photos in the office. Maddie apparently believed in the separation of home and work.

"Isn't that why you're here?" Maddie prompted.

Yes, it was. But suddenly Ash was no longer sure.

"I want to know who owns the house," she said slowly, stalling.

Maddie looked at her for a moment, clearly unsure of where the conversation was going.

"A local man. His name is Frank Boudreaux."

Ash looked out the picture window, her gaze following two women joggers dressed in neon running pants—one in green, one in pink.

"How long has he owned it?" she asked.

Maddie followed her gaze but all she saw were two joggers. The river was blue under the September sun, but she could see frost on the north facing bank.

"Almost ten years," said Maddie. Then, impulsively, she added, "Why?" In the seven years she had been managing this property, no one had ever asked about owners.

Ash smiled at her, but it was a perfunctory smile, one of those placeholder smiles you used until you could think of what to say.

"I'm interested in the house," she said. "I'm interested in its history. What can you tell me about it?"

Maddie Bowen leaned back in her chrome and black leather chair, her gaze fixed on Ash's face. Ash couldn't tell what she was thinking.

Then Maddie smiled. "I could make you a copy of whatever information I have on file," she offered. "The house is a hundred years old. It's had a number of owners."

Ash smiled in return.

"Thanks, I'd like that. I can swing by and pick it up when it's ready."

Maddie waved a hand. "Nonsense. I'll drop it by. Probably tomorrow. When do you work?"

"Ten to two every week day." Ash had been surprised to learn that Charlotte and Max didn't open on weekends, but maybe it wasn't so surprising, after all. Their clientele was the business crowd, mostly, and they had a small catering business on the side. They were busy.

Maddie nodded. "Yes, that's their busy time. Charlotte and Max are good people," she added. "They've been in that spot for over twenty years. They're an institution in this town."

That almost sounded like a warning. Ash stood up and stuck her hand out. Maddie stood up, too, and shook it.

"Thanks for indulging my curiosity," said Ash. "I'll see you tomorrow. Maybe we can have tea."

Maddie smiled. "Maybe we can."

As Ash walked out of the realtor's office, she found herself baffled at her own behavior. She had reread the lease that morning. When she had first arrived at Albans Realty, she had fully intended to hand over a draft for the penalty amount and walk away from the house, but the resignation on Maddie's face had sparked something in her.

She just wasn't sure what it was yet.

CHAPTER 8

After work, Ash returned home and made a stew. Judging by the amount of food Charlotte pressed on her at the end of every shift, she must have thought Ash couldn't afford to buy her own groceries. But while soup was great for after work, for dinner she wanted something a little more substantial. She needed protein to build up her muscles.

While the stew simmered, she stepped out onto the deck. It was still cold out, only a few degrees above freezing, and she stood there shivering in her plaid flannel shirt. The sun was already close to setting, even though it was barely four o'clock. Maybe tomorrow she would hike down to the river.

No, wait. Maddie was coming by after work.

Below, leaves on the oak and maple trees fluttered gold and rust red. The sky was darkening with thin, orange-tinted wisps of clouds floating on the wind. That same wind stiffened her cheeks and turned her fingers to ice. She crossed her arms and tucked her hands under her armpits.

What was she doing here? This wasn't home. Vancouver was home. She had no friends here. No family.

You have no family, no matter where you go, she reminded herself.

And if she had no friends here, well, she had no enemies, either.

Still. The years stretched out ahead of her—long, empty. Lonely. *Oh, quit feeling sorry for yourself.*

She liked Albans. It had a community college and a small university. Maybe she could go back to school, finish her Bachelor of Arts. Find something meaningful to do with her life. She was only twenty-four. This wasn't a bad place to start over.

To start, period.

The tears caught her by surprise. Her throat closed up and she swallowed, trying to keep them at bay, but they rolled down her cheeks despite her determination. She wasn't even sure why she was crying. For herself, sure, and the vast loneliness that filled her days. For the loss of her parents, still so young, in that car accident. Even for Calum, whom she had loved and who, in a weird way, had filled the void in her life, even if it was with fear.

But mostly she wept for her grandmother, whose love and foresight had given Ash the means to escape Calum.

She wiped at her cheeks, ashamed of herself for the second time today. Grandma hadn't rescued her so that she could stand around feeling sorry for herself. There was a small shed at the bottom of the yard. With any luck, there would be a rake in it. She could spend an hour or so raking up the leaves while the stew simmered.

But first, she would put a sweater on. Shivering, she turned her back on the glorious view and headed for the French doors that led into the dining room. Just as her hand reached for the handle, however, a movement in the glass caught her eye and she looked up.

There, staring back at her from the other side, was the blonde-haired woman she had seen six days ago, while she waited for Maddie Bowen on the front porch.

Then, as Ash watched, the woman faded and disappeared.

◊ ◊ ◊

Dear God in Heaven.

Hands shaking, Ash stood on the deck for long minutes, staring at her own reflection in the French door. The handle was freezing cold in her hand, but still she didn't turn it.

The woman had been there. She had been *there*.

Ash wasn't crazy. She had seen her. Six days ago, and now today.

But she had disappeared.

She tried to take a deep breath but she could only manage small gasps.

There was no such thing as ghosts. Was there?

But she had seen the woman. Twice. And she had heard her crying at night. Every night. And last night, she had heard someone fall down the stairs. Was it the woman?

In the background, past the roaring of her thundering heart, she could hear car doors slamming and kids playing in the street. People were coming home from work, from picking up the kids at daycare or at school.

The wind poked a cold finger under her heavy braid and a massive shiver shook her. She couldn't stay outside.

She forced a deep breath into her lungs, then another one, and another.

People who believed in ghosts were troubled. Delusional. She had always believed that. But she didn't think she was delusional.

As if of its own volition, her hand finally turned the handle and pulled the door open. At once the savory smell of simmering stew enveloped her and she stepped into the dining room, glancing around nervously.

No one.

Closing the door behind her, she automatically went to the stew and stirred it, then placed the lid on the pot and turned the heat down. She filled the automatic kettle and set about making herself a pot of ginger peach tea. When the tea had steeped, she poured a cup and went into the living room to sit, staring at the cold fireplace.

Every few seconds she glanced around, but she remained alone.

She sipped and thought, considering, then rejecting, notions. Now she regretted not taking Maddie Bowen up on her offer to let her out of the lease. Clearly, it wasn't the first time a tenant had wanted out. The problem wasn't the house itself—it was wonderful. The problem was that it was already occupied.

She could move out. Go back to the motel on the highway. Find another place to rent.

That would be the smart thing to do. She would certainly sleep better somewhere else.

But she found herself resisting the idea of moving out. She was so sick of running. Besides, she liked this house. Liked the neighborhood. And the... presence... hadn't been hostile.

Not yet, anyway.

She needed more information. Tomorrow she would buy a computer and get herself hooked up to the Internet. If she had a computer, she wouldn't have to wait for Maddie Bowen to bring her information; she would be able to research it herself.

Until then, there was the library.

The Sarah Michaels Memorial Library was in a historical building on Main Street, only a few blocks from Soup 'n Such. It was a two-story building made of limestone, with white marble columns in front and two glowing, round lights on pedestals at the foot of the wide stone staircase. Fallen leaves on the small lawn on either side of the walkway glowed in the light from the globes. In this part of downtown, the city had replaced the industrial-looking light standards with Victorian-looking ones. Every time Ash saw them, they reminded her of British bobbies.

At seven fifteen at night, there was little traffic on Main Street. Cars were parked near La Souche, the three-star French restaurant—the only French restaurant in town—and on the side streets near The Playhouse—which hosted a local amateur theater troupe—but otherwise, Ash could park wherever she wanted. Deciding a little walk would do her good, she parked in her usual spot on the side street closest to Soup 'n Such and headed for the library.

As she turned the corner onto Main Street, the wind caught her, tearing a gasp from her. Scarves. She definitely needed to invest in scarves. And gloves, she thought, sticking her hands in her coat pocket. She passed a middle-aged couple heading into La Souche and two teenaged girls just leaving the library with school books under their arms. She climbed the steps and pushed open the old-fashioned oak doors with long, narrow, glass insets. The library's hours were stenciled on the glass. It closed at nine o'clock on weekdays, and five o'clock on Saturdays and Sundays. There was another set of doors on the inside and Ash pushed them open, too, then stood for a moment, shivering in the warmth and getting her bearings.

The library was much bigger than she had expected. It smelled like every library she had ever been in, a little musty, a little dusty. She always wondered if she was breathing in mold whenever she walked into one.

Straight ahead was a staircase leading upstairs. The carved wooden sign above it read "REFERENCE." The steps were made of wood and had obviously been partly covered by a runner for a long time, as the middle section was darker than the edges. It looked dark up there.

Rows of wooden bookshelves filled the back of the room. She was willing to bet that these same bookshelves had been there a hundred years ago. In front of the shelves were half a dozen scarred wooden tables, with carved legs and old-fashioned, leather-covered captain's chairs arrayed around them. If it weren't for the four computers set on modern computer desks complete with pull-out keyboard trays in the corner, she might have felt she'd stepped back in time. She counted ten people—mostly teenagers—at the work tables, and each computer was in use.

Damn.

Exhausted, discouraged, she almost turned around. She could come back tomorrow. Then an older man walked into the library and had to edge around her as she blocked the way. She sidestepped with a murmured apology. The main desk was to her left. Two women were behind it, one a thin, older woman dressed in black slacks and a white shirt, working on a computer, and the other a woman about Ash's age, dressed in a paisley turtleneck tunic top and black yoga pants. She was using a wand to scan the spines of books in the double-decker trolley next to her. Ash headed for her.

"Hi," she said, interrupting.

"Can I help you?" asked the woman, smiling.

"I hope so," said Ash. "Can I book time on one of the computers, or is it first come, first served?"

The woman shook her head. "Sorry, you have to book ahead, and there are no slots left tonight. Do you want to come back tomorrow?"

By tomorrow, Ash would have her own computer. Damn it. She didn't want to go back to the house no further ahead than she had been when she left. The thought of that ghostly crying set her hands to shaking, and she stuck them back in her coat pockets.

"Are you the reference librarian?" she asked impulsively.

The girl shook her head and turned to the older woman, who stopped what she was doing to look at Ash.

"The reference desk closes at six o'clock," said the older woman. She was probably around thirty-five. Or maybe forty-five. She was pretty enough, with her graying, thick blonde hair up in a loose bun. She had large blue eyes with sweeping eyebrows, a straight nose, and an upper lip that was longer than her lower lip. She smiled. "Maybe I can help?"

Ash smiled back, but it was automatic. There was sadness in this woman.

"I'm looking for information about an old house in town. Do you have any information like that?"

This time, the woman's smile was genuine. "We certainly do. The Albans Historical Society published a book about ten years ago about all the historical properties in and around Albans. Would that help?"

Ash grinned. "It's a good start."

"Hang on," said the woman, rounding the desk. "It's upstairs in the reference section. I'll be right back." She headed for the staircase and, a moment later, the lights went on upstairs.

When she returned, she was carrying a heavy coffee table book and a few regular-sized hardcovers.

"Which house are you interested in?" she asked, setting the books down on the desk.

"I don't know if it has a name," said Ash. "But I think it used to be a farmhouse."

The woman scanned the table of contents page of the coffee table book, *Historical Albans*. Her finger slid down the page. "There's a map," she said. "From there, you can figure out where your house is."

Not my house, thought Ash, controlling a shiver. Definitely not my house.

"You can't take these out," warned the librarian as she handed the books over to Ash. "They're for reference only."

"That's okay," said Ash. "I'll look through them here."

"All the tables seem to be occupied," said the younger woman, joining them. "But there's a comfortable reading nook just past the new release section." She pointed to the back corner, past the work tables.

The reading nook consisted of four leather-bound club chairs set around a low, wide coffee table. An elderly man still wearing his coat sat in one chair, reading a copy of the day's Globe and Mail. He looked over his glasses at her and nodded, then went back to his reading.

Ash set the two smaller books on the table and sat down with the large one on her lap. She riffled through it. It was full of archival pictures of houses and warehouses and public buildings. She found the map the librarian had mentioned and took a few minutes to figure out where the house was. Once she found the library on the map, it was easy enough to trace the streets back to the house on Hawk Street. She checked the legend and found that the house was identified as the McTavish Farm. Flipping to the right page, she opened the book to find a scratchy picture of a pretty farmhouse on a knoll, surrounded by a barn and several outbuildings. A flower garden was on one side of the walk and a vegetable garden on the other. She couldn't be sure, but she thought those were tomatoes growing up the trellis.

The front door was different, and there were shutters on the windows in the picture, and the porch running the width of the house was deeper. Minor differences. It was the same house.

The caption said the photo had been taken in 1903. She read the sparse information below the photo.

The McTavish farmhouse was built in 1890 by Alistair McTavish and his wife, Isadora. They worked the hundred-acre farm until Alistair's death in 1915, after which the farm passed out of the family's hands.

That was it? She flipped to the next page, hoping for more pictures, but there was nothing. How had it passed out of the family's hands? Had Isadora sold it? Were there no children to leave the farm to?

Was Isadora haunting the place?

For the first time, she realized she had no idea what the ghost had been wearing.

She had a vague sense of a long-sleeved shirt and a skirt, but it could have been an old-fashioned dress.

Wait. That didn't make sense. It couldn't be Isadora—nobody would renovate a haunted house. The ghost has to be more recent.

She picked up the other books.

One, *A Brief History of Albans 1850 to 1950,* also mentioned the McTavish farm, but only as an example of how the area's valuable farmland was being whittled away. The Crown gave Alistair McTavish the acres in 1888 as thanks for his services, though the article didn't specify what those services were. Over the years, as McTavish cleared more and more land, he added dairy farming to the corn, wheat, and barley he grew. By the time he died in 1915, the farm supplied milk and butter to Albans and sold its wheat on the open market. In 1918, the book said, the widow sold off ten acres. When she died in 1923, the farm went to a distant relative, who sold the ninety acres to another local farmer. In 1941, a runway was built on the land to accommodate a flight school training pilots to send overseas.

The second book, *The Changing Face of Cox County 1880 to 1950,* was of even less use. Sometime after World War II, the flight school was closed and most of the land sold off to accommodate housing for the returned soldiers.

Ash looked up, trying to remember what Maddie Bowen had said. Something about the surrounding area having been farmland up to about ten years ago.

With a tired sigh, she closed the book and stood up. The books weren't much help. They even seemed to contradict each other. One said the McTavish farm passed out of family hands in 1915 when Alistair died, while another said the widow kept it until her death. Hopefully Maddie would have more recent information when she came by tomorrow.

She made her way to the desk and returned the books to the older librarian, who had taken over scanning the spines of the books on the trolley. The younger librarian was nowhere in sight.

"Did you find what you were looking for?" asked the librarian politely.

Ash shook her head. "Not really."

The other woman's hands stilled as she looked at Ash. She had pretty eyes.

"Why don't you leave me your number?" suggested the woman.

"If you tell me exactly what you're looking for, I can check with the reference librarian tomorrow and call you if she finds something."

Ash hesitated. The only person who knew her cell phone number was Grandma's lawyer. She hadn't even given it to Maddie Bowen, preferring to drop in on her instead when she wanted to talk. Even Charlotte and Max didn't have her phone number.

The phone was prepaid, and not on any plan. Mr. Caldwell, the lawyer, had given her strict instructions to not share the phone number with anyone. It hadn't been a problem until now. If she was going to settle in Albans, she might have to consider getting her own phone, under her own name.

A chill settled in the pit of her stomach at the thought. Calum was an investigator for a law firm in Vancouver. He knew how to dig out information. Her hand drifted to her abdomen. She had to stay under his radar.

"That's all right," she said finally. "I'll come back when I have more time."

And she escaped into the night before the librarian could offer more help.

When she got back to the house on Hawk Street, she sat in the idling Volvo for long minutes, staring at the house. It looked exactly as she had left it. The porch light was on, as was the light over the side door. A light shone inside from the back of the house, where she had left the kitchen light on. It looked so peaceful. So inviting.

Most of the porch lights along the street were off, but there were lights on inside the houses. No one was outside, however. The temperature had dropped while she was at the library and the wind had risen. She could feel it buffeting the Volvo, as if trying to find a way in.

She shivered. She couldn't spend another night in the back seat. It was too cold, for one thing. And she wasn't a ten-year-old girl, for another.

She kept staring at the window in the front door, waiting for a figure to materialize. After ten minutes, she turned the engine off and got out of the car, dragging the backpack with her. The wind immediately caught at her braid, sending icy fingers down the back of her neck. She hunched her shoulders, then closed and locked the door before heading to the side door of the house.

She liked the house. She'd liked it from the first time she'd seen it.

It had looked... safe. A good place to stop running. A good place to hide from Calum.

Inside, she took her shoes off and left them by the door, and hung up her coat on one of the brass hooks. In stocking feet, she padded to the kitchen and stood there, listening to the silence. To-morrow, she would buy a radio.

Everything was as she had left it, including the dirty dishes in the sink. The savory smell of the stew still hung in the air.

She wandered past the stairs and left her backpack on the bottom step before going to the living room and turning the light on. There was no overhead light in this room and the light switch connected to the floor lamp in the corner by the fireplace. It cast a soft glow on the room and made it inviting. A roaring fire would make it even more inviting. Hadn't Maddie said something about providing a cord of wood...?

She'd ask her tomorrow.

Had there been an overhead light when the farmhouse was built and someone removed it in later renovations? Had there even been electricity when this house was first built? Her history was a bit fuzzy. She tried to picture what the furniture might have looked like in 1890. The ceiling height would have been the same but the rooms would have been smaller. Maybe the kitchen had been two rooms. Maddie had said that the laundry room was a later addi-tion. Had there been a wood stove to heat the house and cook?

Stop stalling.

Switching the living room light off, she returned to the kitchen, made sure the mud room door and the patio doors were locked, then checked the front door before turning the hallway light off and making her way upstairs. She glanced into the other three rooms and briefly toyed with the possibility of trying to sleep in one of them.

Finally, she turned away and headed for her bedroom. With her luck, any room she picked would be haunted by a different ghost.

Ten minutes later, she crawled into bed and pulled the blankets over top of herself. She lay there in the lamplight for long silent minutes, debating. Finally, she sat up in bed and, clutching the blankets to her chest, she spoke to the empty room.

"Look." She stopped, trying to marshal her thoughts. "Look," she started again. "Can we take a break tonight? Please? I'm very tired and I need some sleep." Would a ghost care? If it was a ghost and not her imagination?

Her extremely vivid imagination?

"This was probably your room," she said softly. "I'm sorry you're not alive anymore."

She thought of what else she might say, then finally gave up. With a sigh, she turned the light out. She lay back on the pillow, wide awake, and listened for the sound of crying in the night.

CHAPTER 9

The third time Charlotte caught Ash humming, she glanced significantly at her brother, who was eating his soup at the far end of the counter. Oblivious. Typical.

It had been a particularly busy lunch rush, and Charlotte had only just locked the door behind the last of their customers, half an hour later than usual. The restaurant looked like a hurricane had swept through it, leaving dirty dishes piled up in the plastic tub, tables still needing to be cleared, and the floor a mess of mud and leaves.

The day had dawned cold and crisp, but within a few hours, clouds had moved in, bringing with them a cold autumn rain. Max hated the cold and complained all winter long, but it was perfect weather for soup and sandwiches.

Despite the crush of people who had come in over the past four hours, Ash had remained cheerful and bright, moving efficiently from table to table, laughing with the customers, and even keeping a baby amused while his mother went to the washroom.

Charlotte had seen a number of male gazes lingering on her waitress as she waltzed by. Was that what had put the sparkle in the girl's eye? A man?

It wasn't that Ash was normally surly. She was always pleasant and efficient, but there was an aloofness to her that kept her customers at arms' length. And there was a watchfulness about her, as if she was always on guard.

Ash smiled as she passed by Charlotte, carrying a tub full of dirty dishes to the dishwasher in the back.

Charlotte had seen that watchfulness only once today, when Jake Slater, in his police uniform, came in to pick up his order— corned beef sandwich on rye, with a cup of pea soup. But as soon as he walked out, Ash smiled and relaxed.

That couldn't be good.

"What are you doing?"

Startled, Charlotte looked at her brother. She was about to say something when Ash came through the swinging door with the empty plastic tub.

Charlotte smiled at her brother and shrugged. "As soon as those tables are cleared, we need to wash the floor."

Max grunted and returned to his beef stroganoff. "What else is new?" he grumbled.

Ash laughed out loud and began to wash down the tables in preparation for flipping the chairs on top of them. Even Max stared at her as she hummed happily.

When she got back home, Ash stood on the back deck eating her pea soup and enjoying the view of the forest spreading before her, and beyond it, the city. The rain had finally cleared off leaving behind the smell of wet earth, composting leaves and, faintly, wood smoke. It was still pretty cold—she could see her breath—but she had a warm coat and hat on, and her bare fingers were wrapped around the large mug containing the soup. Clouds scuttled by, chasing another rainstorm probably, and the sun peeped through occasionally.

She still hadn't had a chance to explore the woods or do much raking. She'd found out from Charlotte about a good internet service provider and she'd found where the cable entered the house, so hopefully someone would come out in the next few days to hook her up. She still needed to buy a laptop, but maybe tomorrow she'd get a chance to shop.

She'd left everything behind when she ran. All her clothes, her computer, cell phone, her bank card and credit cards... anything that Calum could use to track her. For six months, she'd eluded him. As far as Mr. Caldwell, her lawyer, could tell, Calum still had no clue as to her whereabouts. She'd been careful.

But now... Now she wanted to stay put. Last night she had slept soundly, with no weeping, no tumbling down the stairs. When she'd woken up and realized she felt rested for the first time in a week, she'd whispered "thank you" to the empty room.

"Hello?"

Ash jumped, her hands clenching on the soup mug, and looked down at the lawn, where Maddie Bowen stood staring up at her. She wore black pants and her red plaid coat, but no hat or gloves. Even from the deck, Ash could see the woman's ears were red from the cold. She had an envelope in her hand.

"Hi," said Ash.

"I knocked," said Maddie, a little reproachfully. She was freezing her tail end off.

"Sorry," said Ash, with no hint of repentance in her voice. "I just got home. Come on up."

Maddie climbed up the stairs and followed Ash inside. The warmth found her ears and hands, and she shivered. Ash removed her shoes at the door and Maddie followed suit, wishing she had worn socks instead of pantyhose.

Ash went to the counter and filled the kettle with water. "Have a seat," she said over her shoulder.

"Thanks." Maddie shrugged out of her coat and hung it on the back of the nearest chair before sitting down. Thankfully, she had worn an angora wool sweater with a matching silk scarf, so she warmed up quickly. Except for her feet. "I pulled the ownership history of the house," she said as Ash puttered in the kitchen.

The girl looked much better today than she had yesterday. Or at any time, really. The dark circles weren't as pronounced today, and with her cheeks pink with the cold, she looked healthier. She didn't look quite as gaunt, either.

In the seven years Maddie had managed this property, she couldn't recall anyone ever looking better after moving in.

She pulled the printed sheets out of the white envelope with the Albans Realty logo and address in the upper left corner.

"Records from the 1800s are pretty thin," she began. "In fact, I don't have anything before 1952."

In the kitchen, Ash sighed softly.

Oblivious, Maddie read on. "Back then, this was all still farmland. After the war, the government bought most of it to build homes for returning soldiers. The farmhouse was already here, of course, on twenty acres. A John Priestley bought it. Then the records show it changing hands in 1969, to an Amos Priestley." She looked up as Ash brought the teapot over to the table, along with two cups.

"Amos was probably John's son," said Ash as she sat down.

Maddie shrugged. "Or brother, or nephew." She set the pages down and watched while Ash poured. The peppery smell of ginger tickled her nose as she pulled the mug toward her, wrapping her still-cold hands around it. It was definitely time to pull out her gloves.

"How long did Amos have it?" prompted Ash, pouring tea for herself.

"Let's see." Maddie traced the information down the page with her forefinger. "Here we are. In 1985 title was transferred to Theresa Bonnefoy."

Ash nodded and sipped from the tea. Everyone Maddie had listed so far had kept the farmhouse for years, sometimes decades. That didn't have to mean anything, of course. Just because they owned the place didn't mean they were able to live in it.

After all, the current owner didn't live in it.

"And then?" she said when Maddie didn't go on.

"Theresa Bonnefoy kept it until Frank Boudreaux bought the place, in 2006."

A cold draft whispered against the back of Ash's neck. She refused to shiver or turn around, refused to assign any meaning to it. This was an old house. There were bound to be drafts.

Still. Something in the way Maddie had spoken alerted Ash.

"Do you know Frank Boudreaux?" she asked.

"Yes, of course," said Maddie promptly. "I manage his property." Her hand fluttered as if to indicate the house, but quickly landed back on the mug's handle.

Ash stared at the woman in silence until Maddie sighed and looked at her.

"I went to high school with him."

Ash nodded, trying to understand Maddie's reluctance. She tried a teasing smile.

"Was he your sweetheart?"

"God, no."

Realizing the denial was a little vehement, Maddie looked up at Ash. "He wasn't my type." Still isn't. "Besides, he had a girlfriend from almost the minute he arrived at school."

A faint sob sounded from the bedroom upstairs and Ash stopped breathing. She glanced at Maddie, but the older woman clearly hadn't heard anything.

Ash sipped her tea, trying to ease the dryness from her mouth. "What was her name?" she asked finally.

Maddie blinked in surprise. "Frank's girlfriend?" At Ash's nod, she said, "Odette Wirth. She was in a few of my classes." Odette had been a pretty girl, small, blonde, with huge blue eyes. She'd been so timid, it had surprised Maddie that she ended up with Frank Boudreaux, who was big and loud and an ass. Her head tilted a little as she studied Maddie's face, which had gone white. "Why do you ask?"

Ash remained silent for a moment. "Did they end up married?

Or living together?"

Now Maddie's eyebrows rose in surprise. "They got married right out of high school."

"Are they still together?"

A shiver coursed its way up Maddie's spine. "No," she said slowly. "Odette left him a few years after they bought and renovated the house. He's remarried now." Or at least living with someone.

Before Ash could ask any more questions, the doorbell rang, startling them both. Ash's tea spilled on the battered pine table and she jumped up as if it had scalded her.

Maddie laughed, breaking the tension. "I'll wipe it up," she offered. "If you want to answer it...?"

Ash nodded jerkily and took a deep, calming breath. It was just the doorbell, for Pete's sake. She hadn't heard it yet, and it had surprised her. Wiping her suddenly damp hands on her jeans, she padded over to the hallway. The floor was pretty cold, she suddenly realized. She needed to ask Maddie about firewood.

She could see a dark figure through the glass panel of the front door but she didn't realize until she opened the door that it was a police officer, and worse, it was the police officer she had seen at Soup 'n Such earlier in the day.

He seemed as surprised to see her as she was to see him.

"Yes?" she asked politely. It was the only thing she could squeak out. Why was a police officer at her door? Had Calum sent him?

"Ma'am," said Jake Slater, gripping his regulation cap in his hands. He stared at the young woman in front of him, frowning. Where had he seen her before?

"Can I help you?" asked Ash. Her heart thumped loudly against her ribs and she was afraid that he would be able to hear it in the silence. Behind him, kids were playing street hockey and daylight was beginning to fail. It was later than she had thought.

Jake shook himself mentally. "Sorry," he said with a grin. "I'm

Sergeant Jake Slater of the Albans Police Depart—"

"Jake?"

He looked up to see Maddie walking down the hallway toward him. He'd known she was here, of course. He'd seen her car parked out front. It was the only reason he had dropped in.

"Hey, Maddie." He grinned at her. "I saw your car and thought I'd check in." He nodded at the new door handle and lock. "I see you changed the locks. Have you had any more issues?"

The young woman stared at him, her green eyes wide. If he didn't know better, he would think she was afraid. He looked to Maddie for help.

True to form, Maddie stepped into the breach.

"You'd better come in before my feet freeze off," she said, pulling Ash gently away from the door. With Jake inside and the door closed, she formally introduced them.

"Jake, this is Ash Gantry, the new tenant. Ash, this is my old friend, Jake Slater. He's the one I called when you saw the woman in here. He checked out the place."

Ash visibly swallowed, then gave him a shaky smile. "Thank you," she said. "No, I haven't had any more issues."

There was a moment of awkward silence, then Jake leaned down a little. "Miss Gantry, have we met? You look awfully familiar."

The blood left her face and for a moment, he thought she was going to pass out. He made a move to support her but she regained control of herself and shook her head.

"No, I don't think so."

Maddie glanced from Ash to Jake, not understanding what was going on. "Ash works at Soup 'n Such," she said. "You might have seen her there?"

Jake snapped his fingers and grinned. "That's it. Today. I saw you when I came to pick up my order."

She smiled back. "It was busy today. Sorry, I didn't notice."

Maddie's eyebrow rose but the other two didn't see. She doubted that Jake Slater in uniform could pass by any woman without being noticed.

"Well, I need to get going," said Jake. He fished a business card out of his jacket pocket and handed it to Ash. "If you have any concerns, feel free to call me."

Maddie almost rolled her eyes. When he talked like that, she always thought of those western movie heroes who punctuated all their sentences with "ma'am" before riding off on their horses.

Jake opened the door and stepped out onto the deck, placing the cap back on his head.

"I see you have Alberta plates on your car," he said casually, nodding at the Volvo in the driveway. "Don't forget you need to change your license and registration within three months of moving here."

With a final nod, he walked down the steps and onto the walk, heading for the patrol car.

Something was up with young Miss Gantry, he decided. Maybe he should look into her.

CHAPTER 10

The moment Ash got rid of Maddie, she put on her shoes and coat and drove to the nearest Staples where she planned to buy a laptop but was instead persuaded by the sales clerk—who couldn't have been older than sixteen—to buy a tablet. Then he spent an hour showing her how it worked.

"Try it out tonight," he said, handing it over to her in a bag.

"I don't have the Internet set up yet," she told the boy. Marcus, according to his name tag.

He shrugged. "Technically, you don't need it. Go to any coffee shop with WiFi."

Ash grinned at him. This, more than the cell phone or the car, made her feel like she was finally, truly, independent. Calum couldn't snoop through this tablet, or her calls, or check the mileage on her car.

This was hers.

Clutching the box to her chest, she left the store, bumping into an older guy in the doorway.

"Sorry," he said with a smile before disappearing inside.

She glanced over her shoulder at him. She was beginning to recognize faces around town. A lot of people came into Soup 'n Such. And then there was Barney's Gym. She'd even had a few people greet her when she was walking downtown.

Albans was beginning to feel like home.

The wind found a gap in her collar, prodding her to head for her car.

There were quite a few cars left in the parking lot, even though it was almost closing time. The Staples anchored a small mall that contained an Independent Grocers, a liquor store, and a small shawarma takeout restaurant. The restaurant and grocery store stayed open until nine o'clock every night, but the other stores closed at six.

Dried leaves swirled next to the curb, stirring an odd nostalgia in her. Fall had been Mom's favorite time of year. It always reminded her of new beginnings. Dad would just look at her as if she was crazy.

Smiling, Ash unlocked the car door, tossed the box with the tablet onto the passenger seat and the backpack on top of it, then slid in behind the wheel. She started the engine and pulled up the collar of her wool coat. She needed to keep a pair of gloves in the car.

As the Volvo's heater poured warmth into the car, she considered her options. She still had stew left over from last night. But... she really wanted to start researching, so it was either go home, eat, and head out to the library, or go to a coffee shop, order something to eat, and start figuring out how to research on her new tablet.

She grinned at herself in the rearview mirror and put her seatbelt on. Coffee shop it was.

The egg salad sandwich was definitely not up to Max's standards, but it filled Ash's hunger and the coffee wasn't bad.

She'd found a seat in the corner, by the fake stone fireplace and facing the plate glass window that gave onto Main Street. Albans Beans was maybe six blocks from Soup 'n Such, in a cluster of small shops that sold everything from hats to fishing tackle.

The place smelled of roasted coffee and baked cookies. There were only three other customers in the coffee shop and one left before she even got her coffee. The chair was plush and comfortable and no one bothered her as she tried to remember the store clerk's instructions. She poked and slid a finger along the screen, baffled by some of the icons that popped up, but eventually she found the keyboard and ended up on Google.

Fingers hovering over the virtual keyboard, she tried to marshal her thoughts.

Maddie had said that Frank Boudreaux was the current owner, and had been for ten years. As she thought about him, she shivered, remembering the cold touch of a draft on the back of her neck. Some perverse urge made her ignore her instincts, however, and she decided to start with the previous owner, Theresa Bonnefoy, who had owned it from 1985 to 2006.

A search for her name brought up too many links, so she added "Albans" to the search parameters. That immediately narrowed it down to a hundred or so. Images popped up among the links and she surfed through them, eventually finding one that identified a plump, older woman with fly-away white hair and blue eyes as "Albans Artist Theresa Bonnefoy." A click on the link led her to an Ottawa gallery website.

The pictures on the website depicted bold, geometric shapes in deep, rich colors. Definitely not to Ash's taste, but appealing. A short bio of the woman said that she had become an artist late in life, after teaching high school for thirty years.

Suddenly she remembered the painting that hung in the living room. It depicted the town of Albans as seen from the back deck of the farmhouse, with the forest in the foreground. Maybe Theresa had painted it?

But why would she have left the painting behind when she sold the house?

Ash kept exploring and eventually found the answer. Theresa Bonnefoy had died in 2006. Ash studied the photo of the artist.

She couldn't be the one haunting the farmhouse. The ghost was much younger.

She opened another search page and typed in "Odette Boudreaux" and "Albans." To her surprise, the search engine didn't come up with any hits. She set the pad down and sipped from her coffee. It was almost impossible to believe that anyone today would have no presence on the web. Unless she was a hermit.

She shifted in her chair and put the coffee down. Maybe Odette Boudreaux had been in hiding, just like her. After all, Ash wasn't the name she had used most of her life. Mom and Dad had named her Elizabeth Bourne. She'd gone by Beth all her life. Ashley had been Grandma's name, and when Ash decided to run, that was the name she chose. She hadn't dared keep Stevenson, or Bourne. Calum was sure to look for her under a number of names connected to her family. Instead she picked the name of a street that she came across in a small town outside Calgary: Gantry.

Mr. Caldwell had helped her legally change her name, working with the Registrar of British Columbia and the federal government to provide her with a new identity, driver's license, and health care card, none of which could be traced back to her original name, Elizabeth Stevenson.

There was no way for Calum to discover her new name.

She stared at the screen. Odette Boudreaux had been married to Frank Boudreaux. Maybe she had a web presence under her maiden name.

Ash pulled the backpack onto her lap and rummaged through it, looking for the envelope Maddie had left with her. When her fingers didn't come across the familiar hard shape of her phone, she looked more closely. Had she lost the phone?

Then she remembered. She'd left it to recharge on her kitchen counter.

It wasn't as if anyone would be calling her.

She pulled out Maddie's envelope and took the sheets out. The information had to be on the last page. She scanned through it but, to her disappointment, Odette wasn't even listed on the paper.

She leaned against the tall back of the chair, discouraged. Had Maddie mentioned Odette's last name? She tried her mother's old trick of going through all the letters of the alphabet and assigning a name that started with that letter. It often nudged the name right to the surface.

Closing her eyes, she began with Adams, Bastion, Chalmers. She was all the way to Sorenson when the right name popped into her head.

Wirth. Maddie had called her Odette Wirth.

She typed the name into the search engine. Odette Wirth had been part of the volleyball team at St. Vital High School, and she'd been pretty good. Ash scanned old sports reports and old newspaper photographs that were too grainy to make out any faces.

Then she found the St. Vital High School yearbook page and smiled in triumph.

The baristas started wiping down the tables near Ash and she looked around in surprise. She was the only one left in the coffee shop. She glanced at her watch. Almost nine o'clock. How had that happened?

She hesitated. She desperately wanted to dig deeper into Odette's life, and it looked like the yearbooks were her best lead, but she would have to explore several years' worth of them before she found the right year for Odette. She would need more time than she had available.

Damn.

With a sigh, she powered the tablet down and put it and Maddie's envelope away in her backpack. Now she would have to wait until tomorrow after work. Maybe the library kept a collection of the yearbooks.

She shrugged into her coat and slung the pack over her left shoulder.

"Goodnight," said the barista. Ash smiled and let herself out.

◊◊◊

It didn't surprise her when the soft weeping woke her up at three-forty-three. She lay in bed, listening to the crying, and for the first time, she felt tears rising up in her own eyes.

"Shhh," she whispered, longing to give comfort. "Shhh... It's going to be all right."

The crying stopped. Ash held her breath, waiting to hear the terrible sound of someone falling down the stairs. The silence pressed around her ears and down on her chest.

Was it over? Was that all the ghost needed?

The air suddenly stirred around her and her heart stuttered in alarm.

Whatever—whoever—had been crying by the dresser was now keenly aware of her, as if a vast gulf had just been crossed.

Ash shuddered. Then a cool draft wafted over her cheek and was gone. She was alone again.

CHAPTER 11

Jake pushed back from his desk and stood up to stretch. His office at the Albans Police Department was small, barely big enough for his desk and chair, a filing cabinet, and a chair for guests. But it had a window that opened onto McGinty Park and he could close the door. Not that he ever did.

He'd spent most of the morning sitting on his butt and now he needed to move before it started growing into the chair. He was ready for another cup of coffee, if someone had made a new pot. That last one had been left over from the night shift and his wife could probably have used it as nail polish remover.

Chief Kapinski stuck his head in. "You got those reports for me?"

Kapinski was crowding sixty, but looked closer to fifty. He had come to Albans after a solid career in the military police and made a point of keeping himself fit. He and Jake often played handball and sometimes even ran together. Jake was faster but they were even in staying power.

"I just sent them to you," said Jake, nodding at his computer screen. If he'd known how much paperwork was involved in going up the ranks, he would have seriously reconsidered accepting the promotion to sergeant. He loved the day-to-day work of the patrol officer, and sometimes he wondered if he was wasting himself in what was more often than not a desk job.

But he was a good detective, with a nose for the hinky. Now he had the resources to investigate the hinky, and there was definitely something hinky about Miss Ash Gantry. He just couldn't put his finger on what. It had been bothering him since he met her yesterday.

"Anything the matter?" asked Kapinski, stepping into the office and bringing a waft of his aftershave with him. Jake was pretty sure it was Old Spice. Behind the chief, the sound of phones ringing punctuated the hum of the duty room.

Kapinski's navy uniform trousers were pressed to a knife edge and his long-sleeved, pale blue shirt looked like it had just returned from the dry cleaners. Jake always wanted to check the shine on his boots when Kapinski was around.

He was a good boss and a good police chief. For a moment, Jake considered confiding in him, then decided against it. He liked Kapinski, but the guy was by-the-book. He didn't much care why a person broke the law, only that they did. "Let the courts figure it out," was his motto. And he wouldn't approve of Jake wasting time and resources on a gut feeling... not when the department's budget was up for review with city council next month.

What Kapinski didn't know, he couldn't forbid.

"I think my butt is numb," he said and Kapinski laughed.

Jake didn't know if Ash Gantry was in trouble with the law, but he was willing to bet a month's pay that she was in some kind of trouble.

It was her eyes. Something about the wariness in her eyes reminded him of Odette Boudreaux.

It had rained overnight, but morning had dawned cold and clear, and now the sidewalks gleamed wetly in the sun. It wasn't nearly as warm out as it looked, judging by the number of people who had walked into Soup 'n Such rubbing their hands for warmth. Still, the cold meant good business and Ash's four-hour shift flew by.

When only a few people remained at the tables, and Max sat at the counter eating chicken stew with dumplings, Ash and Charlotte began clearing up.

Ash was placing the dirty dishes from table three onto her tray when something made her look up. She squinted into the glare from the window. Cars and trucks passed by on Main Street. She could hear the hissing of the tires even through the picture window. Pedestrians hurried past, hands deep in their pockets, ears red. She scanned the scene for a few seconds and was just about to go back to work when a figure standing across the street caught her eye.

He—definitely a man—stood in front of Dave's Art Supplies, leaning against the streetlight. His face was turned away, as if he was waiting for someone to come down the sidewalk. He wore jeans and a heavy Carhartt jacket, like so many of the workers who came into Soup 'n Such. Something about the way he stood bothered her.

"Everything all right?"

She jumped and turned toward Max. She hadn't heard him come up behind her.

"Sure," she said, smiling. She glanced back at the street but the man was gone. Probably whoever he was waiting for had shown up. Or maybe he'd been waiting for a lift. "Just a little distracted," she added.

He patted her shoulder and returned to his chicken stew and Ash finished clearing off. She glanced surreptitiously out the window every once in a while, but didn't see the figure again. Something about the man had her on edge, but it could be the night she'd had making her nervous.

She had spent the rest of the night huddled under the blankets, trying to understand what had happened. It had been unsettling to realize that the ghost was focused on her, but she'd known about the ghost from her first night in the house. The difference was that the ghost hadn't seemed aware of Ash, not until Ash tried to console her. But even then, the ghost had done nothing to frighten Ash. Not really.

The night before, she'd even let Ash sleep through the night.

Or, maybe, Ash had been so exhausted that the crying hadn't woken her.

The ghost had even materialized a couple of times. She'd stared right at Ash, first through the front door window, then from the other side of the French doors in the dining room.

The ghost had seen Ash then, so what was so different this time?

She carried the laden tray back to the kitchen and piled the dirty dishes next to the dishwasher, in preparation for scraping into the compost bin.

As she worked, her thoughts chased each other. She'd seen the ghost, yes. And even, sometimes, she'd thought the ghost had looked at her. But what if she hadn't? What if the ghost had been going through actions she had done while she was alive? Actions that had imprinted on her?

Ash had never felt as if the ghost was trying to connect with her. It was as if the ghost would have taken the same actions whether or not Ash was present, like a movie playing in an empty room.

But last night...

Last night, for the first time, she had felt the ghost's awareness of her.

Water splashed over her hand as the water glass shook in her unsteady grasp. She put it down and gripped the front of the sink to steady herself.

Last night, the ghost had come to stand over her as she lay in bed. Ash had felt a sense of otherness, of being the object of the ghost's attention.

Was it because she had shown sympathy? By trying to comfort

it, had she somehow connected with it?

"What's the matter, Ash?" asked Charlotte, walking into the kitchen with the plastic basin full of dirty dishes. "You're skittish today."

Ash took a deep breath. Pull yourself together, she ordered herself firmly.

"I missed my workout this morning," she said with a smile. "It usually keeps me centered."

And she had missed it. She'd been so exhausted she'd fallen asleep as first light began to creep into her room. She'd barely made it to work on time.

"Well, we've got this under control," said Charlotte as she began to rinse the dirty dishes. "You can take off a little early if you like."

Ash glanced at the big clock on the back wall by the door to the alley. It was quarter to two. Only fifteen minutes shy of quitting time. "I can stick it out a few more minutes," she said with a smile. "Thanks."

◊◊◊

"You're short," said Paul, "but that doesn't have to be a disadvantage."

Ash nodded, still breathing hard from their session. She'd called him on her way home and he'd agreed to meet her at Barney's Gym after he finished work. So far, she'd landed on her bum more often than on her hip, and even though she was putting weight on, she could still feel her bones much too close to the surface. Paul had been trying to teach her how to break a fall by spreading the impact on her hip, leg and arm, but so far all she'd managed to do was wind herself and give herself a nice little collection of bruises. So he decided to teach her how to flip a bigger opponent.

The gym was starting to fill up as people came in for a workout after work. Barney was in the office, arguing with a contractor over the cost of replacing the roof. To Ash's surprise, a couple of women had shown up fifteen minutes earlier and set up in the boxing ring.

"Flipping is never your first choice," continued Paul. He wore a faded gray tee-shirt with some kind of insignia on the front and a pair of green sweatpants.

Ash nodded again. First choice was always to avoid a confrontation. Second was to walk away, if she could. If she couldn't, engage with everything she had.

She swallowed. That was the part she had trouble with. Going from maybe to attack.

"And that hair of yours," said Paul, eyeing her French braid critically. "It's like giving your opponent a handle."

She nodded. Barney had pointed out her hair, too, but she resisted getting it cut. Calum had never once used it against her.

Paul had taught her a few moves—how to get out of a choke hold, how to flip an attacker who came at her from behind, how to turn the attacker's longer reach to her advantage. It all seemed easy when she was practicing in the gym.

But if Calum were to show up?

"And if he gets you in a clinch," said Paul, oblivious to her doubts, "this won't work. You have to have room to maneuver. Okay?" At her nod, he said, "All right, try it."

He reached for her and she automatically stepped into his reach, turning a little sideways. She grabbed his shirt and thrust her hip behind his and shoved him off balance. He struggled to regain his balance, his arms windmilling, and she swept her leg behind his. He twisted as he fell to land on his side, his hand slapping the mat. At once he sprang back up, smiling at her.

"That was pretty good," he said. "But you telegraphed your intentions. Now, let's try it again, but this time, look scared."

In spite of herself, Ash grinned.

◊ ◊ ◊

The exercise had done her good, just as she'd known it would. By six o'clock, she was at the library. She'd eaten lunch late—some of Max's wonderful chicken stew—and she wasn't hungry.

The older librarian was there, busy with a patron, so Ash

asked the young man who was working at the desk if the library kept yearbooks of the local high schools.

Fifteen minutes later, to her surprise, she was upstairs, seated at a big oak table, with a pile of thin, hard-covered St. Vital High School yearbooks stacked up next to her. The last time she'd been at the library, the second floor had been closed, but tonight, the downstairs tables were fully occupied, so maybe they decided to open the second floor.

The room felt cozy, in spite of its size, and it smelled of furniture polish. A wall of glass separated the main section, with its five tables and hard oak chairs, from the archives. The lights on that side of the glass were off, and the glass reflected the main reference stacks back to her. Two people sat at the farthest table, a middle-aged woman with an elderly man. They were poring over a book and scribbling on a notepad.

There were three high schools in Albans but last night's search in the coffee shop had told her that Odette had gone to St. Vital High School. She figured Maddie Bowen had graduated twenty years ago, give or take a few years, so she had asked for the yearbooks for five years on either side.

Yearbooks showed individual pictures of each student, and she wanted to get a good look at Odette.

She pulled the first book toward her. It had a forest green cover and a gold crest stamped on the front under the name of the high school and the year. She started to flip through it.

This was probably a pointless exercise anyway. The ghost probably had nothing to do with Frank Boudreaux, the owner of the house. But he had renovated the place, and she couldn't imagine anyone doing that unless they planned to keep living there. The renovations were too... personal. Someone had given a lot of thought to what tiles to put in the backsplash, what color to paint the living room, what type of table to use in the dining room. It was personal. The person whose personality was reflected in the house had planned to live there.

Over the next half hour, Ash flipped through one yearbook after another, peering at all the young faces until they blurred in front of her tired eyes.

The head librarian wandered by at one point, clearly curious about what Ash was doing, but she didn't say anything, only nodded as she walked by.

Almost an hour into her search, in the sixth yearbook, a face suddenly leaped out at her.

The picture was that of a young woman with thick blonde hair pulled up in a ponytail, and bangs covering her forehead. Her eyes were dark blue and she had full lips and a straight nose.

Ash stared at the young, happy face, and chills chased each other up her arms.

This was her ghost.

Oh, her ghost was older, but there was no mistaking those eyes.

Her gaze dropped to the caption under the photo. Odette Wirth.

Her ghost was Odette. It had to be the same Odette who had married Frank Boudreaux.

Ash stared blankly at the photograph for a full minute before her next course of action occurred to her. She grabbed the yearbook for the previous year and quickly flipped through it, looking for a picture of Frank Boudreaux. He most likely was older than Odette and would have graduated before her. Ash had been looking for female faces, not male ones. She still didn't find it but now that she was paying attention, she found a small paragraph at the bottom of the last page of photographs: Missing from the photos: Abel Carter, Amanda Dandignon, Joel and Elizabeth Baxter, and Frank Boudreaux.

Disappointment stabbed through her. Then she shook her head at herself. It didn't matter. She had confirmation of what Odette looked like, and confirmation of who her ghost was.

And then it hit her. That meant Odette was dead. She had to be.

And Maddie didn't know. Did that mean that no one knew? Was that why Odette was haunting the house?

A young woman came up the stairs, carrying a small backpack slung over one shoulder. She had black curly hair that rioted all over her head and brown eyes under a sweep of eyebrows. Her features were more arresting than classically beautiful, and Ash blinked when she realized she'd been staring. She smiled apologetically at the girl and got a grin in return.

The girl found a table at the far end of the room and pulled out a laptop from her backpack.

Ash called herself a fool and immediately pulled out her tablet. She punched in Odette Wirth's name into Google and was rewarded with over a thousand hits. She added "Albans" into the search parameters and the number reduced to just over one hundred.

With a sigh, she started sifting through them again. If she'd been smart last night, she would have flagged the pages with Odette's pictures.

Odette had been a volleyball player in high school and there were photos of her with her team in the Albans Daily Sun write-ups of her winning the point for her team in regional championships. There was one of her holding up a trophy, surrounded by her teammates, grinning. She was shorter than her teammates, so maybe five feet four? Five feet three? Wasn't that short for someone playing volleyball? Ash had never played. Her high school had been into basketball, where height was a definite advantage.

"Are you finding what you need?"

Ash jumped and turned in her seat to find the older librarian standing next to her.

"Yes, thanks," she replied automatically. She realized she was clutching the tablet to her chest and forced herself to relax.

"Anything I can help you with?" The librarian's eyes were alight with curiosity and friendliness, but Ash suddenly felt wary.

"Thanks," she replied, "but I have to go." She turned the tablet off and stuck it in her backpack. The librarian took a step back when Ash stood up.

"So you're done with these?" she asked, waving a hand at the yearbooks sprawled over the table. Her gaze lingered on the last one Ash had been reading.

Ash reached over and flipped the book closed, then piled the books together.

"Yes, thank you." She didn't know why she didn't want the woman to know what she'd been looking for, but she didn't. She practically ran out of the library, only to stop when she hit a wall of rain and wind outside the door. Night had settled in while she was inside and the wind and damp crawled under her coat to lay clammy hands on her flesh.

Shivering, she hurried to where she had parked the Volvo, glancing at the back seat out of habit to make sure it was empty before dropping the backpack into the passenger seat. She unlocked the door, slid in behind the wheel and started the engine, waiting and shivering for the heat to come on.

What now? Odette was dead and haunting Ash's house. Judging by Maddie's reactions, other people had seen Odette, too, or they wouldn't have wanted to get out of the lease.

Had Maddie given her any details about Odette? She'd mentioned something about the house being for rent for a few years—how long, exactly?

The information just wouldn't come. She was tired and hungry, and reluctant to return home. For the first time, she wondered where Charlotte and Max lived. Were they married? If so, they probably lived in different homes with their respective families.

A wave of longing swept over her as she sat in the Volvo, and she leaned her head against the steering wheel, helpless to keep the tears at bay.

She'd had a family once. It was just her and Mom and Dad, and Grandma, but they'd been close, and happy.

Dad had liked Calum, had invited him for dinner a few times, but Mom had had reservations about him. Grandma never met Calum while Mom and Dad were alive, since she lived in Saskatoon, but Ash had told her all about him. She had sensed the same reservations in Grandma that Mom had had, and had resented them.

Then Mom and Dad died in the car crash, and after a while Grandma had to go back home. But Calum had been there.

Calum had always been there, solicitous. Caring. Loving. And Ash had so needed to be loved...

She sighed and sat up straight, digging through her coat pockets for a tissue. What use was there in crying?

She had parked on a side street, facing Main Street, and for a while she sat watching as cars drove by, splashing through puddles and spraying water in their wake. The Volvo was beginning to warm up, but the windows were fogging up thanks to the humidity from her breathing.

The air filtering into the car smelled of wet pavement and spilled oil. There was a faint waft of coffee from somewhere nearby, and the unmistakable smell of pizza.

Her stomach growled in response and she sighed. All right. She had more of Max's chicken stew waiting for her at home, but she decided to save it for tomorrow. She'd get something to eat—something warm—and she'd make a list of what she knew and what she still needed to know. Then tomorrow she'd go see Maddie again.

◊◊◊

She found the source of the heavenly smell—Angelo's Pizzeria—and sat at a table near the kitchen while they cooked her pizza. To her surprise, Angelo's had WiFi. In the hubbub of the busy kitchen and among the tables filled with couples and families eating a quick meal before heading to soccer, or home or even back to work, she sat back and stared at the screen of her tablet, trying to decide what she would search for next.

Finally, she typed "Frank Boudreaux" into the search box and then, on reflection, added "Albans."

As the smells from the kitchen did their best to distract her, Ash scrolled down the page, looking for a likely link. The first few brought her to Albany, New York and Alban Boudreaux in New Brunswick. The third link took her to Boudreaux Contracting.

She scrolled down the page looking at photo after photo of houses. Frank Boudreaux built houses, apparently. She went to the "About" section of the site and found herself staring at a head shot of a man in his forties with dark, crew-cut hair sprinkled with gray, and dark eyes. He was handsome enough in a lean, tanned way, but the smile that showed off his even white teeth didn't go anywhere near his eyes. He wore a blue shirt, open at the collar.

She looked at his eyes again, frowning. Had she seen that face before? She immediately thought back to the stranger she had seen across the street earlier that day, but she didn't think it was the same man, although really, that man had been quite a ways away.

"Miss, your order is ready," said the young waiter, sliding the pizza box onto the table in front of her.

Ash smiled up at him and put her tablet away. Time to go home and eat.

Even though she really didn't know if she wanted to go back to that house.

Even as she thought it, she felt an unfamiliar stubbornness rising up. It was her house, for now anyway. She liked the house and she liked Albans. She would figure out what was up with the ghost and lay it to rest, or whatever it was one did with ghosts.

She wasn't ready to run again.

◊ ◊ ◊

"Look," said Ash, standing in the middle of her bedroom. She wore long pj bottoms and a long-sleeved tee-shirt that she had decided would be warmer than her regular tee-shirt.

She turned in a circle, but the room looked like an ordinary bedroom.

"Odette," she said softly, feeling her skin creep up. She was addressing a ghost. Either she was crazy, or the world was an even stranger place than she had believed.

"I know you're dead. I know you want me to do something for you."

At least, she hoped that was what Odette wanted. What was left of a person after they passed? It was possible only the best or the worst of them remained. But why stay behind at all? They couldn't all stay behind when they died–the world would be over-run by ghosts. So, was it true that only the ones with unfinished business stayed behind? If so, what was Odette's unfinished business?

Her throat tightened and her eyes prickled with unshed tears. She wrapped her arms around herself and glanced around the bedroom. She loved this house. Loved its creaks and its quirks. Loved the street it was on and the town it was in.

She didn't want to leave—again—but she couldn't live like this. Her hand strayed to her belly. It could have been so different. If Calum had been a different man...

She sighed and rubbed her eyes. Pointless, pointless, point-less.

Something cool feathered against her cheek and she whirled, her heartbeat spiking in alarm.

Nothing.

"What do you want?" she shouted into the empty room. She slammed her teeth shut on the words that wanted to spill out be-cause she didn't know if they would be words of entreaty or defi-ance.

Either way, they would be the wrong ones.

She didn't know who Odette was, except the now-dead wife of Frank Boudreaux. Ash was assuming that the ghost wanted her to do something, but for all she knew, Odette Boudreaux had been a mean woman in life and was now carrying this through in death.

She looked down at her bare feet and took a deep, steadying breath. She needed to find out who Odette had been in life, but that would have to wait until tomorrow. Right now, she had to get through the night.

"Odette," she said softly, "I think you want my help. I'm trying to figure out what happened to you and help you. But you have to do something for me, too. You have to stop coming to me at night."

Otherwise, I'll have to leave and you'll have to start over with someone else.

But maybe that was what Odette wanted.

CHAPTER 12

Maddie Bowen was out at a showing when Ash showed up at Albans Realty, so Ash accepted a cup of coffee from the receptionist and sat down to wait. It was two thirty and she was hungry. She'd hoped to come before her shift, but the cable guy had shown up just when she got back from her workout and by the time he finished, she'd barely had time to shower and change before she had to leave for work.

But now she had access to the Internet from home. She might even get a television.

If she decided to stay.

The chairs in the waiting room faced the picture window and the view of the river. The sky was an aching blue and the few clouds reflected in the river as if posing for a postcard.

It was even a little warmer than it had been. It was only September, after all, even though it was marching quickly toward October.

Ash sipped—the coffee even smelled insipid—and enjoyed the view. She had slept, thank goodness. No visits in the night, no strange noises. She'd awakened feeling rested, but aware that she'd had strange dreams, although she couldn't remember any of them.

A man pushed through the front door, calling, "Hey, Olivia, any messages?" before noticing Ash.

"Oh, hello," he said with a smile. His glance took in her jeans, her red crew neck sweater, and her hiking boots. He looked at the backpack on the chair next to her, then at her braid before coming back to her eyes. Ash felt assessed and dismissed in the same glance.

"Who are you waiting for?" he asked.

Before Ash could answer, the receptionist spoke without looking up.

"This is Ash Gantry," she said. "She's renting the Boudreaux place. She's here to see Maddie."

Well. Wasn't that a lot of information to share.

The man's eyes suddenly narrowed and Ash had a feeling that he wanted to take a step back.

"Well, I'll leave you to it, then," he said and started to turn away.

"And what's your name?" asked Ash. He so clearly wanted to be shut of her that she perversely wanted to force him to stay. Besides, he needed a lesson in manners.

"Oh!" He blushed. Actually blushed. "I'm sorry," he said. He stepped toward her, his hand outstretched. "Dave Maddison. I own Albans Realty with Maddie."

Ash stood up to shake his hand. She was a little shocked at herself, but pleased. Six months ago, she would never have done that, called someone on their rudeness.

He was an older man, older than Maddie, probably. He wore jeans and a white shirt and a dark blue Gore-Tex jacket. He still had all his hair, but it was pretty gray.

"Maddie is on her way in," said the receptionist and he took that as his cue to disappear inside his office. Ash sat down again. She should have eaten before coming over.

The place smelled of old burnt coffee and wet soil. Probably the plants had just been watered. The floor in the waiting room was some kind of laminate while the offices were carpeted.

Five minutes later, Maddie waltzed into the office, pink-cheeked and windblown. Ash automatically glanced out the window. Sure enough, the trees along the river were leaning toward the water, leaves fluttering like an audience applauding.

"Ash!" said Maddie, catching sight of her. Then her expression tightened. "Is everything all right?"

Ash stood up and smiled reassuringly. "Yes, of course. I just had a few questions for you."

Maddie hesitated a moment longer, then nodded Ash into her office. She dropped the leather-bound portfolio she was carrying onto her glass desk, then shrugged out of her red coat and hung it up on a coat tree by the door.

"Have a seat," she said, indicating the chairs in front of her desk. She plopped down on her own chair and ran her fingers through her loose hair, trying to put some order into it. She relaxed a little and leaned on her elbows, lacing her fingers under her chin.

"What can I do for you?" she asked.

Ash licked her lips, suddenly unsure of how to go about this. Maddie knew she was interested in the history of the Boudreaux house—maybe that was the way into the conversation. The phone rang in the reception area and the secretary answered. Fresh air seemed to swirl around Maddie, as if she'd brought it in with her.

"I'm still doing a little research on the house," said Ash, feeling her way into the topic. "I would love to talk to Mr. Boudreaux, or his wife, Odette. His former wife, I guess."

Maddie's eyebrows rose in surprise and she sat back in her chair. This young woman was a source of constant surprise. Why on earth did she want to talk to Frank? And Odette?

"Well, you certainly don't need my permission to talk to Frank," she said slowly. "If his phone number isn't in the phone book, I'm sure you can contact him through his company name, Boudreaux Contracting. I don't know how to get hold of Odette, however. I haven't seen her since she left."

She never left, thought Ash.

"What about her family?" she asked.

Maddie shook her head. "Her mom died when she was young and her dad died the year she graduated high school. Her only living relative is an aunt, who took her in when her dad died. She moved to Edmonton when Odette married Frank."

The color drained from Ash's face and she looked down at her knees. Odette Wirth had had no one to look out for her. *Just like me.*

"The aunt might still be in touch with Odette," added Maddie quickly, seeing Ash's reaction.

"What's—?" Ash cleared her suddenly dry throat. "What's her name?"

Maddie thought hard for a moment, trying to dredge the name up from the depths of her memory. "Lily? Lisa?" She stood up suddenly, startling Ash. "Hang on just a sec." She left the office and went to talk to the secretary at the reception desk. They conferred for a few minutes, then the secretary typed into her computer and they studied the information on the screen. Finally, Maddie returned to her desk and sat down.

"Liesel Wirth," she said triumphantly. "She was Odette's aunt on her father's side."

"Liesel Wirth," repeated Ash, planting the name firmly in her mind. Edmonton. She would see what she could find out. She picked up her backpack from the chair next to hers and prepared to stand up. "I have an email address," she said, suddenly remembering.

Maddie blinked, then grabbed a pen and pulled one of the Albans Realty notepads toward her. "Okay."

"It's gantry332@gmail.com. No capitals."

Maddie nodded. "Got it. Will you be getting a telephone?"

Ash smiled and stood up. "I'll let you know if I do." That reminded her. She should call Mr. Caldwell for an update. He had promised to keep track of Calum. "Thanks, Maddie," she said as she made her way to the door. Maddie stood up and walked toward her, almost bumping into Ash when she stopped suddenly. Ash turned to face her.

"You said Odette was in a few of your classes… what was she like?"

The two of them stood less than a foot apart and Ash could smell the faint perfume of Maddie's shampoo. The older woman stared back at her, her blue eyes a little bloodshot. Finally, she sighed softly.

"She was a sweet girl. Kind. A gentle soul." No one who should ever have ended up with the likes of Frank Boudreaux. At least she'd gotten away from him. Wherever she was, Maddie hoped she was happy. "Pretty, too," she added as an afterthought. "Not much taller than you, with blue eyes and hair that really looked like gold. She was the real deal."

Ash waited to see if Maddie had anything else to add, then nodded her thanks and left.

◊ ◊ ◊

By four thirty, Ash had filled three big garbage bags full of leaves and she had only raked half of the front lawn. She straightened from tying off the last bag and groaned. In spite of her daily workouts, the raking was making itself felt in her lower back.

She stretched her back out and took a deep breath of the sharp air. Wood smoke. Grandma always had a wood stove in her house. It was one of Ash's earliest memories—walking up the long driveway to Grandma's house, holding Mom's and Dad's hands, and smelling the wood smoke.

It was almost time to go inside. The sky to the east was as purple as a bruise, and while the western sky still held some hints of pink and orange, the light was fading fast. Besides, her hands were cold. She was definitely going to need heavier gloves.

"Well, you've lasted longer than most."

Ash turned to squint in the fading light. A woman stood on her driveway, not ten feet away.

"What do you mean?" asked Ash uncertainly. She glanced at the street but there was no car parked in front of her house. The woman had walked here.

She was old, maybe in her sixties, and she wore a heavy blue coat, thick woolen gloves, and a scarf wrapped around her neck. The scarf looked like it was hand knitted. She was carrying something flat and round. She shrugged.

"Usually they stay a few days, maybe a week. Not many have stayed as long as you have. None, actually."

Leaving the bags full of leaves behind, Ash walked over to the woman.

"Why?"

Again the shrug. She looked directly at Ash, as if trying to gauge her mettle. "Who knows?" she said. "But since it looks like you're going to stick around," said the woman, "I thought I'd bring you a welcome gift." She pushed the package she was holding into Ash's hands. It was a plastic container and it felt warm to the touch. Ash opened the lid to find muffins inside. The smell of blueberries wafted up to her.

"Thank you," she said. For a moment, she couldn't think of anything else to say, she was so touched. Then she remembered her manners.

"My name is Ash Gantry," she said, holding out her hand. The woman took it in her own gloved hand and they shook.

"I'm Beatrice Stratford," she said. "I'm your next door neighbor." She hooked a thumb over her shoulder at the house downslope from Ash's.

"Nice to meet you, Mrs. Stratford."

"Beatrice," corrected the older woman. "Bea."

"Bea," repeated Ash with a smile. "Please call me Ash. Would you like to come in for some tea? We could enjoy your muffins."

But Bea Stratford was shaking her head. "No, thank you, dear." She glanced up at the windows on the second floor. Her eyes were brown or dark blue, it was hard to tell in the gloaming, but her white hair, cut below her chin with a fringe of short bangs, seemed to capture whatever light there was and shine. "I have to get back home. Why don't you come by tomorrow for dinner? Say, around six o'clock?"

Emotions suddenly flooded Ash, robbing her of words. She nodded and smiled, and Beatrice Stratford, who reminded Ash of her grandmother and a time in her life when she'd been happy, patted her hand and left.

Ash watched the older woman cut across the driveway and carefully pick her way down the knoll to the small rancher next door. When Bea turned to wave, Ash waved back. Then Bea disappeared inside the house, and Ash turned back to her own home, clutching the plastic container of muffins.

A movement drew her eye and her gaze went to the upstairs bedroom window, where a pale, translucent figure stared down at her.

Inside, she made herself a cup of ginger peach tea and headed for the living room where she lit a small fire in the fireplace. The logs had been delivered earlier in the week and she'd spent a happy hour stacking a pile of them on the deck, within easy reach of the French doors.

The dry logs caught right away, crackling and smoking before she remembered to open the damper. She set the screen in front of the opening and sat down on the sofa across from the fireplace. She was hungry and would have to eat something soon, but first she wanted to call Mr. Caldwell, Grandma's lawyer. Well, her own lawyer, really. From her back pocket, she pulled out the phone he had given her before she left Vancouver. When she turned it on, she saw that he had been trying to reach her for a week.

That couldn't be good.

It rang three times before being picked up. As usual, he didn't say anything, but she could hear him breathing at the other end. She reminded herself to use the name her knew her by, her married name.

"Hello, Mr. Caldwell. It's Elizabeth Stevenson."

There was a sharp intake of breath at the other end of the line, and Ash heard his chair squeak as the lawyer stood up to close the door to his office. She wrapped her free hand around the mug of tea, hoping at least part of her would warm up.

"Ms. Stevenson," he said finally, keeping his voice low. Every time she checked in with him, she imagined him glancing furtively out the window of his tenth floor office in downtown Vancouver to make sure he wasn't being overheard. It was almost six o'clock in Albans, which made it three o'clock in the afternoon, Vancouver time.

"Are you all right, my dear?"

Ash blinked at the painting of Albans in the living room, dismayed at how he had couched his question. As if he had a reason to worry that she might not be all right.

"Yes," she said calmly, refusing to get rattled. "Has something happened?"

"I've been hoping you would call," he said. The chair squeaked again as he sat down. Mr. Caldwell was a small, dapper man who wore tailored suits and shoes that dazzled in the sunlight. The few times she had met with him, he had been clean-shaven and his thinning gray hair had been freshly trimmed. She thought he was younger than Grandma, but he had an old-fashioned courtesy about him that made her wonder. She could never imagine him anywhere but behind his big desk, in his office building.

"Is anything wrong?" she asked.

"I'm not sure," he said at once, and her heart sank. She took a deep breath and caught the scent of burning maple. The flames in the fireplace licked higher and higher among the logs. She should close the damper a little but she kept sitting, waiting for him to go on.

"There was a break-in," he said finally. "In our offices. Whoever it was was very careful. As near as we can tell, nothing is missing. But the filing cabinets were opened and run through, according to

Miss Palmer."

Ash set the mug down on the coffee table in front of her and leaned forward, elbows on her knees, clutching the phone to her ear. "I thought we agreed you would keep no files on my case." Calum was an investigator for a lawyer in Vancouver. If a file existed anywhere on her, he would find it.

It's what he did.

"We did," agreed the lawyer. "I didn't." He took a deep breath. "At least not an electronic file. Too easy to hack into. I do have a paper file on your case, in a hidden safe that wasn't touched. But..."

She closed her eyes. "But...?"

"I had your phone number written on a sticky note in my day book," he said quietly. "No name, just the phone number. It was moved and then replaced, but I could tell."

"When?" she asked. "When was the break-in?"

"Eight days ago."

For the space of a few heartbeats, Ash just breathed. Finally, a thought pulled out of the maelstrom of fear that threatened to overwhelm her.

"Did you report it to the police?"

"Of course," he said. "They even checked for fingerprints, but I doubt they will find any that don't belong."

No. No, they wouldn't. Calum was very careful. Very patient. Very methodical.

"Ms. Stevenson?" The lawyer's voice was gentle but insistent. "Are you listening to me?"

"Yes, Mr. Caldwell," she said automatically.

"You must take the chip out of your telephone and destroy it. Then you must leave wherever you are and find a new home."

Suddenly she was standing up. Her knee knocked the coffee table on the way up and the tea sloshed over the rim of the mug.

"Ms. Stevenson?"

She heard his voice as if from far away. "Yes, Mr. Caldwell?"

"Did you hear me, my dear?"

She nodded, then realized he couldn't see her. "Yes."

"Do you remember where we first met? Just say yes or no, don't name the place."

She headed for the kitchen, where she had left her backpack. She pulled the pack up from the chair on which it had been sitting and clutched the strap. Night pressed in against the French doors that led to the deck and she suddenly felt exposed and vulnerable. She quickly drew the blinds and sat down at the table. It was colder in the kitchen and she shivered as she put the phone to her ear again, realizing that he had been speaking at the other end.

"Ms. Stevenson, are you still there?"

"Yes."

"Did you hear what I said?"

She nodded. "You want me to get rid of the chip in my phone."

"I want you to destroy your phone, and buy a new one. Then call the place where we first met and leave a message for me with your new number. Don't call me on my work phone anymore. Once I have your number, I'll call you and give you a new number to use. But before any of that, you need to relocate. Now. Today. That should keep you safe."

When she didn't answer, his tone grew sharp. "Ms. Stevenson. Do you understand?"

"Yes," she said, and before he could add anything else, she cut the connection, opened the back of the phone and pulled the GPS chip out. Then she returned to the living room and dropped the chip into the flames.

It didn't matter. Calum had had her phone number for over a week. Had he found a way to track her down? No. If he'd tracked her down, she'd be dead by now. Or maybe he was biding his time. The stranger she had seen across the street from Soup 'n Such suddenly popped into her mind but she'd known even then that he wasn't Calum.

But maybe he was someone Calum had hired.

She tried to think it through. Her phone had been off for over a week. Probably Calum hadn't been able to track her even though he had her number.

But she'd had the phone on tonight. No more than ten minutes. Eight minutes, maybe. Was that long enough for him to discover where she was?

Oh, God. Her hands shook and she wrapped her arms around herself. Oh, God. He was coming for her.

How long did she have? She should pack her things and leave now. The earliest he could get to Albans—if he flew—was tomorrow. If she left now, she would have almost a full day's head start.

The fire crackled in the grate and she automatically moved closer to the heat. She glanced around the room with its bay window and wood floor and soft lighting. Beyond was the kitchen and the dining room, with the staircase wall closing off the view.

It was strange, how much she liked this house. The moment she had seen it, she had felt at home, much more so than the house she had shared with Calum. That place had been a prison. A place of danger.

But this place echoed of danger, too. She only had to remember the baseball bats placed strategically throughout the house. Maybe there was no safety anywhere.

A cool breeze wafted over her and she felt a gentle caress on her cheek, as if a hand had brushed her in passing.

Ash started to pack, then stopped. She put two slices of bread in the toaster, then put them away.

Damn it.

He was doing it to her again. No—she was *letting* him do it to her again. She'd worked too long to free herself from him to let fear toss her right back at his feet.

In the end, she forced herself to bake a filet of salmon and make a Greek salad to go with it, then sat down and forced herself to eat every bite. She was slowly regaining weight and building muscle and didn't want to backslide. She had taken to drinking a protein smoothie in the mornings, at Barney's recommendation. He didn't like it when she came to the gym on an empty stomach.

This place. This town. From the moment she arrived here, she had felt the town wrapping itself around her, accepting her. She didn't want to leave, despite Mr. Caldwell's advice, despite what logic dictated.

She was so tired of running. Odette's house felt like home.

The wind buffeted the house and she heard raindrops splatter against the kitchen window. She had drawn all the blinds, all the curtains, and while this made her feel safe from prying eyes, it also left her blind to anything—or anyone—who might be out there.

As she ate, she pulled up Google on her tablet and punched in "Liesel Wirth" and Edmonton. A few hundred hits came up and she sat back in her chair. It would take some time to figure out which Liesel Wirth was the one she was looking for.

And then it occurred to her that Liesel might have married and no longer use the last name Wirth.

With a sigh, she began scrolling down the list of links. It soon became clear that they were all for the same woman. Apparently Liesel Wirth was a city councilor in Edmonton. Her name was as-sociated with council decisions and announcements. A number of recent photographs showed Liesel Wirth as a heavyset woman in her early to mid-sixties, her hair a solid gray worn in a short French braid in most pictures. There was intelligence in her eyes and humor, judging from the laugh lines around her mouth and eyes.

Was this the same Liesel Worth who took Odette in?

Ash pushed the empty plate away and pulled the tablet closer to her. She googled Liesel's name in the white pages for Edmonton and a number popped up immediately.

Could it really be that easy?

She jotted down the number on a receipt for groceries that she had stuffed in her jeans pocket, then reached for her backpack. Only then did she remember that she no longer had a phone.

She couldn't remember seeing a pay phone in her travels in Albans, but surely there had to be one. She glanced at the clock on the stove. Almost seven thirty, which would make it almost five thirty in Edmonton. She could afford to drive around town a bit to find a pay phone.

She quickly washed the dinner dishes and set them to dry in the rack. Judging by the sound of the wind, it was cold and wet out there. She put on her heavier coat and skimpy gloves, reminding herself yet again that she needed to buy a hat, scarf, and thicker gloves. She would have time on Saturday.

If Calum hadn't found her by then.

She slung the pack over one shoulder and headed for the side door in the laundry room. Before turning the knob, she hesitated.

"Keep an eye on things," she said softly. "I'll be back soon."

Then she walked out into the rainy night and closed the door behind her.

Cold, fat raindrops splattered her face as she ran for her car, and she quickly unlocked it and slid behind the wheel—still taking the time to check the back seat before she did so. As the car warmed up, she stared at the living room window, glowing with diffused light with the curtains closed. She half expected to see Odette waving at her.

She suddenly realized that she was no longer afraid of the ghost. Maybe it was a question of picking her battles. She had a murderous husband to worry about, after all. Calum was more likely to do her harm than Odette was.

She closed her eyes. This wasn't how she had pictured her life, back when Mom and Dad were still alive and she was at university. For a moment, a longing for how things used to be welled up in her and tears pricked her eyes. She shouldn't have to live this way. No one should.

It took half an hour of driving around, but she finally found a pay phone downtown, on a side street in front of the Bell office. Of course. To her relief, it was one of the old-fashioned phone boxes that protected the user from the elements. She parked at the curb next to the phone booth and ran to it, closing the door on the rain. As she did, the booth lit up and she suddenly felt exposed, as if a beacon were shining on her. The street consisted of business offices and parking lots, all of which seemed deserted. One building down the block had lights on, on the third floor.

She pulled the receipt out of her pocket and picked up the phone. She punched the zero for the operator and waited.

"Operator," said a man's voice after a moment.

"Operator, I need to make a long distance phone call," said Ash. "How much will it cost to call Edmonton?"

The operator remained silent for a moment, but she could hear him punching a keypad. "It will be two dollars for the first three minutes, then fifty cents for each additional minute."

"All right," said Ash. "I want to use cash."

"Do you have a credit card?" asked the operator. "You could just slide it in the slot—"

"No credit card," said Ash firmly. "No debit. Cash."

"Very well," said the operator. "Number, please."

Ash read off the number and pulled coins out of her jeans pocket while the operator dialed.

"Please insert two dollars," said the operator.

Ash placed a toonie in the slot, then two loonies, all the change she had. "I think I'll need more than three minutes," she said.

The phone rang at the other end and Ash's hand tightened on the receiver. She didn't know what she hoped to get from talking to this woman—if she even was the right woman. As the rings continued, she suddenly realized that she hadn't prepared what she was going to say. She couldn't just—

"Hello?" said a woman's voice at the other end of the line.

Ash jumped and almost fumbled the receiver. Her hands were getting cold.

"Hello," she said quickly, aware that she had a time limit. "May I speak with Liesel Wirth?"

"This is she."

Ash's mouth was suddenly dry. She swallowed and tried to compose herself.

"Can I help you?" asked the woman at the other end. Her voice was still polite, but there was an edge to it. She probably got a lot of crank calls.

"Mrs. Wirth, my name is Ash Gantry. I'm looking for the Liesel Wirth who used to live in Albans, Ontario."

There was a long silence at the other end. Finally, Liesel Worth said, "I used to live there up until about seven years ago. What's this all about?" There was another element in her tone now. A tightness that Ash couldn't readily identify.

"I'm sorry to call you out of the blue like this," said Ash. "I'm…" Oh, God, she should have thought this through. "I… I'm trying to find your niece, Odette."

Liesel Wirth remained silent for so long that only the sound of her breathing reassured Ash she was still on the line.

"I haven't heard from Odette since she left Albans," said the older woman finally. "Before I did. She hasn't tried contacting me."

It was Ash's turn to remain silent. That was the reason Liesel Wirth's phone number was so easy to find. And if she had married, she wouldn't have changed her last name, just in case Odette tried to find her.

If Odette had still been alive, she surely would have contacted her only living relative, the woman who had taken her in when her parents died.

"Do you know where she went when she left Albans?" she asked softly.

Liesel Wirth took a deep breath. "Why do you want to know?" she asked. "What's your interest in my niece?"

And here was where preparation would have helped. What could she possibly tell this woman that would persuade her to talk? Ash's thoughts chased each other fruitlessly until she worried the woman would hang up.

Tell the truth, then.

Or at least, part of it.

"I don't honestly know, Mrs. Wirth," she admitted. "I'm renting her house, on Hawk Street. It's such a lovely home. I feel her presence everywhere in that house." She choked back a hysterical laugh, disguising it with a cough. "The real estate agent knew your niece and told me a little about her, but lost touch. I was hoping you knew where I could reach her."

Lame. Lame, lame, lame. Liesel Wirth would think she was a wannabe stalker.

If she did, however, she didn't let on. "Is the real estate agent Maddie Bowen?"

"Yes, ma'am," said Ash, the respectful title slipping out from habit.

"She was always kind to Odette," murmured Mrs. Wirth. "Maddie was the only friend from high school who kept in touch with Odette. Frank managed to chase all the others away."

A great stillness filled Ash. She no longer felt the cold. Her entire attention focused on the voice in her ear.

"Why did he chase them away?" she asked softly.

"Because he was an abuser," said Liesel Wirth matter-of-factly. "First he convinced her she was worthless, then he isolated her from her friends. From me. Then he beat her."

Ash finally remembered to breathe. "Beat her?"

She heard a sound at the other end of the line, wood scraping on wood. Liesel Wirth had pulled a chair out to sit down. Ash wished she had a chair, too, because her knees were trembling.

"She would try to hide it with long sleeves and high collars." The older woman's voice was tinged with sadness. Or maybe that was tiredness. "I tried to convince her to leave him, especially after they bought that house. That's when things got really bad."

"You couldn't help?" whispered Ash. Her voice was trapped in her tightening throat.

"I tried," said Mrs. Wirth grimly. "I begged her to leave him, but he had her so brainwashed she was convinced she would never make it without him. I even spoke to the police about Frank, but there wasn't much they could do. The police officer spoke to Odette and she laughed it off. He spoke to Frank, too, but they'd gone to high school together, so nothing was done." There was no disguising the bitterness in her voice.

"What happened then?" asked Ash. Her hand grasped the receiver so tightly it was beginning to cramp. She switched hands. The wind picked up and rain began to pelt the phone booth as if trying to get in. Cold damp crawled down her back.

"I confronted Frank." Liesel Wirth drew a shaky breath. "I told him to leave Odette alone or I would kill him." She laughed mirthlessly. "He laughed at me. Right to my face. Told me I was a bad influence on Odette and he wouldn't allow her to see me anymore. Allow!"

Waves of emotion crashed through Ash, forcing her to hang on to the small metal shelf beneath the telephone. "And then?" she whispered.

"And then she was gone." Ash could hear the tears in the woman's voice but didn't interrupt. "The next morning Frank came to my house, demanding that I let him see Odette, accusing me of turning her against him, of all kinds of things. He sicced his cop friend on me. But Odette was gone. I never saw her again."

An automated voice broke in. "One minute."

It pulled Ash out of her paralysis. She straightened. "I'm running out of time," she said. "Why did you tell me all this?"

"You're the only other person to show an interest in what happened to her."

Ash could hear the shrug in the woman's voice and she could feel the seconds ticking away from her.

"Mrs. Wirth," she asked urgently. "Do you think Odette is still alive?"

There was a long silence at the other end and Ash thought the line had gone dead. But then Liesel Wirth finally spoke.

"No. I think she's dead."

Then there was a click, swiftly replaced by a dial tone. Ash slowly replaced the telephone receiver in its cradle and leaned her forehead against the cold, damp glass of the phone booth.

CHAPTER 13

When she got home, Ash forced herself to walk around the grounds, making sure the side and back doors were still locked and no windows were broken. A normal woman wouldn't feel compelled to do that. A normal woman would feel safe in her home. In control of her life.

The rain plastered her hair to her head and dampened her coat's shoulders, driving the damp and cold through the fabric and into her flesh.

She had driven home as if in a trance, her mind empty of anything but the need to get to safety, when there was no safety for her. Now thoughts crowded her head as if vying for her attention.

Odette was dead. Ash knew it and so did Liesel Wirth. Now what? Nobody else seemed to suspect, or care. They all bought the story that she had left her husband. Because they all liked Frank Boudreaux? Because they were afraid of him?

She couldn't prove anything. And besides, she had her own problems. Calum was on his way, if he wasn't already here.

She stood outside the side door, wet and cold, fumbling with the key and feeling agonizingly exposed. Was he watching her, hidden by a tree, waiting for her to get inside? There were a few cars parked on the street, but most were tucked away in their garages or parked in the driveways. It was getting late, past eight she was sure. Most of the houses had only one or two lights on inside and very few had their porch lights on. It wasn't the kind of night a person expected company.

She hadn't left her porch light on. She hadn't wanted to make herself an easier target than she had to. The key finally slid in and she unlocked the door. She slipped inside and pushed it closed, turning the deadbolt in place.

She shrugged out of her coat and hung it on one of the coat hooks. The house felt cold and damp. She would light another fire and sit in front of it with a cup of tea until she warmed up.

As she unlaced her running shoes, she glanced at the corner next to the door, reassuring herself that the baseball bat was still there. She toed the shoes off and padded into the kitchen where she dropped her backpack on the floor by the counter before plugging in the kettle. She'd left the kitchen light on and it felt like a beacon in the dark house.

She rubbed her arms, trying to get warm, as she waited for the water to boil.

Calum was coming for her. She could feel him coming, like some great shambling beast... she could almost feel his hot breath on the back of her neck.

And she wasn't ready for him.

The front doorbell rang, startling her so badly that she spun around and clapped both hands over her mouth to keep from shrieking. Her heart slammed against her ribs and she gasped for breath. The doorbell rang again and she pulled her hands away and forced herself to take a deep breath.

Calum wouldn't ring the doorbell.

On shaky legs, she made her way to the front door. She could see a tall dark shape through the window, but she couldn't tell who it was. She shook her head slightly. It was a measure of how safe she had felt here that she hadn't given another thought to covering that window after her first tour of the house.

Whoever was out there could see her coming down the hallway, silhouetted against the kitchen light. She felt as if she were walking through molasses, but all too soon she was at the front door, her hand on the doorknob.

She glanced sideways at the baseball bat resting against the wall. It was within easy reach. She flicked the outside light on and suddenly the police officer she had met a few days ago was looking at her through the window. They stared at each other for long seconds before her hand finally turned the knob and she opened the door. The noise of the rain on the porch roof sounded like an ominous drum roll.

"Ma'am," said Jake. He had a little speech prepared but the look her face chased everything else out of his mind. Holy crap. She was terrified.

"Officer," she said. She stood in that doorway, clearly cold, and clearly not intending to let him in. "How can I help you?"

She barely came up to his shoulder and he wasn't that tall. Her eyes were huge and green and he suddenly felt much older than his thirty-nine years. He was almost old enough to be her father.

He cleared his throat. "May I come in?" It was bloody cold out here and he was in his uniform, with his heavy jacket. She had to be freezing in her stocking feet and light sweater. A stray gust of wind blew a splatter of rain against his back, emphasizing the point.

Ash hesitated. She really didn't want him inside her house. She wanted him to go away and leave her alone. However, cops only did that when you really needed them.

But it was cold. And raining. And Mom would roll over in her grave if she kept him out there. She sighed and stepped back to let him in. Fine. But she was damned if she was going to invite him to sit. He stepped through, took his hat off, and wiped his feet on the mat.

Married.

Ash closed the door and reached behind him to flick on the

hallway light, then stepped out of reach. Her hands were frozen and the cotton pullover she was wearing did nothing to keep the chill away. Even her toes were curling in protest against the cold.

"How can I help you?" she repeated, looking up at him. There was a faint shadow on his cheeks, reminding her that it was awfully late for anyone to come calling. Even a cop.

"Ms. Gantry..." He took a deep breath. "That's not your name, is it?"

What little color she had left her cheeks and, for a moment, he was afraid she was going to faint. He almost reached out to take her arm, but some instinct kept him still. She looked down at the flowery runner on the hallway floor. When she looked back up at him, her expression was neutral.

"As a matter of fact, that is my name." And it was. Now.

He nodded gravely and the cap in his hands went round and round as he fidgeted. He was nervous. She glanced at his name tag. Slater. What name had Maddie used? John? Jack?

"But you didn't have that name a few months ago."

Ash's breaths came shallow and quick. She made an effort to slow them, to breathe deeply. What did this man *want*? She hadn't broken any laws.

"You see," continued Jake, "I did a plate check on your car." He wished now he'd driven right by the house tonight and stayed out of her hair. She so clearly didn't want him here. But... He knew he'd hate himself if he didn't try to help her. "You bought the car in Calgary, back in March, and haven't registered it anywhere." Her driver's license was registered in Alberta, too, but the address she'd given was a motel. Whatever information he could glean about her was no older than six months.

That was how long Ashley Gantry had been on the run. Longer, maybe.

"I'll register it here, now that I've found a place," said the girl calmly. Her arms were crossed and her fingers dug into the flesh of her upper arms. He didn't think she'd noticed. "I haven't had a chance yet."

Jake blew a breath out noisily. He was handling this all wrong. Accusing her. He didn't want her to think of him as the enemy. He stopped turning the cap in his hands and stepped a little closer to her, wanting to emphasize his next words.

"Ms. Gantry. Please." He looked away, caught by surprise at the tears pricking his eyes. He swallowed. "I'm here to offer my help."

Ash looked up at the tall, good-looking officer, baffled. What did he mean? Why did he look so miserable?

"What kind of help?" she asked cautiously. Was this a come-on? Was this why he had come so late in the evening? She swallowed nervously. She was alone in the house with a strange man. It didn't matter that he wore a uniform. Maybe it was worse that he wore a uniform.

As if sensing her discomfort, the man stepped back. He reached inside his jacket and pulled out a business card and a pen. Leaning the card up against the wall, he jotted something down on the back, then handed her the card.

"I know I gave you one of these the other day but my cell number's on the back of this one. If he comes for you, call me."

He was staring into her eyes as if he would burn his intent into her soul.

A cool breath washed over her and she looked into the dark living room, knowing what she would see.

Odette stood by the open doorway of the room, five feet away, a barely visible shape against the darkness of the room. She was staring directly at Officer Slater.

Ash's mouth parted and she turned to look at the police officer again. "You knew her, didn't you?" she whispered.

Jake blinked. Odette. She meant Odette. Of course she did.

"She went to my high school," he said slowly, not even trying to pretend. "I didn't help her when I could have. But I can help you." His voice was so low, it was barely audible.

This was the cop Odette's aunt had talked about. The one who had done nothing for her niece. And now he was offering to help her?

Suddenly Odette was next to the police officer and Ash watched, goosebumps chasing each other down her scalp, as the ghost cupped Officer Slater's cheek in her hand.

Jake jerked back at the cold touch on his face. He looked around in alarm but Ash Gantry stood still in front of him, staring at him in shock.

"I'm sorry to have bothered you," he managed to choke out. He placed the cap on his head and made to turn away. Then something in her look stopped him.

They stared at each other in silence as each read the knowledge in the other's face. Then Jake nodded silently and let himself out.

CHAPTER 14

When she woke, there were tears on her cheeks. She'd been dreaming of the baby again. She lay in bed for long minutes, her hand on her empty belly, thinking about the police officer's visit the night before.

He had seen Odette. Or at least, sensed her. He'd been freaked out by Odette's touch, but not surprised. He knew about her. Had experienced her presence before.

And far from seeming angry at him for failing her, Odette had cupped his cheek as if to comfort him. Odette didn't blame him.

It was still dark out. Too soon to get up, but she couldn't sleep anymore. She hadn't slept well. Odette had left her alone after the appearance in the hallway, but Ash had spent a long time thinking about the woman and wondering what had happened to her. Why did she haunt the house? Was it because her body was nearby? The more she thought about Odette, the more she realized the woman had to be buried in the woods in the back.

It only made sense. She had heard Odette falling down the stairs and heard the small sounds she had made as someone choked the life out of her. All Frank would have had to do was carry Odette out to the deck and down to the trees to bury her.

Would that cop believe her if she told him they had to search the woods?

Where did Odette go when she wasn't making herself known? Did she still have the memory of her life? Was the ghost only the expression of her pain? Her fear?

With a sigh, Ash pushed the blankets off and got dressed. It was going to be a long day. After the workout, if she had time, she'd buy another phone. Maybe Barney or Paul could tell her where to find one. Then, after work, she had to pick up a few groceries, including some wine for dinner at Mrs. Stratford's.

Hawk Street was quiet when she finally left the house and stood on the porch, banana smoothie in hand. Mrs. Stratford, next door, was already up, judging by the light in the window on the side of her house, but there were no other lights on in the houses she could see. It wasn't even six o'clock yet. Soon lights would start going on as her neighbors got ready for work and school. But for now, the world was hers—and Bea Stratford's.

Ash was looking forward to having dinner with the woman. Along with the wine, she'd get a loaf of bread from the bakery down the street from Soup 'n Such.

Then she realized that she was thinking like a normal person. A person who didn't have to worry about a crazy husband hunting her down. She glanced around the empty street, suddenly nervous, then hurried down the steps.

It had stopped raining but the driveway was still wet and the grass sparkled where the streetlights found the water droplets. She got into the car, shivering until the heater finally kicked in and chased the fog from the windows. She was definitely getting warmer gloves today.

It was still dark by the time she pulled into the parking lot behind Barney's Gym, but she had passed a few cars on the road. Albans was waking up. Barney's ancient Renault was parked in its usual spot, just below the one light in the parking lot. She was starting to think that Barney actually lived at the gym. She couldn't see Paul Coventry's Focus anywhere. He didn't come every morning, but just because she couldn't see his car didn't mean he wasn't there. She would have to watch herself, having learned the hard way that he and Barney took her survival training very seriously. A surge of affection for the two men filled her suddenly and she smiled a little.

It was good to know that she had it in her to like some men.

She sat in the car for a minute, emptying her mind, trying to center herself for the workout. Finally, she took a last swallow of the smoothie and replaced the plastic glass in the cup holder.

The street next to the parking lot was puddled and the streetlights gleamed back at her from the pavement. There was something peaceful about rain and darkness, as if the rain added an extra layer of cover.

She was getting stronger. She knew she was. And she was learning how to fall without hurting herself, how to get out of holds, how to incapacitate an attacker. But she knew better than to believe any of it would have an effect on Calum. In her mind's eye, she saw again the handgun she had found in the shoebox at the back of the spare room closet back in Vancouver. It had a cylinder and it had been loaded.

Calum hadn't wanted her to know he had it. Maybe he worried she would use it against him. Now she wished she had taken it with her, even though she knew she could never pull the trigger and take someone's life. Even Calum's.

But if she had taken it, he wouldn't have it now.

She closed her eyes and leaned her forehead on the steering wheel. She had her backpack. She could just drive away and keep driving. How far would be far enough? Once she got to Newfoundland, would she be cornered? Better to face what was coming here. At least she felt a little prepared.

The beatings had started once they were married. She had begun to sense a barely restrained fury in her husband. It was as if he no longer had to pretend. Once he found out she was pregnant, the beatings got worse. Over time, she became convinced that one day he wouldn't stop. That he would give in to the hate.

She didn't know why he hated her. Why he had married her. Why he beat her.

She did know that if she had stayed with him, he would eventually have killed her.

Like Frank had killed Odette?

Enough. Time to get on with her day. The windows were fogging up again. She got out of the car, pulling her gym bag and backpack out with her, and locked the door. A car was parked across the street, but otherwise, the street was empty. By the time she came out again, there would be more traffic, more cars would be parked on the side streets as people tried to find free parking close to their offices.

The back door was unlocked, as usual. She glanced inside before entering, to make sure the entryway was empty. Then she pushed open the inside door with enough force to bang it against the wall and stepped through quickly, glancing to either side as she did.

Over by the sparring ring, Barney looked at her, coffee cup halfway to his lips. His eyebrows rose questioningly.

She grinned and shrugged. "Girl can't be too careful."

He laughed. "You got that right. Paul will be here a little later. You might as well do your regular workout first."

She nodded and toed off her street runners before heading for the locker room. Barney hadn't turned all the lights on yet and the gym was gloomy. Minutes later, she emerged in her sweat pants and tee-shirt, picked up a skipping rope from the peg by the equipment wall and started warming up.

Forty minutes later, Paul arrived, unshaven and tousled.

"You okay?" asked Barney, emerging from his office. A couple of young men had arrived in the interim and were sparring in the ring.

"Daughter went out last night," grumbled Paul. "Stayed past curfew. I had to go get her."

Barney slid a glance toward Ash and they silently agreed not to press. Paul's fifteen-year-old daughter was a bit of a challenge to her parents.

Ash kept going with her routine—lifting weights by now—while Paul warmed up with stretches and skipping rope. Finally, the two men in the ring finished and she and Paul took over the space.

Before Ash could do more than turn toward him, he barreled toward her, arms outstretched. She barely managed to duck under his reach and turn before he was coming at her again.

This time she couldn't avoid his reach, so she stepped into it, turned slightly and swept her leg out to trip him. It worked, and he lost his balance, but his left arm swept Ash down with him and she landed hard on her hip before Paul landed on top of her, smashing his forehead into hers.

Pain exploded in her head and hip, stealing her breath. She couldn't even talk, let alone cry out. Paul rolled off her with a groan but she stayed where she was, focusing on taking one breath after another.

"Well, that was ugly," said Barney.

She turned her head slightly, surprised she could move her neck, and opened her eyes. He was standing outside the ring, hands hooked on the top rope, staring down at both of them.

"I think she broke my head," said Paul. She glanced over at him. He was on his back, too, arms splayed, staring up at the ceiling.

Barney sighed. "Stay there, both of you." He left, only to return seconds later with a small flashlight. He climbed into the ring and straddled Ash, bending over so he could shine the light into one eye, then the other. She blinked as she teared up.

"No concussion," he announced. "You'll live."

"Tell that to my head," she groused. He grinned and stepped over to Paul, where he repeated the procedure.

"You're fine, too," he said. Paul was already struggling into a sitting position, his hand over his forehead where a goose egg was taking shape. Ash put her hand to her own forehead. Sure enough, a huge lump was rising over her right eye. Great. Was that going to bruise now?

"Come on," said Barney, putting a hand out to her. She grabbed his big, gnarled hand and he gently pulled her to her feet. But when she put weight on her left leg, pain shot through her hip and she hissed.

Immediately Paul was at her side and he and Barney lowered her to the mat once more.

"I'm fine," she insisted, even as tears of pain pricked her eyes. She was useless at this. Couldn't even fall without hurting herself.

"Just be quiet and let us check you out," said Paul roughly. He moved around to her bad hip and gently flexed her knee. She felt a twinge in her hip but otherwise was fine.

"See?" she said. "I'm fine." She made as if to get up but Barney pushed her shoulders back to the mat. The two guys who'd been using the ring had emerged from the locker room.

"Want me to call an ambulance?" one of them asked.

"No!" said Ash, just as Barney said, "Not yet."

"I'm going to move your leg now," warned Paul and then he pushed her bent leg up, pushing her knee toward her chest and Ash groaned. He pulled her knee sideways toward the mat and this time she told him he was a sadist and she hoped he got a black eye. Ignoring her, he pulled her knee toward her other leg. It wasn't pleasant but it didn't hurt nearly as much as the other way. Finally, he sat back on his heels.

"I think it's a pulled muscle," he said. "There's no structural damage. Nothing's broken, but to be on the safe side, you should go to the hospital."

She was not going to the hospital. It was bad enough she had a cop asking around about her. She didn't need hospital administrators asking for her health care card or identification, or questioning the scars on her body.

Another man, a regular, appeared at the side of the ring and asked if he could help. Barney shooed everyone away, telling them she was fine.

"Just help me up, please," she said firmly. They did and she tried not to wince when she put her weight on the leg. After a moment, she realized that she could walk and let them help her out of the ring.

"Ash," began Paul when they finally stood on the floor by the ring, "I'm so sorry." The goose egg looked shiny on his forehead.

She grinned up at him. "Hey," she shrugged. "Let's just chalk it up to experience." The words coming out of her mouth surprised her. Grandma used to say that, whenever something unpleasant happened. As far as Grandma had been concerned, everything was a learning experience.

"I think you're done for the day, girl," said Barney. He looked worried. "In fact, I think you shouldn't come back until next week. Give the leg a rest but do some stretches, alternate heat and cold—you know the drill."

"Yes, sir," said Ash. Right now, that sounded like very good advice. She let them help her into the locker room and Barney helped her into her coat. Paul carried her bag in one hand and supported her around the back with his other arm. He grabbed her outdoor shoes on the way out.

"Let me drive you to the hospital," he offered.

She shook her head. "Nope. I think I need to keep moving or this hip will stiffen up." And she wasn't going to the hospital. She slung her backpack over her free shoulder and, with his support, hobbled to the Volvo. He took the keys from her, unlocked the doors and placed her gym bag and backpack in the back seat before helping her into the car. She hissed a little as her hip accommodated her sitting position.

"You all right?" he asked worriedly.

"I will be," she assured him. "Stop worrying. If I were you, I'd put a cold compress on that goose egg."

His hand went to his forehead and he felt gingerly around the swelling. "Holy crap." Then he looked at her critically. "I could say the same for you. Go to the hospital, get them to check you out. Okay?"

"Please stop worrying," she said. "I'll see you on Monday." She gently pulled on the door and he reluctantly let it go. She wanted to get home as soon as possible and take a bath before her hip seized up completely. She didn't want to have to cancel her shift at Soup 'n Such.

She drove carefully. It was still too early for most people, but it was no longer night. The sky in the east was pink with dawn and darkness was fading into early morning gray. She drove slowly to determine the range of motion in her hip, taking side streets and going around the block several times until she was sure she could drive home without causing an accident.

The second time she turned the corner onto Third Avenue, she noticed it. A car was following her. She did another circuit of the block just to be sure. It was the same car that had been parked on the street outside Barney's. A navy blue, newer model SUV-type car. She couldn't tell what make.

At once the pain in her hip became secondary. Someone was following her. Was it Calum? It wasn't Calum's car, but it could be a rental. He wouldn't risk using his own car.

A pain in her jaw told her she was gritting her teeth. She stretched her neck out, trying to loosen the tension that threatened to freeze her in place.

It might not be him. It could just be a coincidence. She coasted to a stop at the stop sign, then turned onto Main Street. She kept an eye on the rear view mirror and to her relief, the SUV turned the opposite way. She shook her head at herself. Was it always going to be this way? Was she always going to have to watch her back?

Nobody could live like that.

When she got back home, she made sure all the doors and windows were still locked, then made herself coffee while the tub filled. She didn't have any bubble bath foam, but the heat would do her good. Getting up the stairs with her cup of coffee was tricky and took forever, but she finally got to her bedroom and stripped, leaving her clothes on the floor. With the cup in one hand and using the baseball bat she kept by her bed as a cane, she limped to the bathroom and managed to get into the tub without killing herself.

She groaned as the hot water closed over her chilled flesh, then reached forward to turn the tap off. Finally, she leaned back and slid down until the water was up to her chin.

Holy geez, that felt good.

CHAPTER 15

Maddie looked up from her computer screen to take in the scene across George Street. The day had dawned wet but the sun was up and it was going to be a nice day.

Cars drove past her building, but not many. George Street wasn't a main road and, usually, only clients or business owners drove by during the day. On weekends, people would park farther down the road in the municipal parking lot and stroll down the path along the river, or cycle, in summer.

Across from George Street, the river flowed past, steel gray in the morning light. The water looked almost thick, as if it were beginning to freeze, but the river rarely froze all the way across. The ice would start to form along the river banks in November but that was pretty much it.

A few brave souls jogged along the path, most wearing running jackets and gloves. On the other side of the river, the forest marched up the bank in a parade of greens, yellows, and reds.

Every year at this time, she remembered why she and Dave had picked this place to set up Albans Realty. Every winter, as the wind rattled the windows and drafts made her crank up the heater under her desk, she cursed the decision.

She shivered and reached for her mug of coffee, wrapping her fingers around it and breathing deeply of the rich steam.

She had walked from home today. It was under a mile, and Steve needed the car to take Helen to gymnastics after school. If she needed a car, she could use the realty car. The walk had been pleasant, if cool. Everything smelled fresh and clean after the rain. She'd even caught a whiff or two of wood smoke, which had reminded her that she and Steve needed to place their order for a couple of cords of wood for the fireplace.

She sipped from her cup, enjoying the silence in the office. Olivia only came in at nine thirty, and Dave was in Toronto today and tomorrow on personal business. She had a lot of work to do—not to mention housework, judging by the layer of dust on her glass desk and the droopiness of the impatiens plant on the filing cabinet—but for now, she wanted to enjoy the quiet before all the craziness started.

A silver Honda CRV pulled up in front of the building, drawing her eye. She knew that car. Sure enough, as she watched, Frank Boudreaux got out of the vehicle and headed for the door to Albans Realty.

So much for Zen time. With a sigh, she set her cup down and went to unlock the front door.

"Maddie," said Frank as he walked in. Fresh air swirled in with him, making Maddie glad of the angora sweater she'd worn today.

"Hi, Frank," said Maddie cordially, locking the door behind him. "Did we have an appointment today?"

He was wearing a lined Carhartt jacket, open, with a heavy gray woolen shirt underneath, and jeans and work boots. On his way to work, then.

"No," said Frank. He had big, work-rough hands. They always surprised her when she noticed them. Nothing in high school had prepared her to think of him as hard-working, but his contracting company seemed to be doing well, and she'd heard others praise his work ethic and professionalism.

"I'm on my way to work," continued Frank. "Thought I'd pop in and pick up the new keys."

"Oh, right," said Maddie. She'd completely forgotten that she'd had the locks changed on the Hawk Street house. "Come on in," she said. "Do you have time for coffee?" She offered out of courtesy, hoping he would refuse.

"Sure," he said. "I'll have a cup."

"Black, right?"

"Yep. You always had a good memory, Maddie."

Maddie smiled perfunctorily and waved him into her office while she went to the tiny kitchenette and poured him a coffee. She reminded herself firmly that he was a good client.

"Here you go," she said as she set the cup down on the desk. He'd been standing by the picture window, looking out at the river. Now he turned back to the desk and sat down. Maddie sat down, too. She reached for the small wooden cabinet tucked under the glass desk and pulled open the top drawer. The shiny new keys to Ash's house gleamed back at her. The locksmith had threaded a small round tag on a string through the key ring and noted Ash's address on it.

Maddie's hand closed over the keys and she hesitated for a moment. She was curiously reluctant to turn the keys over to Frank, even though he was entitled to them. After all, he owned the place. She glanced at him and saw his almost-black eyes studying her dispassionately. He was a good-looking guy, in his own way. In high school, he had kept his black hair shoulder length, but now it was in a half-inch buzz cut that emphasized the lean cheeks and weathering of his skin. He had deep grooves on either side of his mouth, and a few deep lines on his forehead, but she could see how he would be attractive to some women.

But put him in a hoodie and he would look like a thug robbing a Seven Eleven.

She pulled out her hand and closed the drawer, then pushed the keys across the desk toward him. She forced a smile on her face.

"How's..." for a moment she drew a blank on his common-law

wife's name, but then it came back to her. "...Kathleen?"

He smiled tightly and pocketed the keys. "She's fine," he said. "Busy with work."

Maddie nodded politely. Just how busy could a librarian get? Even a head librarian?

"So, how's the new tenant?" asked Frank.

Maddie blinked, suddenly aware that this was the real reason Frank had dropped by. He wanted to know about Ash.

"What do you mean?" she asked cautiously. Frank might be her client, but Ash... well, Ash needed someone on her side.

He raised an eyebrow and looked at her quizzically.

"Well, is she a keeper?" he asked. "It's not like we've had much luck with that place."

Maddie relaxed a little. This might be a good time to bring up the possibility of selling—

"I was thinking of maybe selling the place," continued Frank. "I'd hoped it would be a solid rental property but..." He shrugged. "What do you think?"

Wow. Maddie nodded enthusiastically.

"I've been hoping you'd come around to my way of thinking," she said. "You're losing money every month you don't rent it. Of course, the new tenant seems to like it there, and she does have a six-month lease," she reminded him.

He shrugged and finally picked up his coffee. "I can wait." He sipped and nodded his appreciation. There was something about him... like he was all coiled up or something... "Do you think she'd want to buy it?"

He'd never shown any interest in any of the tenants before, but maybe it wasn't surprising, seeing as he hadn't been keen to sell before.

"I don't know," said Maddie truthfully. "She's certainly been interested in it."

Frank's eyebrows rose. "How do you mean?"

Maddie shrugged. "Oh, you know. Asking about how many

previous owners, how old the place was, when it was renovated. That kind of thing." She looked down at the desk and picked up her own cup, more to avoid that brilliant dark gaze than because she wanted to drink. She hadn't lied to Frank. Not exactly. But there was more to Ash's interest in the house than Maddie had let on.

When Frank didn't reply right away, she glanced at him. He was studying the cup in his hand.

"Did you check her references?" he asked, looking up.

Maddie tried to keep her dismay from showing. She no longer cared about references. She'd stopped asking after the first dozen tenants walked out. She looked Frank in the eye.

"No, Frank. I didn't ask for references. I thought full payment in advance for the six months was a good enough reference."

Frank grinned and put a hand up in a "whoa" gesture. "I know," he said, "and I'm not questioning your work ethic."

Except that it sure felt like he was.

"But," he continued, "I'd like to know who I'm dealing with if we're going to approach her about possibly buying the place."

Maddie leaned back, frowning. "I think it's too soon," she said honestly. "She's only been in there for a couple of weeks. Not even a couple of weeks. I think we need to see if she's interested in staying, first." She shrugged. "And if she's not, we put the house on the market. It's a gorgeous house, Frank. Someone will want it."

Until they didn't anymore. She stifled a sigh and looked at him expectantly.

Frank swallowed more coffee, then winced as it went down. "But she's got a job here, right?"

Maddie nodded. "At Soup 'n Such. She seems to be settling in well, Frank. Just give her a bit of time. I can always talk to her if you want."

"Maybe you're right," he said, standing up. He loomed over the desk and looked at her intently. "But if I'm going to put the place on the market, I need to do something about that cellar."

Maddie nodded slowly. "It is creepy."

Frank laughed humorlessly. "It could stand a few more lights. And I want to pour concrete down there, give it a proper floor. Fix the steps. You know, make it a good storage space."

"That'll certainly improve the value," agreed Maddie.

"I'd like to get the work done as soon as possible," said Frank. "Next week, if possible." He stuck his hand in his jacket pocket and pulled out car keys. "My guys will have some down time until we can get inspections done on my current project, so it would be a good time. Can you ask her?"

"Sure."

"All right," he said finally. "Let her know that my guys can work around her schedule, not bother her any more than they have to. Thanks for the coffee, Maddie. I've got to get to work."

"Frank..."

He looked down at her. "Yes?"

"The house is in your name and Odette's. She's entitled to part of the proceeds of the sale." That was much harder to say than she had anticipated, but it had to be said.

All the friendliness evaporated from his face, leaving the underlying hardness exposed, like soil eroding away from a rock face.

"You worry about the house, Maddie, and let me worry about Odette."

And with that, he strode out of Maddie's office and into the lobby. A moment later, she watched him climb into his CRV and drive off.

She stood up finally to take his mug to the kitchen. Instead, she paused in front of the picture window and stared unseeingly at the view.

Now, what the hell had that been all about?

CHAPTER 16

Ash went to Mason's Pharmacy on Fourth Avenue before her shift started to buy a heating pad and an ice pack—and bubble bath foam—and to her delight, discovered that they sold cheap telephones and telephone cards. Then, as a bonus, she found a bin with warm gloves by the cash register.

So she was smiling as she limped into Soup 'n Such. A patron held the door for her on his way out. There were only four people in the restaurant, seated at separate tables. Two were older men, seated by the window, reading newspapers. The other two, a teenage girl and a young man, were each focused on their smart phones.

Max was wiping down the counter with a dishcloth in one hand and holding a plastic tub with a few dirty cups and plates in the other. He looked up as she walked in.

"What happened?" he demanded. Every head in the restaurant turned toward her and she felt herself blush.

"Things got a little enthusiastic at the gym," she said with a smile. "It's superficial."

Charlotte, hearing her brother's question, came in from the back with a tray of cooling banana walnut muffins. She stopped in her tracks when she caught sight of Ash. A lump on the girl's forehead seemed to catch the light no matter how she turned her head. Charlotte squinted. The lump was a faint shade of blue.

"Did you put a cold compress on that?" she asked as she slid the tray into place in the display counter. "Come here," she ordered, ushering Ash behind the counter and shooing Max into the kitchen with the other hand. When they all stood in the kitchen, she took Ash's chin in her hand and turned her head this way and that. What a doozie. The kid would be lucky if she didn't get a black eye out of it.

"What happened?" Max asked again and Charlotte could feel him bristling next to her. She understood. They both liked this girl, even though they knew almost nothing about her. Clearly, she was running from something, but until she was ready to tell them, they wouldn't ask.

Ash grinned in embarrassment. "Just an accident," she said. "My sparring partner has a matching one." She touched her forehead gingerly. "How bad does it look?"

"Not bad at all," comforted Charlotte, just as Max said, "It looks like hell." Charlotte glared at her brother. "Why don't you get the frozen peas out and a clean cloth."

He shrugged and went to the upright freezer in the corner. Moments later, Charlotte had forced Ash onto a stool and pressed a cloth-covered plastic bag of frozen peas against her forehead. Wisps of hair floated around the girl's face, which was still pink with embarrassment at all the fuss.

"Now," said Charlotte. "What's wrong with your leg?"

Half an hour later, satisfied that Ash would live, Charlotte and Max finally decreed she was free to take her shift or, better yet, go home and rest. Ash insisted on finishing the shift. The exercise would help keep her hip from seizing up, she assured them, grabbing an apron and an order pad and trying not to limp as she walked to the dining room.

She was right. Staying on her feet and moving around did help keep her hip from stiffening, but it was also exhausting. And while she would never admit it, she had developed a headache, no doubt thanks to the enormous lump over her eye.

Most of her patrons winced in sympathy when they noticed the lump and some tactfully ignored it, but she noticed her tips were much larger than usual.

"Well, that's that," said Charlotte with satisfaction as she closed the door on the last patron and flipped the sign on the window to "closed." She'd worn pants today because it was so chilly out, and her favorite blue flannel shirt. It was time to put her dresses away until spring. She turned to face the room, hands on hips, and studied the mess. Ash had given it her all, but she just couldn't move as fast with her sore hip and she hadn't been able to keep up with clearing the tables. Charlotte watched her carry a gray plastic tub to the counter, her limp much more pronounced now that there were no more patrons. The girl's face was pale and her lips were pressed tight with pain.

"Go home," said Max, coming in from the kitchen to grab the tub. "Take it easy this weekend. Ice. Heat." He looked over Ash's head to Charlotte, his gruff face creased with worry. She nodded at her brother.

Ash just smiled, picked up an empty bin and turned back to the tables by the window. "As soon as we're done clearing up," she said. Holy geez. She couldn't wait to get home and take another bath. But she still had to pick up the wine and the bread before she could go home. Right now, the thought of more shopping was overwhelming. She tried not to sigh as she picked up the dirty glasses and cutlery and placed them in the tub. A flash of light caught her eye and she looked up from the dirty dishes.

The sidewalks had dried and while there were still puddles in the street, mostly the pavement was dry. The sun shone down from a partly cloudy sky, adding to the glare from the window. There were lots of people out and about, and there was a kind of excited energy in their movements that reminded her it was Friday afternoon. People were looking forward to the weekend.

Another flash drew her eye and she looked up and down the street, trying to figure out what was flashing—something metallic, twirling in the breeze, maybe? She glanced at Dave's Art Supplies, expecting to see something in the display window, but then her eye was drawn down to a familiar, dark blue SUV parked in front of the art supply store. It looked a lot like the car she had seen twice before today.

Seeing the same care twice might be a coincidence. Seeing it three times wasn't.

The car's windows were tinted and reflected the day back at her so that she couldn't see inside, but the driver's side window was partly open and as she watched, the lens of a camera emerged from the darkness to rest on the open window's edge.

It was aimed right at her.

She stumbled back, hissing in pain as the sudden movement stabbed through her hip. Immediately Charlotte's hand was on her elbow, steadying her.

Charlotte scanned the street and sidewalk outside her window, looking for what had freaked Ash out. In a moment, she saw it. That car... and was that a camera lens?

"Come on," she said, pulling Ash gently back and out of sight of the car. They retreated to the kitchen, where Charlotte pushed the girl down onto the same stool she had used at the start of her shift. She gave her brother the eye and Max silently went to the freezer and pulled out the frozen peas again. When the wrapped package was pressed against Ash's forehead, Charlotte took a deep breath, gave her brother a warning look, and crossed her arms over her chest.

"I think it's time you told us what's going on, Ash."

Max glanced at her but she ignored him. She knew her brother well enough to know he would follow her lead.

Ash looked at her employers out of her left eye, the right one being obscured by the frozen peas. She felt guilty, suddenly, as if she had been lying to them. She hadn't. She just hadn't told them much about herself—why drag them into her problems? Nobody wanted to get involved in these ugly realities.

She didn't want to be involved in this ugly reality.

Max stepped forward and placed a big hand, scarred from many cuts and burns in the kitchen, on her shoulder.

"It's time, Ash. We can help."

The tears came so quickly she had no time to stop them. The first hot tears began to roll down her cheeks and suddenly Charlotte wrapped her arms around her, pressing Ash's head against her breasts, holding her as she sobbed.

Max's hand rubbed her back up and down as Ash cried uncontrollably, for herself, for her grandma, for her parents, for her baby.

After a while, the sobs slowed to an occasional hiccup and Charlotte gently released her. Max handed her a clean tea towel to wipe her face and she buried her face in the clean-smelling towel, wishing the floor could open up and swallow her whole.

"I'm so sorry," she said around a hiccup, her voice muffled.

The towel was tugged away from her face and she found herself looking up at Charlotte. Her blue plaid shirt had a huge dark splotch where Ash's tears had soaked it. Charlotte was absently patting the spot dry with the tea towel.

Max moved away from Ash and went to stand by his sister. They both looked at her, their identical blue eyes filled with concern.

Ash took a deep, shuddery breath.

"I ran away from home," she said, trying on a smile. It wavered and fell away. "My husband..."

Charlotte cocked her head to one side. "Your husband what?"

Ash found herself wondering what had happened to the peas. But Charlotte and Max stood waiting, looking as if they were ready to wait forever if they had to.

"He beat me," she said finally. "My grandmother warned me

about him. My mother didn't like him. But I knew better. I loved him, you see. Then Mom and Dad died in the crash and Grandma invited me to come live with her... Instead, I married Calum."

Now that the dam had broken, she couldn't seem to stop the words. She knew they were coming out disjointed, disorganized, but Charlotte and Max just stood there and listened, letting her get them out in her own way.

She told them about Vancouver, about Grandma living in Saskatoon, about being suddenly orphaned at nineteen, about cutting short university to marry Calum, despite Grandma's qualms. About the beatings. Grandma's death. The baby.

Then she told them about Mr. Caldwell and Grandma's plan to rescue Ash.

"And that's how you ended up here," said Max. His face had grown harder as she told them about Calum's abuse. His ruddy cheeks stood out beneath his crew cut salt and pepper hair. "And now...?"

Charlotte glanced through the doorway to the dining room. "And now you think he's found you." Her face was red, too. "Is that who's in the car across the street?"

Max's head came up sharply and he made as if to go into the dining room, but Charlotte put a staying hand on his burly arm.

"Let's hear her out first," she said grimly.

Ash took a deep breath. The tears were out of her system now, she hoped. She hated the weakness that had led to them, but was also realistic enough to understand that the combination of stress over Calum's discovery of her phone number and possibly her location, coupled with the pain she was in, and—oh yes—the fact that she was living in a haunted house had probably left her more shaken than she had thought.

"I don't know who's in the car," she admitted. "I don't think it's Calum—I don't think he would have had time to take a flight out here from Vancouver, rent a car, and locate where I work."

The brother and sister looked at each other, then back at Ash.

It was Charlotte who voiced their concern.

"Maybe not. But he could have hired someone to follow you around. Why else take pictures of you? Your husband would want proof."

Ash nodded. That's what she thought, too.

"We should call the police," said Charlotte firmly.

Max grunted. "Why don't we just confront the guy in the car?"

Charlotte glanced at her brother, considering it. Finally, she shook her head. "Probably not a good idea. But we could get his license plate number and turn it over to the police."

Before the words had finished coming out of her mouth, Max grabbed an order pad from the pile on the shelf by the door, plucked a pen from the cup next to the pile, and left out the back door.

Ash swallowed as the damned tears threatened again.

"No time for that," said Charlotte crisply, noting the trembling lip. "We'll drive back to your place and you can pack a few things. Then you're coming home with me."

Ash couldn't help herself. The tears began to leak out and she reached for the damp tea towel in Charlotte's hands. She wiped her eyes with more force than necessary, angry at herself for drawing her employers into her private nightmare.

"No," she said finally. She took Charlotte's hand as the older woman opened her mouth to object. "No, Charlotte," she repeated firmly. "I'm not running any more. Let him come, if that's what he wants."

And in that moment, a ball of rage so huge it threatened to choke her rose in her chest, and she saw herself smashing Calum's head in with one of her baseball bats.

Shocked at the violence of the image, she blinked and released Charlotte's hand. At that moment, Max returned, entering through the alley door.

"Got it," he said grimly, waving the pad at them. "Bastard drove off when he saw me."

"She refuses to come home with me," said Charlotte, turning

to her brother.

Before Max could add his arguments to his sister's, Ash put up her hand. "That man has alienated me from friends and family. He's broken my bones, given me bruises and concussions. He's killed my baby." Her breath caught on the word and she took a moment to control herself. Then she looked up at both of them. "I will be damned if he's going to chase me out of my home."

Her hands flexed, and she longed suddenly for the baseball bat. "Besides," she continued more calmly, "the police are watching out for me." She pulled Officer Slater's card from the back pocket of her jeans and handed it to Charlotte.

Charlotte took the card and glanced at the name. She nodded and handed the card to Max. "I know Jake Slater," she said. "Good man. Max will call him and give him the license number."

Ash was about to object, then realized she was being foolish. There was no need for secrecy any more. Albans was where she would stand up to Calum. She watched as Max moved away to make the call. Things were coming to a head now. People knew about Calum. If something happened to her, they would go looking for him.

Unlike Frank Boudreaux, who had gotten away with murder.

CHAPTER 17

The liquor store buzzed with activity as people swung by after work to pick up wine and beer for the weekend. Ash waited patiently for her turn to pay, glad she had taken a basket. She'd picked up three bottles of white in the end, deciding it was a good idea to have some on reserve. As she waited her turn, she imagined smashing one of those bottles over Calum's head.

The cashier looked at her as she placed her bottles on the counter. He was an older man, thin to the point of gauntness, with bushy gray eyebrows to match his mustache. He raised an eyebrow as he scanned the first bottle.

"I hope the other guy looks worse."

Ash blinked at him in confusion until she remembered the lump on her forehead. It had turned a pale blue while she was at work. There was no hiding it now.

"He looks pretty much the same," she assured the clerk and handed him money.

The woman behind the counter at the bakery had had the same reaction when Ash stopped earlier to pick up some bread. There hadn't been much left by the time she got there and she ended up getting some fruit tarts instead.

She left the dim busyness of the liquor store, bag in hand, and

limped through the full parking lot to her car. The sun was beginning to go down and it sent long shadows across the pavement.
People hurried past her, first in sunshine, then in shadow, as they
headed for the various stores in the little strip mall. There was a
sushi place two stores down that seemed to be popular.

She tried to scan the other cars as unobtrusively as possible,
looking for the navy SUV, but she didn't think it had followed her
here. She'd taken a circuitous route from Soup 'n Such, watching
her rear view mirror and doubling back often.

She unlocked the door to the Volvo, then put the wine in the
back before tossing her backpack onto the passenger seat. Then
she gingerly folded herself into her seat, trying not to jar her hip,
and sat there for a few moments, enjoying the sunshine on her
face.

A woman walked by, holding a toddler by the hand and talking
on a phone, and suddenly Ash remembered Mr. Caldwell's instructions. She pulled the backpack toward her and fished through it to
find the cell phone. It was a cheap thing that flipped open, and the
clerk at the drugstore had assured her it didn't come with a GPS
chip. She dug around at the bottom of the pack until she found the
card, then remembered she didn't have the phone number for the
little diner on Georgia Street where she and the lawyer had first
met.

She leaned back in her seat, clutching the phone to her chest.
Was it only a few months ago? It felt like she had been on the run
for years. But it had only been a little over six months since she
found out about Grandma.

Calum hadn't wanted the expense of a land line in the apartment when they moved. He'd refused to let her have a cell phone.
Too expensive, he'd said, especially while they were saving to buy
a house.

The apartment he'd found was near Surrey, in a neighborhood
filled with South Asian businesses and stores that sported signs in
Punjabi, with much smaller English lettering beneath.

Their one-bedroom apartment was above a restaurant that specialized in Indian cooking. The choice had baffled her, at first. It was much too far for her to keep her job at the insurance agency in downtown Vancouver, and while she had walked up and down the streets of the neighborhood applying for a job, no one would hire her because she didn't speak Punjabi.

Eventually it had dawned on her that this was Calum's way of isolating her even more. She had no money, no telephone, no car, while he had a cell phone and drove their car—his car—to work every day. There were no public phones anywhere near the apartment.

He had pulled her out of her own neighborhood, forced her to quit university, then moved her away from friends and neighbors...

It had taken her a long time to see it, but Calum wanted to control every aspect of her life.

But she'd had Grandma.

When Mom and Dad died, she began writing to Grandma every week. Calum didn't know. She always mailed the letters without his knowledge.

And when they moved to this neighborhood, she had befriended the owner of the corner store down the block—as much as she could when the woman didn't speak English and Ash didn't speak Punjabi—who would let Ash use the phone in her little cubby of an office at the back of the crowded store to call Grandma collect.

But in the last few months, there'd been no answer when she called, and she hadn't received a letter in weeks.

Then, one February afternoon when the watery sun shone through her kitchen window, a courier arrived at her door with a letter. It was addressed to her.

Calum was still at work, or he would have been angry. She signed for the letter, her heart thudding in dread. When the courier left, she turned the envelope over in her hand. It was a business-sized envelope, a good quality paper, cream colored. The return address was from Saskatoon, but it wasn't in Grandma's neat block letters. It had a printed return address in the corner, from Kors, Avens and Bateman. With trembling hands, she tore open the envelope and pulled the single sheet out.

"Dear Ms. Stevenson,

It is with deep regret that I write to inform you that your grandmother, Morgan Ashley Wagner, has passed away. It is my understanding that you had not seen your grandmother in a number of years, and may not be aware that she had been suffering from breast cancer. A few months ago, the cancer metastasized and on January 4th, she died.

As her attorney, I have been entrusted with her last will and testament, which names you as sole beneficiary. I have attempted to find a phone number for you, to no avail. I have also written several times to the address Mrs. Wagner had for you, but have not heard back.

If you receive this letter, please call my office at 555-637-4597, collect, at your earliest convenience so we may discuss the terms of Mrs. Wagner's will.

Yours respectfully,
Andrius Kors"

Ash stood in her empty kitchen, staring unseeingly at the letter, trembling all over. She had written Grandma a month ago, telling her that she was pregnant, knowing it would make her happy. But Grandma had already been dead. Grandma would never meet her great-grandchild. Ash would never see her again.

Through her tears, she reread the letter. Why hadn't she received the lawyer's letters? She looked up, staring unseeingly through the kitchen window to the alley beyond. Calum. He couldn't intercept her mail, since she was home to receive it. No. He had had her mail re-routed.

The bastard.

He had known for weeks that Grandma was dead, and he

hadn't said a word. He'd only met Grandma once while Mom and Dad were still alive, then again when they died. Grandma had taken an instant dislike to him, and Ash suspected it had been mutual, although Calum never said so.

When Calum left that first time, Dad had asked Grandma what she thought of him. Ash had caught the look between Mom and Grandma, but Grandma had only shrugged.

"He reminds me a lot of James."

Dad had blinked at her uncertainly. Ash didn't know the whole story, but she'd heard enough over the years to suspect that James, Grandma's husband and Ash's grandfather, had been abusive. He had died in the car accident that stole Grandma's ability to walk.

Dad had laughed and gone on to explain that young Calum was a great asset to the law office where he worked.

Grandma had nodded silently but the look she had turned on Ash had been troubled.

Ash's hands fell to her side and she almost dropped the letter. From below came the smell of frying chicken and sesame oil. Someone in the kitchen dropped something and it clanged noisily.

Finally, she staggered to the door, barely remembering to grab a jacket, and, still clutching the letter, ran to the corner store three blocks away.

Amar stood behind the counter at the store. She was a small Indian woman whose age Ash had never been able to guess, but whose warmth had drawn Ash to her. Amar looked up in surprise when Ash entered. Ash mimed putting a phone to her ear and Amar smiled and nodded her to the back of the store.

Amar's store was actually her family's store. It carried everything from bread to coffee cream, with spices and Fair Trade coffee thrown in. Her office was at the top of three rickety wooden steps at the back of the store, and it was barely big enough to contain the small table that she used as a desk. Piles of paper littered the surface of the table, and a white mug half filled with tea had been abandoned on top of a precarious pile.

Ash placed the cup on the wooden surface of the table before sitting down in the wobbly rolling chair. She suspected Amar had gotten it at an estate sale and Ash never felt very safe sitting on it. Of course, at a hundred pounds, she probably outweighed Amar by fifteen pounds. Maybe Amar felt very safe on it.

After digging the phone out from under loose invoices, Ash placed the collect call, which, after some confusion, was accepted, and finally she spoke to a Ms. Lanigan, who apparently was Mr. Kors' assistant.

"I'm sorry," said Ms. Lanigan. "Mr. Kors is busy with a client right now. May I take a message?"

Ash stared down at a pamphlet in Punjabi. It had a picture of a shelf unit on the front.

"No," said Ash. "I'm... it's difficult to reach me. He sent me a letter..."

"What was your name again?" asked the woman at the other end, her tone sharp.

"Elizabeth Stevenson. He's my grandmother's attorney."

"Please hold, Ms. Stevenson. Do not hang up." There was a click, and soft music reassured Ash that they hadn't been disconnected.

A moment later, the music cut out abruptly, to be replaced by a gruff male voice.

"Hello, this is Andrius Kors." He had a faint British accent, as if he'd been in Canada for many years and it had faded.

"Mr. Kors, this is Elizabeth Stevenson," she said. "You've been trying to reach me."

"And you've been very difficult to reach, my dear," he said, frustration lacing his voice. Then, as if remembering, he softened his tone. "Please allow me to express my condolences. Your grandmother was a fine woman. I was very sorry to learn of her passing."

Ash's throat tightened, and she swallowed. "I hadn't even known that she was sick," she managed to whisper. "I hadn't received any news of her in ages."

"All her letters were returned," said Mr. Kors.

The tears began to roll then, and Ash couldn't keep them from her voice. "Oh, Grandma."

Mr. Kors cleared his throat. "Your grandmother hinted that you might be in a... a difficult position," he said. "Is it safe for you to talk?"

Ash stared at the phone in her hand. She felt herself flush in shame. Of course Grandma had known.

Ash looked around, suddenly aware of the time. A clock on the wall behind her read four thirty, already.

"For now," she said. "I can only spare a few more minutes before I have to get back."

There was a pause at the other end, then Mr. Kors began to speak.

"Very well," he said. "In that case, let me give you all the information you need at the moment. While your grandmother's letters were returned, my letters to you were not. You must assume that they were read. Your grandmother left you everything. She instructed me to sell her house and all her assets and place the money in an account under your name. Do you have a piece of paper and a pen?"

The question was so sudden that at first Ash didn't realize what he was asking her. Then she looked around the small office and found an empty envelope in the trash bin under the table. She plucked a pen from the holder and said, "Go ahead."

He rattled off a series of numbers, then had her repeat them to him.

"That's the account number," he said. "It's with the Toronto-Dominion Bank, in Saskatoon. Here's the address." He gave her the address, then the routing number for the bank.

Amar popped her head through the door and Ash held up a finger to indicate she needed one more minute. The woman nodded and withdrew, leaving a waft of ginger in her wake.

"After selling her house and liquidating all her assets," continued Mr. Kors, "you have approximately seven hundred and fifty thousand dollars to your name."

Ash blinked.

"Pardon?" she finally asked.

"Yes, it's quite a lot," agreed Mr. Kors. "I tried to prevail on her to invest the money, but she wanted the cash available to you. In case you needed to get away."

Ash's breath caught. In case you needed to get away.

"Thank you," she whispered. "Oh, thank you." She didn't know who she was thanking. Then a thought intruded.

"Your letters to me," she said hesitantly. "Did you say any of this in them?" Did Calum know that she had money now?

"No," said Mr. Kors. "My letters all said essentially the same as the one you received today."

So. Calum knew that Grandma was dead, that she had left everything to Ash. He must suspect that there was some money involved. The fact that he hadn't told her meant he was either hoping she would never find out or he was trying to figure out how to acquire it himself.

The fact that she could even consider this surprised her. A year ago, she would have accepted everything he did as being in their best interests.

But now she suspected Calum only ever had his own best interests at heart.

"There is a great deal more to discuss," continued Mr. Kors. "If you will allow, however, I will entrust a colleague in Vancouver to carry through with your grandmother's wishes. His name is Hamish Caldwell and you may count on his discretion."

"Yes, that's fine," said Ash. She felt overwhelmed by the information that suddenly she had the money to leave Calum if she wanted. Thanks to Grandma. A rush of grief caught her by the throat as she realized how impossible it all was. "Wait," she began. "Wait. I don't know how... My husband won't..." She stopped, suddenly unable to speak her shame.

She could hear Mr. Kors breathing at the other end. "Please don't concern yourself, my dear," he said gently. "Say nothing of this to your husband. Hamish and I have dealt with these situations before. He will contact you. Discreetly. You are, of course, free to call me at any time. My assistant has instructions to interrupt me when you do."

He hung up and she sat there for a minute until the dial tone finally intruded on her shock. She replaced the handset on the cradle and shakily walked back to the front of the store, folding the letter into the back pocket of her jeans, along with the precious piece of paper with the account number.

Amar was restocking cans of pop in the tall cooler by the back wall. Ash went over to her.

"Thank you," she said.

Amar nodded and smiled. Then she placed a small hand on Ash's abdomen and patted it.

"Baby?"

Ash looked down at her swelling belly and took a deep breath. She would do it. She would leave Calum. For the baby's sake, if not her own.

"The baby's fine," she said with a smile, then went home.

She was making pasta when Calum came home thirty minutes later.

"Hello, sweetheart," he said, coming up behind her and wrapping his arms around her. He buried his face in her neck. "And how was your day?"

"Fine," she said casually. And then, obeying an impulse over which she had no control, she said, "Isn't it odd that we never get mail?"

She felt him stiffen behind her, then he moved away. She stopped stirring the sauce and turned to look at him. Every once in a while, his good looks caught her by surprise. He kept his blond hair short and it curled up in the front, giving him a boyish look. He had a wide forehead above deep-set green eyes, a straight nose, and a generous mouth. He kept himself fit. At six foot two, he drew the eye of every woman he passed.

She used to feel so lucky that he was hers.

"We get all our bills electronically," he said.

"I know." He got all the bills electronically. She never saw any of them. "But I haven't seen a letter from Grandma in a while." She shrugged casually and turned back to her sauce.

She was walking a tight line between idle conversation and confrontation. If he decided she was challenging him, he would hit her.

"Maybe she's been busy," said Calum, moving away from her. He would go to the bedroom now and change into his jeans and a sweater.

Or maybe she's dead.

"Maybe I could call her," she said, then held her breath. A small part of her wanted to take the saucepan and hit him with it, but she knew better.

"You know we're saving our money." He was back in the kitchen, only a few feet away from her. He hadn't had time to change. Was there a tightness in his voice? She desperately wanted to turn around, but didn't dare. He would see the grief in her eyes. The rage.

"I know," she said softly. "For the house."

"You don't sound so sure," he said, suddenly inches away from her, his breath, smelling of coffee, brushing the hairs over her ear.

She forced a smile on her face, hoping he would hear it. She still didn't dare turn around. "I'm sure. I want a house, too."

She heard a familiar sound, the cracking of his vertebrae as he twisted his head, and she braced herself. Oh, God.

Suddenly his hand was on the back of her neck and he pushed her face toward the simmering sauce.

"Really?" he asked gently even as she resisted his push. "Really, Lizzie? Because to me, it sounds like you have doubts."

"Calum, please!" she cried as bubbles popped in the sauce,

splattering her face with burning bits of tomato sauce and oil.

He suddenly yanked her away from the stove, sending her crashing into the kitchen table. She twisted to protect the baby, turning away from him.

"After everything I do for you," he said calmly, grabbing her by the arm and flinging her against the wall, "you have the nerve to question me."

Her head rang from colliding with the wall. She tried to keep her balance but he pushed her down to the floor.

"You ungrateful bitch."

And then the kicking began.

Six hours later, she woke up in a bed in the emergency department, with Calum hovering over her solicitously and holding her hand as the doctor told them that she had lost the baby.

"I'm so sorry," said the doctor, an older woman with gray hair and warm brown eyes. She squeezed Ash's free hand, then released it. "I want you to stay overnight. We need to make sure you haven't suffered any more damage in the fall." Her gaze remained fixed on Ash, as if she refused to look at Calum.

It was only much later that Ash realized Calum had told the doctor she had fallen down the stairs.

Calum stayed with her for hours as she lay in the bed, bleeding and numb. He talked the whole time, though she couldn't make out a word he was saying.

When they finally found a bed for her, she found herself in a room with three other women. Calum stayed with her, holding her hand, whispering to her so the others wouldn't hear while she kept her face turned away from him. Eventually, his words began to penetrate.

He was sorry. So sorry. He didn't know what had come over him. He promised he would never hit her again. He promised he would make it up to her.

His words finally penetrated the ice encasing her dead heart. Something hot and prickly filled her chest.

She turned to face him, then. "Will you bring my baby back to life?" she asked in a clear, ringing voice.

His hand tightened painfully on hers and she stared at him, daring him to try.

He had wanted to kill her baby. The only thing that had kept her sane in the last few months, and he had stolen it from her.

He twisted his head around, cracking the vertebra in his neck. That was always the signal that he was about to lose it.

But he was in public now. All she had to do was scream and help would arrive. And he knew it.

And so what if he did hit her? What could he do to her that he hadn't already done, except kill her?

For four years, she had justified all his actions, blaming herself when he lost control.

She had to make sure there was no reason for him to be jealous.

They couldn't afford another car, or the Internet, or a land line, since they were saving up for a house, in a better neighborhood.

He loved her. He just had a temper. He would change. She needed him.

But now he had killed her baby.

There was no justification for that.

He left then, promising to return in the morning. She turned her head away, refusing to look at him, watching the darkness outside her window.

When a hand gently shook her shoulder, she started and twisted in bed, but it wasn't Calum. It was a stranger, a young man with short, curly black hair and dark eyes.

"Ma'am," he said softly.

Ash looked around, but the room was dark and silent. The women in the other beds were sleeping. Only then did she realize how late it was. Had she been sleeping, too? The only light in the room spilled in from the open doorway. Even the hallway outside the room was quiet.

"Who are you?" she asked. Should she be alarmed? Her head

throbbed with pain.

"My name is Sam," he said quietly. "Mr. Caldwell sent me."

She blinked up at him, trying to make sense of what he was saying. Then the name dredged up from earlier in the day, a lifetime ago.

"The lawyer," she said. "How did he know...?"

The man shrugged. "He sent me to your address—the neighbors told me you'd been hurt." Then he leaned down slightly. "Ma'am, do you want to stay with your husband?"

The hot tears came surging up from her broken heart, almost choking her. She shook her head.

"Then we need to get you out of here now," said the man. Sam. "If we wait, it'll be more difficult. We have a safe place where you can heal."

Ash wiped at her face, her shoulders screaming at the movement. Her ribs ached just from breathing and she had cracked two. No other broken bones, but she doubted she could walk.

"All you have to do is get dressed," said Sam reassuringly. "I have a wheelchair waiting for you."

Ash stared up at him, this stranger even younger than she was. Could she trust him? *Should* she trust him?

And suddenly she realized that it didn't matter. She was never going back to Calum. No matter where she ended up if she went with Sam, at least she wouldn't be with her baby's killer.

"All right," she whispered. "Help me up."

He pulled the curtains around her bed closed and turned back to her. It was painstaking, but he had clearly done this before, and soon she was sitting up, her legs dangling over the side.

"Did he take your clothes?" asked Sam, bending to peer below the bed.

Alarm suddenly spiked through Ash. The letter from Mr. Kors was in the pocket of her jeans, as was the account number. The letter wasn't a big deal–after all, Calum had intercepted earlier letters from the lawyer. But if he had her account number and bank information...

"Here we go," said Sam, pulling a plastic bag out of the small cabinet at her bedside. Someone had sealed it with tape, almost like an evidence bag. Sam tore open the plastic bag and pulled out her clothes. His hands clenched on the blood-soaked shirt and bra. That would be from the cut on her forehead, she thought dispassionately. Calum was usually so careful about not marking her face.

But this time, he hadn't been in control of himself.

In the end, Sam had to help her get dressed. She tried not to cry, as it hurt her taped ribs. After what seemed like a long, long time, he finished tying her shoes and helped her into a wheelchair that he pushed next to the bed.

A wave of dizziness swept over her, and she closed her eyes and hung her head, breathing deeply.

A warm hand on her forearm brought her back.

"Just hang on," he whispered. "We're almost out."

She nodded and he pulled the curtain open. For one wild moment, she expected to see Calum on the other side but the room was still quiet, the other occupants still breathing rhythmically in sleep.

"The nurses—" she said suddenly. The nurses would never let them go.

"Don't worry about it," he said with a grin. "They won't stop us."

And then they were rolling down the wide hallway toward the elevators. She caught a glimpse of a clock as they rolled past it. Two thirty-five. The lights were dimmed and the nurses' station at the far end of the hallway was empty. She tried to look back at Sam, but her neck and shoulders protested. Where were all the nurses?

The only sounds were from the rubber wheels on her wheelchair whispering on the linoleum and the faint regular beeping coming from some of the rooms. There was a faint smell of coffee but she couldn't tell where it came from. There were none of the regular medicine smells she always associated with hospitals.

To her surprise, Sam rolled past the bank of elevators, turning right into a side hallway that had only one light on, at the far end by another elevator. As they approached it, a figure emerged from the shadows.

"You're set?" she asked Sam, and only then did Ash recognize the doctor who had examined her in the emergency room. She wore a white lab coat over a pair of black pants and a flowered pink and green shirt.

"I got it, doc," said Sam. He stuck his hand out and they shook, then the doctor pressed on the button to call the elevator. She turned to Ash.

"You have cracked ribs and serious bruising. A mild concussion. I've read your file. It's not the first time you've visited us after a 'fall.' You can choose to go back to him, if you want, but another concussion could do you serious harm."

Ash nodded, then winced as the pain in her head swelled.

The elevator dinged softly and the door opened. Sam wheeled her in and turned her around to face the doctor.

"You need rest," said the doctor. "Sam will take care of you. You can trust him. Now go. I hope I don't see you again."

The door slid closed and the elevator whisked them down to ground level. To her surprise, the door opened onto a deserted hallway.

"It's a staff entrance," explained Sam. "No security guard." He produced a key card and slid it through the reader by the push bar, then opened the door when the light turned green.

And then they were outside the hospital and in the employee parking lot. Sam wheeled her out from under the door's sheltering overhang and over the wet pavement. It had rained earlier and there were puddles. The air felt cold and damp on Ash's skin and her hands ached. She began to shiver, gasping as the involuntary movement jarred her ribs. She had no idea where her coat was.

Then she realized it was probably still at home.

Home.

"Here we are," said Sam, stopping by an older model four-door sedan. It looked yellow under the sodium lights of the parking lot. He helped her into the back and made her lie down before he covered her with a blanket. Immediately she felt better. Moments later, he slid behind the wheel and started the engine.

And just like that, she escaped Calum. Sam brought her to an apartment in downtown Vancouver and before he left that night, he gave her a cell phone.

"It's untraceable," he told her. To her surprise, he removed the wig that had covered his fair hair, and popped the colored lenses that had turned his blue eyes brown. He placed the lenses in a small plastic container and stuffed the wig in his coat pocket. "You can call your husband if you want," he said, "or you can dial the number you'll find in the directory list. It's Mr. Caldwell's number. He'll be able to help you get free."

He no longer looked as young as she had thought in the hospital. There were fine lines by his eyes and what she had taken for peach fuzz was actually a reddish beard coming in. She wondered how many times he had done this.

She was sitting on the leather couch in the living room. The sliding glass doors revealed a view of the lights of downtown. She looked around at the plush carpet, the huge television, the glass shelves.

"Whose place is this?" she asked.

Sam shrugged. "It belongs to the law firm," he said. "You're not the first client who's needed a safe place to hide." He waved at the kitchen and toward the back of the apartment. "The bedroom's in the back and the kitchen is stocked with food. The front door has two dead bolts that can't be picked." He waved at the sliding glass doors. "We're on the tenth floor. Nobody's going to get you here unless you let him in."

He stood looking down at her, clearly waiting for a response.

Ash had sat on the comfortable couch and looked at the view of the world outside. Despite her physical pain, she felt at peace for the first time.

"Who's paying for all this?" she asked suddenly.

Sam laughed. "Don't worry about it. I'm sure it's a tax write-off." Then he sobered. "What do you want, Elizabeth?"

She looked up at him, absolutely sure of her answer.

"I want my life back, Sam."

He nodded with satisfaction. "All right, then. Where do you keep your important papers?"

She blinked at him. "Pardon?"

"Birth certificate, passport, marriage certificate… all those papers. If you're going to start a new life, Mr. Caldwell is going to need them."

"How are you going to get them?" she asked, more out of curiosity than alarm. She realized suddenly that she had no doubt he would be able to get them from the apartment in Surrey.

He grinned. "That's my specialty," he said. "Breaking in."

And breaking people out, she thought. She told him where her papers were kept and asked for her purse, too. At that, he shook his head.

"He'll notice if your purse is gone. He won't notice if your birth certificate or passport goes missing. At least, not for a while. What you need now is time to heal and make plans. Call Mr. Caldwell tomorrow. I'll check in with you. I'll always knock five times, then three."

And with that, Ash's new life started.

CHAPTER 18

As she sat in the Volvo in the liquor store parking lot, Ash considered the new life she'd found so far. Always on the move. Always careful not to share too much information about herself.

She put the key in the ignition and started the engine. The sun beat in through the windshield. From the back seat, the smell of sweet pastry and cream rose enticingly and her stomach growled. Her hip hurt and her face—she glanced in the rearview mirror—her poor face not only hurt, it looked like hell. But she knew hurt—understood pain. She knew she could stand it, could put up with it as long as she had to.

What she couldn't stand any more was running and hiding.

She glanced from side to side, then pulled out of her parking spot. The sun was already low in the western sky. The air vent brought cool air into the car, air laden with the smell of rain and exhaust and various food smells as the restaurants in the vicinity got ready for the dinner crowd. She took a deep breath as she negotiated the streets of Albans, heading for home. She watched for a blue SUV but saw no sign of it. Either she had lost it in her travels or the driver already knew where she lived.

Her hands clenched on the steering wheel at the thought.

Fifteen minutes later, she turned onto Hawk Street and slowly drove toward her driveway. Kids were already home from school and playing shinny on the street. As she drove up, a pair of girls quickly moved the hockey net out of the way to let her pass. She smiled and waved at them and they waved back.

She pulled into the driveway and carefully got out, wincing when her foot caught on the lip of the door opening, jarring her hip. Backpack in hand, she fetched the tarts and wine from the back seat and slowly made her way to the side door. She practiced walking normally, if slowly, putting her foot out and gently rolling her weight from heel to toe, reminding her hip how it was supposed to move.

As she walked, she found herself studying her backyard. The grass was too long, as was the grass in the front yard. She had to find a lawn mower somewhere, or hire somebody to cut her grass. Maybe Max or Charlotte would lend her a lawnmower.

Then her attention caught on the view that rolled away from her backyard.

The strip of forest at the bottom of her yard exploded with color, thanks to the rain and the cold nights. Bright yellows and ambers in the poplars vied with the pink underbrush and scarlet maple trees, interspersed with the occasional dark green fir tree. Glints of light peeked between the trees as the setting sun caught the St. George River.

Odette's resting place was beautiful.

She looked around suddenly, aware that she was being watched. Bea Stratford was watching her from the side window. When she realized that Ash had seen her, she grinned and waved a wooden spoon at her. She was getting dinner ready. Ash freed a hand and waved back.

She would be going over soon, but before she did, she had a few things to do.

She finally went inside, locking the side door behind her. She crossed over the trap door, feeling it give gently under her foot, and placed the wine, tarts, and backpack on top of the washing machine. She wouldn't even put the wine in the fridge until she walked around and made sure the house was still secure.

It was slow going, and she broke into a sweat negotiating the stairs, but the house was empty, with no sign anyone had been there. As she peered into the small ensuite, she eyed the bathtub longingly, but there would be no time. It was already almost five thirty and Bea expected her at six.

She fetched the wine and put the entire bag in the fridge, next to the tarts in the square box with string keeping it closed. Then she pulled her backpack to the table and eased herself down onto a chair.

She fished the tablet out and began searching for the phone number of the little diner where she and Mr. Caldwell had first met. Georgia's Sweets. She had the phone out and was dialing when it suddenly occurred to her that she could just call Mr. Caldwell at his office and leave him the information. After all, it didn't matter anymore if Calum was tapping his line. She no longer cared if he found out where she was.

Did she?

In the end, she completed the call to Georgia's Sweets. It was one thing to choose not to hide anymore. It was another to give the man an invitation.

"Georgia's Sweets," said a woman's voice on the phone, startling her.

"Hello," said Ash. "I'd like to leave a message for one of your customers."

"Which one?" asked the woman.

Ash could hear cutlery rattling in the background and two male voices talking desultorily, even though she couldn't make out the words. The diner was decorated in a retro '50s look, with a long counter and padded red stools in front and a series of booths in matching red leather lining the wall. Windows over each booth gave an unfettered view into the parking lot. Behind the counter, a pass-through gave a glimpse into the shiny, modern kitchen.

"Hamish Caldwell," said Ash.

"He's not here right now," said the woman, but her voice had sharpened.

"Yes," said Ash. "He asked me to call and leave a phone number with you. Is that all right?"

There was a hesitation at the other end and, for a moment, Ash thought the woman would refuse, but then there was a soft click and the background noise disappeared.

"All right," said the woman. "Go ahead."

Ash suddenly realized the woman had gone into a private room. The bathroom? The office?

She gave the woman the phone number for her new cell phone, then, impulsively, she gave her the address of the house in Albans.

Mr. Caldwell would know she had stopped running.

"I'll make sure he gets this when I see him," promised the woman before hanging up.

Ash sat at the table for long minutes, staring at the sky outside her French doors. The sun was setting in a wash of oranges and reds, setting the tips of the trees at the bottom of her yard on fire. In another hour, the sky would darken to purple and soon after, the stars would start coming out.

She sighed and put the cell phone down, then pulled the card Officer Slater had given her out of her pocket. Max had jotted the policeman's number down and promised to call him with the plate number of the SUV that had been following her. Now she would send the officer an email and tell him everything. That way, he would have everything he needed if he had to go after her killer.

A sharp rap at the front door startled her out of her morbid thoughts and her head jerked toward the sound. She couldn't see the front door from where she sat. She hadn't bothered turning lights on as she searched on her tablet and then called Georgia's Sweets, and now she sat in gloom. Whoever was at the front door wouldn't even know that she was here.

Except for the Volvo parked next to the house.

She found herself very reluctant to open the front door. Whoever was there could easily push her back into the hallway and none of her neighbors would be the wiser. Silently, she pushed herself up from the table and grabbed her cell phone before heading for the laundry room. She would go out the side door and around the house to see who was there. If whoever it was tried something outside, she would scream the dead awake.

She glanced around, surprised at not seeing Odette, who always seemed to appear when Ash was scared. At the side door, she picked up the baseball bat before easing the door open. It was still light enough to see. She took the steps one at a time, wincing every time her hip jarred. She could hear the kids calling to each other in the street as they moved the net out of the way to let a car by. Bea's kitchen window glowed with light, though Ash couldn't see her. Across the street, a woman closed the door of her car with her hip, as her hands were busy with cloth grocery bags.

She could hear someone knocking insistently at her front door as she eased her way to the corner of the house. Then she spotted the familiar police car parked in front and stuck her head around the corner to see Officer Slater lifting his fist to pound at her door.

"You're going to break my door down," she told him, unable to disguise the relief in her voice.

Jake whirled toward her, his right hand slapping to the weapon at his belt before he recognized Ash Gantry. His relief at seeing her sharpened his voice.

"Why didn't you answer the door?" he demanded.

Her eyebrows rose in surprise and he realized that he was out of line. He sighed. Removing his cap, he ran his hand through his hair. It had been a long day. He'd tried finding out more about Ash Gantry, but the trail started six months ago and the name change information was sealed. He would need to explain to a judge why he needed the information, and no judge would grant him permission when all he had was a bad feeling.

Then Max Strelzow called him with a plate number and a story of a car following Ash Gantry. Jake had done a plate search only to learn that the car belonged to Terry Billingsley, Albans' one and only private investigator. Terry had confirmed that he was on the job but refused to divulge his client's name until Jake warned him that his client was probably an abuser looking for his runaway wife.

"He's a fellow investigator," Terry had protested when Jake confronted him in his tiny office above the bookstore on Sixth Avenue. "He works for a lawyer's office in Vancouver. This is work, not personal."

Jake had stared at the young man whose wispy blond hair needed a trim and who still had pimples on his face, for God's sake.

Had he gotten it wrong? Was Ash Gantry a criminal escaping justice, not a woman running from an abusive man?

Then he remembered the fear in her eyes, the cool touch on his face that had felt comforting even as it scared the crap out of him. No. His gut told him he was right about Ash Gantry.

In the end, Terry gave up his client's name: Calum Stevenson. Back at the station, a cursory search revealed that Stevenson was indeed an investigator working for a Vancouver law firm. He had no formal record, but he'd had brushes with the law, all of them involving violence or threats of violence. He'd been charged twice, but both times the charges had been dropped.

Not surprising when he worked for attorneys who specialized in criminal law.

Then he dug deeper and learned that Stevenson was married to Elizabeth Bourne Stevenson. He stared at the online wedding photo for long minutes. Elizabeth Stevenson was Ash Gantry.

That was when Jake decided to go see Ash Gantry again. He didn't want to waste time doing searches. He wanted to find out the story directly from her—and make sure she was safe.

"If you'd like to come in," said Ash, "come around the side. The front door is locked."

Still clutching his cap, he came down the steps and cut across her lawn—which needed mowing in a bad way—to the driveway. He turned the corner in time to see her limping up the wooden steps to the side door. He saw a baseball bat in her hand before she disappeared inside.

There had been a baseball bat in her front entry last night. His stomach churned at the thought of the fear that she must live with every day of her life. He thought of Sarah, his little girl, and what he would do to a man who put that kind of fear in her eyes.

Then he thought of Odette, and shame flooded him.

He forced himself up the steps and into the darkness of the laundry room that also served as mud room. Light suddenly bloomed and he stood by the door, blinking as his eyes adjusted.

"Do you want some tea?" asked Ash. She stood in the doorway of the kitchen proper, wearing a red woolen shirt tucked inside jeans that were too big for her. Her hair was pulled back in a loose braid and her bangs were a little too long. She should have looked disheveled, and a little childlike. Instead, there was a dignity about her that was new. She looked taller.

He thought again about his daughter Sarah.

"Yes," he said. "I'd love tea."

"Come in, then," she said calmly, turning away. Then she glanced at him over her shoulder. "Don't worry about your shoes."

Something about the exchange struck him as funny and he was smiling when he placed his cap on top of the washing machine. Then he noticed the baseball bat lying on the dryer and the humor seeped away.

The room smelled of laundry detergent and damp earth, reminding him of the cellar beneath his feet. He carefully wiped his shoes on the mat and followed her inside the kitchen.

"Have a seat," she said, waving him to a stool at the counter. He sat down and watched her as she filled the electric kettle and pulled a small Brown Betty down from the cupboard above the stove. That was where his wife kept the things she didn't use often but wanted at hand if she did need them.

Then Ash turned toward the light and he hissed in dismay.

"What the hell happened?" he asked evenly. The side of her face was a little swollen, but it was the purplish bruise on her forehead and over part of her eye that concerned him.

She looked at him in surprise, the lid of the Brown Betty in one hand. Then she blinked and her free hand went to her forehead. She grinned.

"You should see the other guy."

But he didn't smile and, by the look on his face, he was thinking the worst. She shook her head slightly.

"A bad fall at the gym this morning," she explained. "And the other guy has a matching bruise."

He studied her for a moment. There was humor lurking in her eyes. He relaxed a little.

"Did you get yourself checked out?" he asked gruffly.

Ash shrugged with one shoulder. She'd been through worse.

"I don't have much time," she said, glancing at the police officer. He looked big and official, and a little incongruous, sitting there at her kitchen counter. She wanted to smile again, but the grave expression on his face warned her not to. She found the ginger peach tea in the cupboard and put two bags in the teapot, then took down two white mugs from the open shelf above the sink.

"Are you going somewhere?" asked Jake cautiously. It wasn't any of his business, but really, should she be exposing herself?

She flashed a grin at him, reminding him suddenly that she was very young.

"I have a date," she said, then seeing the surprise in his eyes, added, "My next-door neighbor invited me for dinner."

Jake nodded, relieved. That should be okay. He knew Bea Stratford. A practical, capable woman.

"I'm glad you came," continued Ash more seriously. Just before the water in the kettle came to a roiling boil, she pulled the carafe off the heating pad and poured the hot water into the teapot, then into the two mugs to warm them up. She wasn't much of a tea drinker, really, but she'd read somewhere that it was better to pour tea into a pre-heated cup.

The smell of ginger wafted up from the teapot and Jake groaned inwardly. He hated ginger.

"Why?" he asked. After the reception he'd gotten last night, he'd hadn't known what to expect, but he certainly hadn't expected to be greeted with tea and a baseball bat.

"I was getting ready to write you an email," said Ash. She picked up the teapot and swirled the water around in it, then set it down again. Then she wrapped her hands around the round body of the ceramic pot, warming them before the heat made her pull back. Finally, she looked across the counter at him. Even sitting down, he was taller than her.

He sat there patiently, looking at her, waiting for her to speak. For the first time she noticed that there was quite a bit of gray in his short dark hair. She hadn't noticed, either, that he had light gray eyes that somehow managed to look warm. Maybe it was the fringe of dark lashes.

You're stalling, she told herself.

"Maybe I should start," he said suddenly, surprising her.

He looked across the counter at her and tried to pull the right words together.

"Max Strelzow called me a few hours ago," he began. He watched her pour and accepted the mug that she slid across at him. "He told me about the SUV that had been following you." Her shoulders tensed and her fingers tightened on the handle of her own mug. "It turns out it belongs to a local private investigator. He's been hired by your husband, Calum Stevenson, to find you." It still amazed him that she was married. She looked all of sixteen, for Pete's sake.

For a moment, he thought she would break, she seemed so brittle. Then all the tension whooshed out of her in a great sigh of relief.

"Well, at least I'm not crazy," she said finally.

Jake's mouth twisted in a wry grin. That was one way of looking at it.

"The investigator said that he reported your location to your husband."

She nodded, unsurprised.

"Why is your husband looking for you?"

She looked up at him, her green eyes dark despite the cheerful light in the kitchen, and suddenly she looked much older.

"He wants to kill me," she said. "And I'm going to let him try."

Jake just looked at her. This woman. Holy shit.

CHAPTER 19

Ash set her napkin down, a little embarrassed that she had eaten so much.

"That was delicious," she told her hostess sincerely.

Bea Stratford leaned back in her chair across from Ash, one hand in her lap and one twirling the stem of her wine glass. Her hair was a smooth white cap, brushed back behind her ears. She grinned.

"It's good to see such a healthy appetite in a young woman," she said approvingly. "So many are obsessed with carbs or good fats or whatever."

Ash thought about her protruding hip bones and bony chest. She was filling out again, but it was a slow process.

"I didn't have time for lunch," she said with a smile. "And this meal was delicious."

Bea had made chicken breasts with a tasty sauce that didn't seem to have any cream in it but still managed to be flavorful. She'd roasted carrots, yams, broccoli, and leeks with olive oil and garlic, and had made mushroom risotto to accompany everything. Ash had had seconds... and if she hadn't been too embarrassed, she would have asked for thirds.

The table at which they sat was long enough to sit six comfort-

ably, and by the split in the middle, it had leaves that could accommodate more. The table and its matching chairs reminded Ash of
Grandma's oak dining room set. All that was missing was a lace table
runner down the middle to cover the crack.

"This is a nice home," she said.

Bea's house was new—all the houses in the neighborhood had
been built in the last ten years—and the living room and dining room
were open to each other, and the dining room to the kitchen, around
the corner. Pale hardwood covered the floors, even in the kitchen,
which was hidden from the front entrance behind a narrow red wall.

"I like it," said Bea. She wore a white tunic top with long sleeves
and narrow black pants that made her look taller. Ash had been
surprised to find that Bea Stratford was only a hair taller than she
was. Bea just looked taller. A long silver chain had a watch face as a
pendant and she wore small silver earrings.

Ash felt decidedly underdressed in her jeans and red turtleneck.
She really had to get more clothes.

Maybe she'd wait and see what happened with Calum first. No
point in buying new clothes if she was about to die.

From where Ash sat, she could see the fireplace in the corner
of the living room. A sculpted wood box—long and narrow—sat on
wheels next to the fireplace. When Ash asked, Bea told her that it
held the split logs she used in the fireplace. Her late husband had
built it when they first built the place.

"We bought the lot as soon as it came on the market," continued
Bea. She reached over to pick up the bottle of Pinot Grigio and refilled
Ash's glass before refilling her own. "After all," she said, waggling the
bottle, "we're not driving."

Ash laughed. "It's a good wine, even if I do say so myself." She
had taken a long time picking it out at the liquor store and finally
went with the store clerk's recommendation.

"You may indeed say so yourself," said Bea. "It's from a local
winery, just down river." She sipped from her glass. "They offer tours.
I'll take you, if you're interested."

The swell of gratitude took Ash by surprise and she had to look away. Every little kindness threatened to undo her. She cleared her throat.

"That would be nice," she managed. "I've never seen a winery."

"I guess there aren't many out in Alberta," said Bea.

Ash stared at her blankly.

"Isn't that where you're from?" asked Bea, confusion on her face. "Your license plates..."

"Oh!" Ash shook her head. "No, not really. I only stayed in Alberta a couple of weeks. I'm from Vancouver, originally."

"B.C.," said Bea, nodding her head sagely. "Good wines there. Not as good as ours, of course, but good enough."

"Hey!" protested Ash laughingly.

Bea grinned at her, unrepentant, and got up to clear the table. Ash automatically went to stand up and winced as her hip reminded her not to move so quickly. Bea waved her down. "Sit. You only get to help on the second dinner invitation." She gathered Ash's plate and cutlery and disappeared into the kitchen. "What brought you out here?" she asked. "We have winter, you know."

Ash smiled and looked down at the placemat. It was made of heavy woven cotton, blue, with white fringe on either side. It looked homemade. She picked up a crumb and placed it in the palm of her hand. What to say. She had made a decision to no longer hide, but did that mean she had to drag this nice woman into her problems?

"A bad marriage," she said finally. "It was time to leave."

"Ah," said Bea behind her. Ash looked over her shoulder to find the older woman leaning in the kitchen doorway. "I'm sorry."

Ash shrugged.

"No kids?" asked Bea gently.

Ash flinched a little but for the first time, the thought of her baby didn't stab through her.

"No kids," she said softly.

Bea's big, work-hardened hand landed softly on Ash's shoulder and was gone.

"Are you going to join me in coffee?" she asked, "or are you a tea woman?"

"Coffee, please," said Ash.

"Good woman."

While the water heated, Bea placed the tarts Ash had brought on a serving plate and brought it to the table. Ignoring the older woman's objections, Ash helped her bring the cream and sugar and cups and dessert plates to the dining room. She moved slowly, forcing herself to walk normally rather than limp. She'd learned that it was the fastest way to recover from an injury.

When they were finally seated again, with the coffee sitting in the French press waiting to be squeezed down, it was Ash's turn for questions.

"Did you know the owners of the house I'm renting?"

Bea looked down at the wine she was swirling in her glass. Her eyebrows rose.

"Not really," she said finally. "Odette and Frank Boudreaux." She glanced at Ash before looking down again. "They were private people. Then Odette left a few years ago and Frank moved out soon after. I guess he couldn't stand living there without her."

Ash almost snorted, but remembered herself in time.

"Were they happy, do you think?" she asked carefully. She didn't know exactly what she hoped to learn from Bea, but she didn't want to come right out and share her suspicions.

Bea looked at her, head cocked. "What an odd question."

Ash shrugged. "I like the house. I like it a lot. I wonder about the people who lived there before me."

"It used to be a farmhouse, you know. Abraham and I used to drive out here on Sundays. We raised our children downtown, but we always liked this area. We kept an eye on the renovations. The house doesn't look much like the old farmhouse from the outside. I haven't been inside."

Ash's eyebrows rose and she couldn't help but grin. "You're a sly thing, Bea Stratford. Come by for coffee tomorrow and I'll show you around."

Bea grinned back. "I believe I will take you up on that offer," she said. "Speaking of coffee..." She pressed the plunger down on the French press and poured coffee into both their cups, then slid a fruit tart onto Ash's dessert plate.

They helped themselves to sugar and cream in companionable silence and Ash took a sip. Oh, my. Bea knew how to make coffee.

"Good tart," said Bea around a mouthful of blueberries and pastry.

Ash dug into her own tart and had to agree.

"They bought the farm, then immediately subdivided," continued Bea as if there'd been no pause. "At the same time, they started renovations." She sipped from her coffee cup and looked thoughtful. "It changed the character of the place, of course, both the subdivision and the renovation. I kind of got the impression that it wasn't Odette's idea to sell off the land. But Frank Boudreaux doesn't take no for an answer."

Ash's pulse quickened. "Why do you say that?" She tried to keep her tone casual, but Bea's gaze sharpened with interest. She shrugged.

"I could hear him yelling at her sometimes," she said. "Ours is the closest house to theirs and his voice carried. I wasn't surprised when she left him."

"Are you sure?" asked Ash before she could stop herself.

"That I wasn't surprised, or that she left him?" Bea was smiling, but her eyes narrowed in interest. "What's going on, Ashley?"

Ash took another sip of coffee to cover her discomfiture. "Nothing." She looked away. "I don't know."

"You don't know what?" asked Bea.

Ash was no longer interested in her tart. She pushed her plate away. "Nobody's seen or spoken to Odette since the day she left here," she said carefully. "I spoke to her aunt in Edmonton, her only living relative. She hasn't heard from her in seven years. Don't you think that's strange?"

Bea toyed with the handle of her cup but her attention was fixed on Ash. "Maybe they weren't close."

Ash shook her head. "Liesel Wirth raised Odette after her parents died. They were close. She told me that Frank came between her and Odette."

The hands on the cup stilled. After a while, Bea looked up from her abandoned tart.

"What exactly are you saying?" she asked.

There was no disguising the wariness in her eyes and Ash silently cursed herself. She didn't know this woman. Just because they had taken an instant liking to each other didn't make them friends. What was she doing, confiding in her?

"Nothing." She smiled and shook her head. "Just my imagination getting away from me." She pushed away from the table and rose carefully. "It's getting late. I need to take a bath and soak this hip while I can still move."

Bea automatically got up, too, and together they cleared the table. Ash wished she could take back the last fifteen minutes. Their easy camaraderie was gone and Bea moved around her kitchen as if she were preoccupied.

"No, don't worry about the dishes," said Bea when Ash started rinsing them off. "That's why God invented dishwashers."

Ash grinned in spite of everything and headed for the front door and the closet where she'd left her coat.

"Thank you for dinner," she said as she pulled her coat off the hanger. "It was delicious and I had a lovely time."

The smile Bea gave her was genuine.

"I had a lovely time, too. Thank you for coming."

Ash opened the door and stepped out onto the porch. "I should be around all morning," she said, looking at Bea. "I hope you do come over for coffee." To her surprise, tears pricked her eyes and she turned away before the older woman could see.

"That was an unhappy marriage," said Bea suddenly.

Surprised, Ash turned to look at her. Bea was standing in the doorway, arms crossed over her chest against the cold, staring at Odette's house.

"How do you mean?" she finally asked when Bea didn't continue.

Bea dragged her gaze back. "I would see her go to work and come back, at first. Then, after a while, I never saw her outside anymore except to do yard work. Even then, I learned not to talk to her if Frank was around. He would always find an excuse to call her inside. I used to feel so sorry for her. And mad, if you want to know the truth. I wanted her to tell him off. To yell at him. But she never did."

They stared at each other for a long moment as the words settled between them. Finally, Ash nodded.

"Good night, Bea."

"Good night, Ash."

Ash turned and carefully made her way down the stairs.

Bea didn't want to admit it, but she'd known something was wrong between Frank and Odette. There was no disguising the look of guilt in her eyes.

As Ash slowly made her way across the lawn to her own place, she found herself wondering if Bea would have turned a blind eye to Calum's beatings, too.

CHAPTER 20

Taking a bath just about did her in. Getting into the bathtub was tricky enough, but getting out involved getting to her knees in the rapidly cooling water, then slithering over the edge and onto the bath mat. Ash was pretty sure that added a few more bruises to her hip bones, but even as she struggled to her feet, she was glad she'd made the effort. Her muscles had relaxed in the tub and hopefully she'd feel better in the morning.

She quickly dried herself, then rubbed moisturizer all over while standing in front of the mirror. She noted the bruises on her hip, the hip bones and ribs sticking out under her pink skin, the bruising starting to extend down to her eye. She sighed. With her wet hair straggling down her back, she looked like a refugee from the apocalypse. But as she kept rubbing the lotion on, she noted the play of muscles in her shoulders and arms, and the definition in her abdominal muscles, and she smiled.

She was getting there.

She finished with the lotion and slipped into her long-sleeved tee-shirt and pajama bottoms before giving her hair another rub with the towel. She combed it out, then braided it so that it fell in one long braid down her back. She would have crazy hair in the morning, but she just didn't have the energy to dry it tonight.

Tomorrow, if she could move, she would go grocery shopping and buy some new clothes. She walked slowly into her bedroom, taking care to move correctly. The hip felt sore, but as long as she didn't make any sudden movements, it didn't hurt too much.

She knew she was kidding herself. She'd been injured enough to know it would be days before she regained regular movement without too much pain.

But for tonight, it was enough. She pulled the blankets down, made sure the baseball bat was on the empty side of the bed, sat down on the edge, and used her hands to support her leg as she carefully lifted it into bed. Moments later, she was snuggled under the blankets with the lights off. She drifted for a few minutes, contemplating the incredible day. Starting with getting injured, realizing she was being followed, her cathartic confession to Max and Charlotte, telling the police officer about Calum, then dinner with Bea...

It occurred to her suddenly that if Calum could hire a private detective to follow her around, she could hire one, too, if only to have a record of his movements once he came looking for her.

"Don't come tonight, Calum," she mumbled as sleep overtook her. "I'm too tired." Then, just before she sank into oblivion, "Good-night, Odette."

She didn't feel the brush of cool air on her cheek.

◊◊◊

Jake parked on Kestrel and walked around the corner to Hawk Street, heading toward Ash Gantry's house. Night had settled in a few hours ago and the wind had fallen, thank goodness. As it was, the clear skies promised cooling temperatures and he could see his breath. The slight wind from his passage bit into his exposed face and he stuck his cold hands in his jacket pockets. He'd left the house so fast he'd forgotten his gloves, leaving a bemused Gemma in bed with a promise to call as soon as he could.

It was past midnight and all the lights were out at Ash's place, as were those in most of the houses on the street. He'd warned the patrolmen in the unmarked car not to approach the vehicle unless the occupant made a move toward the house. As a consequence, they didn't get plate numbers and he had no idea who he was dealing with.

For all he knew, whoever was in the pickup truck—Calum Stevenson, more than likely—had been watching the house for days. His guys had arrived an hour ago, once the chief finally approved his request and he had a chance to organize the watch, and only realized there was someone in the pickup after they'd been watching the street for a while.

There. A white pickup, S-10, no canopy. There were a few other vehicles parked on the street, but most vehicles were in the driveways. Something moved in the rear window and he hesitated.

He had to be careful how he approached the driver. He didn't want Stevenson making a run for the house, and Ash. And he didn't want the guy to pull a weapon on him.

He pulled out his cell and punched in a number.

"Brixton."

"It's Slater," said Jake to the senior man in the unmarked car. "Approaching suspect vehicle from the rear passenger side."

"We've got eyes on you, Sarge," said Brixton. "You want we should distract him?"

"No," said Jake. "I'll keep the line open. You get ready to move if he makes a break for it."

"Got it," said Brixton.

Jake stuffed the phone back in his pocket without turning it off, then reached inside his jacket for the nine millimeter in his shoulder holster. He pulled it out and slid the action back, then pulled the tiny LED flashlight from his left pocket. He kept his weapon at his side as he ran in a crouch toward the pickup. Then, just as he reached the passenger side window, he flicked the flashlight on and rapped on the window with the butt of his weapon.

The figure inside the cab jumped and Jake heard a muffled "Jesus Christ!" before the window rolled down and Max Strelzow glared at him in the beam of the flashlight. Silver whiskers covered his round face and his crew cut reflected back the light of the flashlight.

"What the hell are you doing?" demanded Max. Jake noticed that his hand was on the crow bar on the seat next to him. He wore a heavy jacket, fully zipped, and warm gloves.

"Max," said Jake patiently, finally lowering the flashlight. "What the hell are you doing here?"

"Jake?" said Max and there was no disguising the relief in his voice. "Besides having a heart attack," he said pointedly, "I'm keeping an eye on Ash."

Jake suddenly remembered Brixton and pulled out his phone, first releasing the slide and replacing the nine millimeter into its holster. He caught the widening of Max's eyes.

"Brixton?"

"Here, Sarge. Everything okay?"

Jake leaned his elbows on the door and aimed the flashlight down. "Yes, all clear. It's Max Strelzow, the subject's employer. He's keeping an eye on her, too."

Brixton sighed. "Is he trying to steal my job?"

Jake laughed. "Nope, your job is safe. Keep your eyes open. How's Bilodeau?"

"Freezing his ass off, he tells me, but all's clear at the back of the house."

Jake laughed again. Bilodeau had drawn the first shift in the woods at the foot of Ash's backyard. It would indeed be cold but the rookie had better learn to dress appropriately.

"All right, signing off," said Jake. He slid the phone back in his inside pocket and turned back to Max.

"Go home, Max," said Jake. "We've got this covered."

Max nodded. "Right. I'd better make a few phone calls first." He pulled his right glove off and fished through his coat pocket.

"Who do you need to call at this hour?" asked Jake.

"Barney Strumgen," said Max. "He runs Barney's Gym. He was

going to take the next shift, starting at one. He can call Paul Coventry and tell him he doesn't have to take his four o'clock shift. Then I'll call Charlotte and let her know she's off the hook for the seven o'clock shift."

Jake stared at the man, at a loss for words. Ash Gantry had only been in Albans for a few weeks and she'd already inspired four people—five, counting him—to band together to protect her. He glanced up at her dark house, fully expecting a pale figure to be staring back at him, but the house remained asleep and quiet.

CHAPTER 21

Ash hadn't responded to the email Maddie sent, so after dropping Helen off at gymnastics on Saturday morning, Maddie popped by the house on Hawk Street. It was only a little past two, and Ash wasn't home.

At least, the car wasn't in the driveway. Maddie parked on the street in front of the house and ran up the steps to the front door. She knocked, just in case Ash's car was in the shop or something, but there was no answer.

She'd only wait a few minutes. Maybe Ash was gone for the day. She was a pretty young thing. She probably had lots of young men hitting on her at the restaurant. Maybe someone had asked her out.

Maddie shook her head at herself. Ash might be young physically, but her eyes were old. And sad.

She sighed and turned away from the house. Despite the brilliant sunshine, it was cold and her thin leather gloves were not cutting it today. She'd wait inside the warm and cozy minivan and drink her coffee. The house was at the top of the hill and the wind seemed to gather speed and viciousness as it barreled up the road toward the high point.

It didn't seem to bother the kids playing hockey in the street.

She watched them for a moment, remembering her own youth. Only the girls didn't play street hockey back then. They played tag or hide-and-seek, or flag.

Pulling the collar of her coat up, she started back toward her car. At that moment, a kid yelled, "Car!" and they hustled the net out of the way to let Ash's blue Volvo by. Maddie waited by the driveway as Ash pulled in and cut the engine. She opened the door and carefully eased herself out of the driver's seat, dragging that ugly backpack with her.

Then the girl turned to flash her a smile and Maddie gasped.

"Dear God in Heaven!"

Ash's smile turned rueful. "I know," she said, closing the driver's door and opening the back door. "I look like I got caught in a gang fight."

She looked more like she'd gone to hell and back, and lived to tell the tale.

"What happened?" asked Maddie, hurrying to help her with the bags in the back seat. There were groceries, but also a few bags from Muncie's, a women's clothing store downtown, and one from Jamieson's, a family store.

"Come inside," said Ash, closing the door. "I bought cookies and different tea. You can try it out while I tell you." The wind was cold and she was exhausted from getting in and out of the car and trying to walk normally when her left hip felt like it was filled with little shards of glass.

Maddie followed Ash up the driveway to the side door. Ash was walking slowly, carefully putting her weight on her left foot and rolling through the movement. What the hell...?

They hauled the bags inside the laundry room and Ash went to fill the electric kettle with water. She glanced at Maddie, who seemed to be having some kind of internal debate. The realtor left the clothing bags on a chair by the table, but brought the groceries to the counter and automatically started putting the perishables away in the fridge.

Ash smiled a little to herself. Maddie had to feel pretty comfortable with her to take that kind of liberty. She pulled the box of assorted herbal teas out and the Earl Grey, and turned to the older woman.

"Black? Or herbal?"

Maddie blinked, then peered closer at the herbal tea box. "Peppermint." She didn't feel like having tea and longed for the coffee she had left behind in the minivan. Oh, well.

Ash nodded and pulled the plastic off the box. As the water heated, she reached into the cupboard above the stove for the Brown Betty, feeling the tightness in her hip. She hadn't done any stretching at all, she remembered guiltily. When Maddie left, she'd do some long stretches to ease the growing stiffness. She pulled out the bottle of Tylenol and swallowed two with some water. Her head was killing her.

"So, what happened?" asked Maddie as she came around the counter to sit down on one of the stools. She'd noticed Ash taking the pills. With a bruise like that, it wasn't surprising she needed pain killers.

So Ash told her about the bad fall and Paul landing on her and banging his head against hers. Maddie winced.

"I'll bet his black eye is even worse," finished Ash.

Maddie rolled her eyes. "It's not a competition, you know. You could have been seriously hurt." Not that it was any of her business.

Ash shrugged. She'd seen worse. Much worse. "So, what brings you around?" she asked. The water finished boiling and she poured some into the Brown Betty, and some into mugs.

Maddie blinked, suddenly remembering that she had come for a reason, not just a visit.

"The owner of the house wants to do some work on the place," she started. "In the cellar." She nodded toward the laundry room. "He'd like to pour a concrete floor, insulate the walls, that kind of thing."

"When?" asked Ash. Could she refuse? What did her lease say?

Maddie laced her fingers together on the counter and cocked her head at Ash. "He says his men would be able to start next week." At the look of dismay on Ash's face, she hurriedly added, "Don't worry. They would only work here while you're away at work. They'd keep their supplies under a tarp on the driveway. They wouldn't start until after you left and would be gone by the time you got home."

Ash poured the hot water out of the mugs and swirled the tea in the Brown Betty, thinking. She didn't like the idea of Frank Boudreaux's men in her house. She glanced around but saw no sign of Odette. Did that mean she didn't mind? Maybe she hadn't heard? Where did ghosts go when they weren't around?

She poured tea into both mugs and pushed one across the counter toward Maddie. "How long will it take?" She shifted her weight onto her good hip and opened the box of shortbread cookies.

Maddie pushed the serving plate closer to Ash and shrugged. "He figures the concrete will take the longest, because it'll need a few days to cure. So, maybe two weeks, tops."

Ash's face was unreadable and Maddie wondered what she was thinking. Frank's request was reasonable, but Ash was within her rights to say no. It suddenly occurred to her that Ash might not know that.

"You don't have to agree," Maddie said impulsively. She plucked a cookie off the plate and took a bite, chasing it with a sip of peppermint tea. "You can say no."

Ash nodded. "I know." All her instincts told her to say no, but the more she thought of it, the more this sounded like an opportunity.

"Why now?" she asked suddenly. "Can't he wait until my lease is up?"

Maddie shrugged and watched Ash walk carefully around the counter to sit on the stool next to hers.

"He wants to put the place up for sale when your lease is up," explained Maddie. "And fixing up the cellar will help sell the place."

Well, it made sense, thought Ash. That cellar was a creepy place. And she could arrange to come home early one day to talk to the workers, innocent-like, and hopefully find out more about Frank Boudreaux.

She shrugged. "Sure," she said casually. "I don't see any problem. He's got the key, I presume?"

Maddie nodded. "Of course. He owns the place." She blew on the tea, wondering why her stomach suddenly felt queasy.

Ash was disappointed that Bea Stratford hadn't come over. It would have been nice to make a friend in her neighborhood, but clearly she had spooked the woman last night at dinner. Oh, well.

She stood on the back deck, looking out at the trees at the bottom of her yard and the carpet of colorful leaves on her lawn. There was no getting out of it. She had to finish the raking. And mow. While the little shed at the bottom of the yard held three rakes, there was no lawn mower. She toyed with the idea of buying one, but it didn't make sense, if she was only here for six months.

But Frank Boudreaux was going to sell. The thought played in her mind, tempting her. She liked the house. Liked the neighborhood. Liked the town.

She could do worse than settle here. And she had enough money, thanks to Grandma. She could settle here—as long as Calum left her alone.

She sighed deeply, aware of the sun on her face and the cool breeze numbing her bare hands.

Calum. Where was he? Was he watching her now?

Did it matter? How much longer was she going to let him control her, even when he wasn't around?

Pulling the thin woolen gloves out of her jacket pocket, she slowly went down the stairs and headed for the shed. Her hip protested, but she knew she was better off moving, slowly and carefully. That way it wouldn't seize up on her. Besides, what was she going to do? Sit on her bum all day?

She didn't bother turning the shed light on. A small window on the side facing the house provided enough light, along with the open door. Shelves lined two walls and on either side of the window, clamps held rakes in place against the wall. A hose caddy had a hose wrapped around it and there were hand nozzles and sprinklers on the shelves, along with plant food and fertilizer in a bag on the floor. Empty terracotta pots filled one entire shelf. The place smelled musty and dusty. She grabbed a rake and closed the door.

She'd finish the front before starting on the back.

An hour later, she had two big piles of colorful leaves ready to be disposed of, except that she had forgotten to buy plastic bags. There had been bags in the house, but she'd used them up a few days ago when she first raked the front lawn. By the time she got back in the car and drove back to the store, the wind would have redistributed the leaves all over her lawn.

Way to plan ahead, Ash.

She didn't think she could handle another trip to the store. Her hip was killing her and all she wanted to do was stretch out. She straightened and wanted to lean against the rake, but the teeth were too flexible and she didn't want to risk breaking them or bending them out of shape.

The exercise had warmed her so well that she had taken her gloves off and was considering taking off her UBC sweatshirt. She pushed the loose hairs from her face and stretched her neck out. Finally, she realized what was making her so twitchy; she was being watched.

She glanced up and down the street. The kids were still playing shinny, screaming triumphantly whenever the ball made it inside the net. Not surprising. It was a perfect fall day, with the sky pale blue and thin, filmy clouds rushing by high up. In spots protected from the wind, the sun actually felt warm. A few neighbors were working in their yards, too. They had all remembered their big orange yard refuse bags. Cars were parked up and down the street. She couldn't see anything wrong, or anyone who didn't belong.

But the back of her neck itched, and she felt like running back inside and locking the door behind her.

"Nice day to work in the yard."

Ash whirled, winced as her hip protested, and saw Bea Stratford standing on the other side of Ash's driveway, at the bottom of the incline, a hand shading her eyes as she looked up.

"Bea," she said with a smile.

"Sorry I didn't come by this morning," said Bea. "My daughter called with an emergency babysitting request. By the time I got back, you'd left."

"No worries," said Ash. "Are you ready for that tour?"

"Sure, but shouldn't you get those leaves off your lawn first?"

Ash glanced at the nearest pile and watched the wind pick up a dozen leaves and swirl them around before dropping them ten feet from the pile. She sighed.

"I forgot to pick up bags," she confessed.

Bea laughed. She had an old-fashioned printed red and white scarf over her head, tied underneath her hair at the back, and wore a pair of black jeans and a blue sweater with the sleeves pushed up. Except for the white hair, she really didn't look old enough to be a grandmother.

"I've got lots of bags," she said, turning away. "I'll go get a few." Then she glanced over her shoulder at Ash. "It's okay to ask for help, you know."

Fifteen minutes later, they stuffed the last of the leaves in a bag and tied it off. Ash straightened her aching back and stood with hands on hips, surveying the lawn and the orange bags. Back in Vancouver, kids used to take the bags and draw Halloween faces on them, as if the bags were really pumpkins. Of course, that was usually about a month later than now.

"That lawn needs cutting," said Bea, standing next to her.

Ash glanced at her but there was no censure in the older woman's voice. She was just stating a fact.

"I know," said Ash. "I don't have a lawn mower."

"Oh, you don't need a lawn mower," said Bea. She hooked a thumb over her shoulder toward the street. "You just need a kid with a lawn mower." She looked at Ash and grinned. "I'll give you a name. Kids are always looking to make extra money. Heck, they'll even rake your backyard for you."

Ash blinked at the older woman, surprised it hadn't occurred to her. "I'll take that name," she said with a nod. "Come on inside. I'll give you a tour. Would you prefer tea or coffee?"

Bea raised an eyebrow. "Personally, I never saw the point of tea."

Ash laughed and led her inside through the side door, leaving the rake leaning against the house. They took turns brushing the crumbling bits of leaves off their clothes before going inside and taking their shoes off.

The next couple of hours flew by as Ash gave Bea the tour of the house and it was almost four thirty by the time they ended up sitting on the back deck, drinking coffee. The sun was low in the sky and cast long shadows on the lawn. Bea watched the wind pluck leaves from the birches and the maples and cast them into the air. The bulk of the old farmhouse protected them from the worst of the wind. She didn't mind that it was starting to get colder. It was so beautiful out here. The farmhouse had the best view of all the houses on the street.

"Well, he may have been a jerk," she said finally, "but he was a smart one."

Ash looked sideways at her neighbor. "Pardon?"

"Frank Boudreaux," explained Bea. "He did a good job of fixing up the house. And he was pretty smart in buying up the farm and then selling off the lots. It gave him the capital to start his contracting business."

Ash nodded, not wanting to interrupt.

"Maybe that's why she stopped working," continued Bea after a while. "They didn't need the money."

When Bea remained silent, Ash tried a little prod. "Where did she work?"

Bea blinked and turned her gaze back to Ash. "At the library," she said. "She was the head librarian." She laughed a little. "Frank Boudreaux must have a thing for librarians," she continued. "I hear he's living with the current head librarian."

Ash smiled perfunctorily but everything in her stilled as she remembered the head librarian at the library. The tall, thin woman with graying blonde hair and big blue eyes—she could have passed for Odette's sister. She had shown a lot of interest in Ash's research about the house—the McTavish farmhouse, as it had been known. And she'd shown a lot of curiosity about Ash's interest in the high school yearbooks.

Had she told Frank? Did that explain Frank's sudden interest in fixing up the house?

"Well, I should go," said Bea, getting up from the top step where they had been sitting. "I have to get supper going. The kids are coming over tonight."

They headed back inside and left the cups on the counter.

"I'll have to call you with the phone number," said Bea. "What's your phone number?"

Ash smiled, absurdly pleased to be able to give it to her. She had to hunt for a piece of paper on which to jot it down, and finally had to rip off a corner of a flyer that had come in the mail. Then she had to hunt for a pen, and finally found one at the bottom of her backpack.

Number in hand, Bea looked at her quizzically. "That was a lot of work."

Ash laughed and walked her out. They stood on the driveway, enjoying the last of the sun's warmth. The kids had been called inside for dinner and the street was quiet, as if resting after a day of activity.

"Thanks for the visit," said Ash. "I'll replace the bags the next time I go out."

Bea shrugged. "No need. I have enough to last for a few years. I'll call you in a few minutes with that number." She patted Ash on the arm and cut across the lawn toward her house.

Ash gave the street one last, lingering glance, then turned back to her own house. Odette hadn't shown up once during Bea's visit. Ash couldn't tell if that was good or bad; if Odette liked Bea, or didn't. But she never seemed to come when Maddie was around, either, and Odette had known Maddie in high school, just like she'd known Jake Slater.

Ash sighed. Her head was beginning to ache again, and she was hungry. She'd taken out the frozen spaghetti sauce, so she'd get that going and while it heated slowly, she'd take a hot bath.

She had just pulled out the sauce pan when her cell phone rang. That would be Bea with the phone number.

She hurried across the kitchen to the table where she'd left her backpack and pulled the phone out. She didn't recognize the number.

"Hello?" she said, expecting to hear Bea's gravelly voice at the other end.

"Ms. Gantry, this is Hamish Caldwell."

Ash smiled. "Hello Mr. Caldwell. You got my message."

"Yes, my dear," continued the lawyer, his tone serious. "I'm not sure it's wise to connect with you openly, so I'm calling from the diner."

"Mr. Caldwell," she began, then stopped, trying to marshal her thoughts. This man had done so much for her... she didn't want him to think she was ungrateful. "Mr. Caldwell, it's time to stop running. I know Calum hired a private investigator to locate me. He knows where I am. And that's fine. I'm not leaving. I've informed the police and they are watching for him."

Hamish Caldwell remained silent for so long that she looked

at the screen to make sure they hadn't been cut off. Finally, he spoke again.

"I understand. You must understand, too. Calum Stevenson is a very smart man, with a highly specialized skill set. He finds people. Now that he knows where you are, I believe you to be in extreme danger."

He wasn't telling her anything she didn't already know, but to hear it laid out baldly made her shiver. She knew Calum would come for her. She just didn't know what would happen when he did.

"My dear, who are you dealing with at the police department?" asked Mr. Caldwell.

She glanced at the cupboard where the mugs were. She'd taped the business card that Jake Slater had given her to the inside of the door.

"His name is Jake Slater," she said, walking over to the cupboard and pulling it open. "Sergeant Jake Slater." She read out the phone number.

"I'll call him," said Mr. Caldwell, and Ash thought she heard discouragement in his voice.

"Mr. Caldwell," she said gently, "I like it here. I like the people, the town, the house I'm in. I'd like to settle down here, go to school, find something meaningful to do with my life. I'm twenty-four. I can't keep running for the rest of my life. This is where I make my stand."

"I understand, Ms. Gantry. Believe me. I just don't want any harm to come to you."

Me neither, thought Ash, and looked around as a flicker in the corner of her eye caught her attention. Odette stood in the doorway between the kitchen and the laundry room, watching her.

CHAPTER 22

She fell asleep thinking about Frank Boudreaux, not Calum. She didn't know what to make of the fact that his new wife— or common-law partner, she supposed—was the head librarian. It bothered her that the woman was blonde and blue-eyed, just like Odette. Was Frank beating her, too? Had she told him that Ash was doing research on the house? On him and Odette?

But she wouldn't know who Ash was looking for in the yearbooks. Not for sure.

In spite of the questions swirling around in her head, she fell asleep quickly and slept well. In the morning, she woke up refreshed and was relieved that her hip felt better, too. Then she caught sight of herself in the bathroom mirror and winced. The bruise was uglier than ever, mottled yellow and green and blue, and that eye was still bloodshot.

Oh, well.

After a huge breakfast of eggs, toast, and bacon, she went outside and started to work on the backyard. Bea had come through with the phone number and Jenny Kavanaugh was coming over in the afternoon to mow the lawn, so Ash had to finish raking.

She took a break for coffee and sat on the top step of the back deck, enjoying the sun on her face. She'd grown up in Vancouver and was used to long, glorious falls, but she hadn't expected that it would be just as glorious—if colder—in the east.

By the time she broke for lunch, the backyard and side of the house had been raked clean. All the leaves were captured in Bea's orange bags and piled on the driveway, next to the house, ready for the next trash day.

She was just washing up when she heard a lawn mower start up outside. She went to the front porch. The girl pushing the lawn mower looked up at her and waved but kept mowing. Jenny Kavanaugh was maybe fourteen years old, tall and rangy, with long red hair caught up in two braids. She wore ratty old jeans and a sweatshirt to match, and heavy work boots, work gloves, and ear protectors. She'd clearly done this before. They hadn't met yet—Ash had only spoken to her on the phone.

The racket chased Ash back inside and she stood in her dining room for a minute, wondering what she should do now. She didn't think she could relax while that noise ratcheted up and down as Jenny moved across the lawn.

Then her gaze caught on the top of the trees at the bottom of the backyard and she made up her mind. She'd been meaning to explore those woods since the first day she moved in. She'd walk slowly and be careful, but she wanted to see the woods that were probably Odette's tomb.

She grabbed her jacket from the back of the chair and went to the French door, then remembered she should let Jenny know where she was. Five minutes later, she found an old receipt at the bottom of her backpack and scribbled, "I'm out back." Then she taped it on the glass of the front door before leaving out the back. She remembered to grab her phone, in case she wanted to take a picture.

A few clouds scuttled by, but the sun was high and warm, and she found herself smiling as she carefully descended the steps. It was ridiculous to feel so happy. Her life could explode at any minute.

But she *was* happy. She liked this town and the people in it.

And she liked Odette's house. It suddenly occurred to her that she could talk to Maddie about buying it. But maybe she'd wait until Frank finished the work in the cellar. If he wanted to sell, she would certainly consider buying it.

The thought of owning Odette's house woke all the butterflies in her stomach. It was outrageous, really. Could she really buy the house from the man who had murdered Odette?

Because he had murdered her. She was as sure of that as she was sure that Calum was coming for her.

Her feet left imprints in the long grass and the drone of the lawnmower drowned out the sound of the wind through the trees. As she entered the shaded woods, she shivered at the sudden coolness. The air even smelled cooler here. Watching where she placed her feet, she went deeper, until she figured she would be hidden from a casual glance from anybody on the back deck. She turned then and studied the lawn, the stairs, the door.

Frank could easily have carried—or even dragged—Odette through the back and into the woods. The only risky part was while he was on the deck. Anyone standing in Bea's backyard would have seen Frank on the deck. But if he did it at night, and there was no moon... No one would have seen Frank drag his dead wife into the woods.

The cool wind played with her loose hairs and she turned away from the house, looking around. The woods consisted mostly of maple trees and elms—at least she thought they were elms—and pine and even a few spruce trees. A few yellow leaves fluttered down as she watched. From this angle, she couldn't see the river, but she knew that if she kept walking in a straight line from the house, she'd find it.

As she walked, she became aware of the smell of the woods, a rich, humus smell, with dank undertones of rotting leaves. She glanced from left to right, right to left, looking for a tell-tale hump that might indicate where a body was buried. Even as she searched, however, something told her she wouldn't find anything. It didn't feel right.

Maybe Odette wasn't here after all.

Her foot landed on an exposed root and she twisted to keep from losing her balance. She hissed as a sharp pain in her hip reminded her to be careful.

Then she heard a twig snap and forgot about the pain.

The sound had come from her right. She slowly turned to study the woods. The sun penetrated haphazardly, leaving mottled shadows on the ground and the trees. Despite the constant drone of the lawnmower, she became aware that the woods had gone silent. It was as if a white noise had suddenly ceased.

Someone else was in the woods. Or something else.

"Who's there?" she called sharply, already backing up in the direction she had come.

Another twig snapped and she heard a muffled curse. She stopped and looked around the forest floor for a stick or a stone to use as a weapon.

There. A branch had broken off some time ago and lay like a gray, bleached bone only a few feet away. Keeping her body turned toward the direction the sound had come from, she sidled over to the branch and leaned over to pick it up. Her hand shook as she grasped the smooth wood, but she felt absurdly grateful for its heft.

As she straightened, a movement caught the corner of her eye and she jumped. A man stepped out from behind a tree, twenty feet away, hands up.

"Sorry to startle you, ma'am," he said gently, not moving.

"Who are you?" demanded Ash, hoping volume would disguise the tremor in her voice. "Why are you hiding in the woods?"

He smiled and slowly lowered his arms, but still didn't move toward her. He wore a heavy denim jacket with a gray wool sweater under it, and a pair of black corduroy pants. Dressed for the weather.

He was maybe thirty years old, with short brown hair and a round face, despite a fit appearance. She couldn't tell what color his eyes were. She didn't recognize him, but that didn't mean anything. She didn't know most of her neighbors. *Was* he a neighbor? Or another one of Calum's hired guns?

"Were you spying on me?" she asked, recognizing how crazy she sounded. Just because he had surprised her didn't mean he was up to no good.

His eyebrows rose and he shook his head. "No, ma'am," he said promptly.

Something about the way he held himself, a wariness, made her jumpy. "What's your name?" She pulled out her phone, ready to punch in 9-1-1 if he made any sudden moves.

He sighed and his shoulders slumped. Slater was going to kill him. He'd specifically told them not to let her see them. "I'm Corporal Daniel Montrose," he said, pulling out a flat leather wallet from his back pocket. He flipped it open to show her his identification. "From the St. Albans Police Department."

Ash was too far to make out his identification card, but there was no mistaking the badge that was pinned to the other side of the wallet.

She lowered the branch. "What are you doing here?" She stared at him expectantly.

He smiled ruefully. "I'm supposed to be making sure you're safe."

Ash finally relaxed. "Officer Slater sent you."

"Sergeant Slater, that's right." Clearly, she knew Slater. His name was enough to reassure her.

She looked around suddenly as another thought struck her. "Are you alone?"

He flipped his wallet closed and stuffed it back in his jeans pocket. "Out here, yes. There's a car in front." He took a few steps toward her, then stopped at the wariness in her eyes. She might trust Slater but she didn't know him. What the hell happened to this woman?

A bird trilled deeper in the woods and another one answered.

A small part of Ash was miffed that Jake Slater had set people to watch over her without telling her, but mostly she was relieved. She hadn't known how tense she had been until just now. It was good to know that he had her back, even if it was his job.

But did this mean he knew something she didn't? Was Calum in town?

She stuffed her cold hands into her jacket pockets. She suddenly felt like bait. If Calum was here, she wanted to know. Needed to know. She might be ready to face him, but she didn't want to be caught by surprise.

"What were you looking for?" asked Montrose, studying her.

She shrugged. She didn't want to tell him she'd been looking for Odette's grave.

"The river," she said. "I can see glimpses of it through the trees from my back deck. It looks closer than it is, I think."

He nodded. "It's a good two hundred yards from here," he said, nodding in its direction. "And you have to be careful. The bank is high and the river has undercut it. It's easy to fall in."

The droning sound of the lawnmower moved closer. Both their heads turned toward the sound. Jenny had finished the front and was now working on the back.

"How did you get the shiner?" asked Montrose.

Ash's hand lifted to her forehead. The skin around her eye and on her forehead was tight and tender. "My sparring partner and I head-butted a couple of days ago."

Montrose felt his eyebrows start to rise and controlled them with difficulty. This tiny thing had been boxing?

"Well, I'd better get back," said Ash awkwardly. She turned and headed toward her backyard. Then she stopped and looked back at the police officer. "Thank you," she said. She paused to get her emotions under control. "Thank you," she repeated, unable to get anything else out.

Daniel Montrose watched her walk away, favoring her left

side. Those had been tears in her eyes.

Ash was making herself a cup of coffee when Jenny knocked at the French doors. Ash waved her inside.

"Hi," said Jenny, and Ash realized they hadn't even properly met.

"Hi," she said. "Thanks for doing this on such short notice."

Jenny shrugged. She was more than rangy—she was all angles. And she had to be at least five inches taller than Ash's five feet two. "No problem. You don't want to keep it long over the winter," she added. "The voles will move in."

Ash wasn't even sure what a vole was.

"How much do I owe you?" she asked.

Jenny removed her work gloves and tucked them under her arm. Ash noted that the girl carefully stayed on the rug in front of the doors. Her jeans had a hole in one knee and the bottoms were covered in grass clippings.

"I'm not done," said Jenny, shaking her head. "I still have to trim the edges, but I can do that after school tomorrow. Then it'll cost you twenty-five dollars."

Ash blinked at the girl. She'd never hired someone to cut her grass, but that seemed a little dear to her.

Jenny clearly saw the look on Ash's face. "It's more expensive because the grass was really long and it took me a long time to cut it. Most people hire me to do it weekly, and then it's only ten dollars a week. This time of year, of course, I don't mow as often."

Ash smiled at the girl, admiring her business sense. "That makes sense," she said. She dug into her jeans pockets and pulled out a few bills. "Let me pay you now," she said. "I trust you to come back and finish the job."

Jenny grinned as she accepted the money, and for the first time, Ash noticed the braces. Suddenly the girl looked much younger.

"You have three more bags for garbage pick-up," said Jenny,

pocketing the money. "I noticed you already have a bunch of bags piled up next to the house. Don't put them out on regular garbage day or the city won't pick them up. I think they're picking up organics next week, but check the city's website."

Ash mentally revising Jenny's age upward again. "Thanks. I will."

With a nod, Jenny let herself out through the deck doors and clambered down the steps to where she had left the lawnmower. It was nearly as tall as Jenny was, and there was a bag attached to the side, which explained why Ash wasn't left with a bunch of clippings to rake. She stepped out onto the deck and watched the girl push the lawnmower around the corner of the house. The air was cool on her bare arms and she pulled the sleeves of her sweater down. She took a deep breath. She loved the smell of a freshly mown lawn. It always smelled like watermelon to her.

The lawn looked great, trimmed in a grid. The trees at the bottom of the yard swayed in the breeze, reminding her that Daniel Montrose was watching from the woods. She almost raised a hand. Instead, she went back inside and finished making her coffee. Then she sat down at the table and called Jake Slater.

Jake dribbled the ball in the driveway, switching hands when River, his ten-year-old son, tried to steal it from him. Sarah, his eight-year-old, watched his moves carefully from the sidelines. That was her way: watch, study, learn. River was more hands-on. The boy darted in and Jake let him grab the ball.

"Ha!" crowed River, holding up the ball triumphantly.

Jake's phone rumbled against his butt and he put his hands up in a time out gesture.

"Phone," he called to the kids.

"Sure, Dad," said River disbelievingly. He had begun practicing a cynical expression. It looked ridiculous on him, but Jake wasn't about to say anything. River turned away and tried to toss the basketball into the hoop. Sarah ran for the ball when he missed.

Jake pulled the phone out of his back pocket. He didn't recognize the number.

"Hello?" he said.

"Sergeant Slater?"

"Speaking," said Jake. Then he recognized the voice. "Ash?" Adrenaline spiked through him and he turned away from the kids. "What's happened?"

"Nothing," Ash hurried to say. She should have realized that he would assume the worst when she called. "I met your officer in the woods, and I wanted to know if Calum is in town."

Jake's lips tightened. Dammit. He hadn't wanted to alarm her. Who the hell was in the woods right now? Oh yes—Montrose. He was usually dependable.

"Sergeant Slater?"

"Call me Jake," he said automatically. Sunlight ricocheted off cars in driveways all along the street. Terence Davies waved at him from his front garden. Jake waved back.

"Jake," said Ash patiently, "I'm sorry to disturb you at home." And he was home. She could hear kids playing in the background and the familiar drone of a lawnmower. It was jarring. She hadn't thought of him as having a personal life. "I won't keep you long. Is Calum here?"

Jake closed his eyes and blew out a silent sigh. "I don't know, Ash. We don't know where he is. All we know is he took leave from his job. We've got a BOLO out for his vehicle but I don't think he'd be driving it. But we can't find where he would have rented one, either."

At the other end, Ash nodded slowly, even though Jake couldn't see her. Calum was on his way, might even be here, in Albans. Might even be watching her house.

"All right," she said finally. "All right."

◇◇◇

She had chicken for dinner, and after she finished with the dishes, she went through the house for the third time, making sure the doors and windows were locked and drawing the curtains so no one could see inside. For good measure, she placed chairs under the door handles of all three outside doors.

She'd wanted to watch the sun set over the woods, but the desire dissipated when she thought of standing on the back deck, exposed. She felt sorry for Officer Montrose in the woods, or who-ever replaced him. It was going to be a cold night and it was all for nothing. Calum would find a way to get to her.

Of that, she was sure.

Besides, as lovely as the woods were, Odette's remains were buried there. Maybe buried there. How could she enjoy the beauty of the sunset, knowing Odette was lying in a cold, lonely grave, unacknowledged, unmourned?

As she headed into the living room with her cup of tea and tab-let, she suddenly realized that she had been making an assump-tion. She had assumed that Odette had been killed in the summer or fall—when the woods were accessible to Frank. He couldn't have dug a grave if the ground was frozen.

She had no idea what time of year Odette went missing. She'd never asked.

She tucked her cold feet under herself as she curled up on the couch and took a sip of tea. The tea was more for comfort than be-cause she really wanted it. She glanced at the time on the tablet. It was a little past eight o'clock. That meant six o'clock in Edmonton. She should wait until morning, but even as she thought it, she was up again and heading to the dining room where she'd left her backpack and Liesel Wirth's phone number.

Moments later, she punched in the number on her cell phone and listened to it ring once, twice, only to be picked up on the fourth ring.

"Hello?"

A man's voice.

"Hello," said Ash. "May I speak with Mrs. Wirth, please?"

"Who's calling?" asked the man. He didn't sound friendly. Had she miscalculated the time difference?

"This is Ash Gantry. I'm calling from Albans in Ontario."

There was a silence at the end and Ash wondered what the man was thinking. She couldn't tell if he was older or younger.

"Just a moment," he said abruptly.

Ash wandered back into the living room as she waited and stood studying the split logs in the fireplace. This would be a good night for a fire, she decided, especially as she couldn't seem to shake off the chill she'd had since coming in from the woods.

"Hello," said a woman's voice at the other end of the phone, startling Ash. "This is Liesel Wirth."

"Mrs. Wirth, this is Ash Gantry. I'm sorry to call so late."

"Not a problem, Ms. Gantry," said the woman. She took a deep breath, clearly audible at the other end of the line. "Has something happened?"

Ash closed her eyes. Of course, she would assume the worst. "No, ma'am," said Ash gently. "But I did have one question for you."

She couldn't tell if the sigh she heard was one of sadness or relief. "What is it?"

"When did—" She stopped herself just in time. She didn't want to use the word 'disappeared.' "When is the last time you saw Odette? Or heard from her?"

Ash could almost feel the tension emanating from the other end of the line, but Liesel Wirth's voice was calm when she finally answered.

"In December, it'll be seven years."

Ash sank down on the couch and stared unseeingly at the logs waiting on the fireplace grate.

CHAPTER 23

In the morning, she removed the chair in front of the side entrance door before heading to the gym. There'd be no sparring or practicing throws today, but she could stretch and do weight training. The gym was practically empty, with only two guys in the ring, sparring, and another woman doing biceps curls by the weights area. The place smelled a little dusty. Barney closed on Sundays and closed down the air circulation.

Barney looked up from a pile of white towels he was folding.

"Hey, Ash!" he called.

She waved at him and headed for the locker room, but he intercepted her, standing in front of her, forcing her to stop.

"Let me look," he said.

Obediently, she tilted her face up to his. He examined the side of her face critically, then nodded. "How's the leg?"

Ash shrugged. "A little stiff. I won't be doing any mountain climbing, but I do have a full range of motion." *As long as I move slowly.*

Barney nodded. His white hair was freshly cropped and she could see pink skin through it. He smelled like Ivory soap.

"You look like hell, but you're moving okay," he finally said. Then he gave her his basset hound grin. "Paul looks even worse."

Ash winced at the thought. Poor guy. It was funny in the abstract, but every time she looked at herself in the mirror, the ugly bruising caught her by surprise and reminded her of Calum. Not that he ever struck her in the face. No, it was always somewhere no one could see. Except for the last time.

She sighed and headed into the locker room to put on her workout gear and indoor running shoes.

Ninety minutes later, she was back home and taking a hot shower. The workout had been a good idea. She felt much better for it and might even survive the day after a sleepless night.

As she made herself breakfast—the smoothie would not last her until the end of her shift—she briefly considered taking coffee out to the watcher in the woods, then decided against it. If Calum was watching, she didn't want to tip him off. Besides, she didn't have a thermos, or even a thermos cup.

As she scrambled some eggs, she looked around the kitchen. It was fully furnished, but there were little things missing, things a real home would have. String. Notepads. Scissors, push pins. Little things that eased day-to-day living. Still, she'd been lucky to find the place, despite the fact that it was haunted. It occurred to her that she hadn't seen Odette since Saturday. Again, she wondered what that meant. What occupied the ghost's time when she wasn't busy haunting?

Frank Boudreaux's guys showed up in two pickup trucks just as she was getting ready to leave for the restaurant. She stood by the side door, squinting in the sun, waiting for them to park on the street in front of the house. The driveway was too narrow to accommodate side-by-side parking and they obviously didn't want to hem her in. Three guys in jeans, ball caps, and Carhartt jackets walked up toward her. The older guy, a man in his fifties with a receding hairline and deep wrinkles around his eyes, gestured at the two younger men to wait while he went ahead.

One of the men who hung back kept his back to her. He had blond hair the exact same shade as Calum's. Her breath quickened as adrenalin flooded her system. Then he turned slightly. Not Calum.

Not Calum.

"Ms. Gantry?" said the older man as he reached her. He was carrying a pair of work gloves in one hand. She dragged her attention back to him. He was trying very hard not to stare at her bruising.

"Yes." She decided she wouldn't bring it up if he didn't.

"My name is Bart Lemay," he said. "I hope we aren't chasing you away."

She grinned at him. He had very nice blue eyes and a big, fat wedding ring on his hand.

"I'm on my way to work," she said. "You've got a key?"

He nodded. "Yes, ma'am."

She unlocked the door and opened it. "Let me show you where everything is."

He followed her inside and she pointed out the trap door. "The staircase is more a ladder than anything else. Bring flashlights because there's only one lightbulb in the cellar and it's hanging off a rope in the middle of the room."

He nodded and she led him inside the kitchen. "Kettle, coffee, coffeepot." She pointed at where she'd left them on the counter. "Sugar is in the cupboard with the cups. Milk is in the fridge. Help yourself."

His eyebrows rose higher with each bit of information she fed him.

"Thank you," he finally said with a half grin. "That's very generous."

She shrugged. "Don't worry about tracking in dirt in the laundry room and kitchen. They're easy to clean. Watch the hardwood floors, though. Oh, and the bathroom is just across from the stairs in the hallway."

The grin was full-blown now. "Ma'am, if you're not careful, we may never leave."

She smiled at him. "It won't be much fun working in that cellar," she warned him. "The least I can do is try to compensate."

Charlotte looked around when Ash entered through the kitchen and her round face broke into a grin.

"There's our girl," she said. Then her grin faded. "Wow. I didn't know human flesh could turn that many different shades."

Ash laughed. Something was simmering on the stove—beef stew by the smell of it. Max entered through the door Ash had just used, hauling a twenty-pound bag of rice under one arm and a crate of coffee cream balanced on one shoulder. He paused in the open doorway, letting in the cold air, and studied her from head to toe. Finally, he nodded and came all the way in.

"You still look like hell," he said gruffly. "You sure you should be here?"

"If I was able to rake my yard yesterday," said Ash, "I can take my shift today."

Max glanced at Charlotte, who shrugged. They'd keep an eye on her. Make sure she didn't do too much.

But by the time two o'clock came around, Ash was feeling pleasantly tired, nothing more. Her hip was definitely on the mend and most of the customers joked and laughed with her about the black eye. She would be happy when it finally disappeared. She didn't like being the center of attention, and the black eye pretty much guaranteed that she would be the center of everyone's attention no matter where she went.

"Busy shift," commented Charlotte as she helped Ash finish clearing off the tables. The girl looked much better today than she had on Friday. Charlotte had popped in to see her on Saturday, but Ash had been gone. Max had told her not to worry, that the cops were keeping an eye on her, but Charlotte still worried. She'd never experienced that kind of violence, but she knew how dangerous Ash's situation was. All she wanted was ten minutes with Calum Stevenson and the business end of her cast-iron frying pan.

Part of Charlotte wanted to force Ash to come home with her, so she could make sure the girl was all right. But... But Ash was a grown woman. Charlotte had to respect that she knew what was best for her.

"All right," she said when the tables were clean and the chairs upended on them. "We'll see you tomorrow."

Ash hesitated. "I still owe some time from when I left early on Friday," she pointed out. "I'll stay and help clean up the kitchen."

Charlotte smiled. "Max won't let you. Don't bother trying." Max had become very protective of the girl, which Charlotte thought was funny. While her baby brother had had several women in his life, he'd never wanted children. Now that he was old enough to be a grandfather, he was developing paternal instincts.

Ash looked around. Surely there was something else she could do? "I'll sweep and mop the floor," she said firmly.

Charlotte shook her head, but Ash had already headed for the broom.

It was almost dinnertime by the time Ash got home. She'd had coffee with Max and Charlotte after the shift, and her two bosses had talked to her about the possibility of working a few of their catering jobs if she was interested. Ash said yes, of course. She liked Max and Charlotte, and she was a good server. It wasn't something she planned to do for the rest of her life, but right now, it worked for her.

She pulled into the driveway and had to park a little farther from the house than usual. Where she normally parked, Frank's men had unloaded lumber and left a tarp half over it, half flapping in the wind. Probably the wind had untucked it.

The wind caught her braid as she clambered out of the Volvo. It was almost dark and all the streetlights had gone on. Along the street, lights were on in many of the homes. No one was playing street hockey tonight. Too close to dinnertime, probably. Too cold, decidedly.

As the wind put blooms of cold on her cheeks, she reached inside for her backpack. It was heavier than usual. She'd stopped to buy notepads and pens, and push pins and scissors, string, and more tape. It made her feel good.

She left the backpack on the top step by the back door and went to tuck the tarp in. In the end, she pulled a two-by-four off the pile and placed it on top of the tarp's edge. The wind might still work it free, but it would have to work harder.

She straightened and paused to take in the view. The freshly mown grass in her backyard still smelled faintly of watermelon, but now the watermelon was tinged with wood smoke. The lawn sloped down, losing definition the farther it got from the reflected light of the streetlights. The woods loomed darkly at the bottom of the yard and she wrapped her arms around herself in sympathy for the watcher. There would be no moon tonight. Those woods would be dark and cold. Officer Montrose had said there was another watcher posted on the street, but she had seen nothing unusual when she drove in. A part of her wanted to call Officer Slater and have him pull his men, but just the thought of them in the dark, watching for Calum, gave her courage. She wasn't alone.

Maybe she had never been alone. Maybe if she had reached out for help when she was in Vancouver...

Beyond the woods, the forest marched on, pierced only by the lights of downtown Albans. She let the backpack hang from the crook of her elbow while she unlocked the door and let herself in. The house still smelled faintly of coffee and sawdust. And something else musty and damp. What had those workers been doing?

She reached behind her to close the door, then flicked the laundry room light on. Blinking against the sudden light, she was about to step forward to drop her backpack on top of the washing machine when something flickered in the kitchen doorway.

Odette. Once she was sure she had Ash's attention, the ghost looked down at the laundry room floor. Ash followed her gaze, then reached out to steady herself against the wall.

She had just about stepped into the open hatch to the cellar.

Holy crap. What kind of men had Frank Boudreaux sent to her house? Furious, she dropped the backpack on the bench below the coat hooks and unzipped it. She was sure she had put the flashlight back in there...

She finally found it in an outer pocket and flicked it on. She would have preferred to just close the trap door and call Maddie Bowen to complain, but she wanted to make sure they hadn't done something worse in the cellar.

She shone the light down the rickety steps but all she saw was packed dirt. Gritting her teeth, she turned around and put her foot on the top step. She hadn't been down in the cellar since the first time she saw Odette staring back at her from inside the house. She and Maddie had searched the house, including the cellar, but found nothing. Of course.

Once at the bottom, she swung the flashlight around, catching glimpses of lumber and pails. The smell of sawdust was strong here. They had had been sawing lumber. She caught sight of the string hanging from the ceiling and headed for it. She pulled and the lightbulb went on, flooding the cellar with weak light.

Judging by the two-by-fours nailed together in the center of the space, they'd been building forms, probably in preparation for pouring cement. She saw two sawhorses, one toppled over, a tool belt that looked like it had been flung away, the hammer and tape measure spilling from its open pockets.

A circular saw sat on the packed earth floor as if it had been dropped there. She glanced into one of the pails. It was half full of hardened cement.

She sighed. No workers treated their equipment or work site that way. That older man she had dealt with this morning—Bart— he hadn't struck her as the kind of man who would allow this. Or who would be easily spooked.

"I really wanted them to finish this," she murmured regretfully.

A faint knock drew her head up toward the steps. Someone

was at her side door. She pulled on the string to turn the overhead light off and climbed the rungs carefully. She emerged from the cellar to see a dark figure standing on the stoop. A man, by the size, but he had his back to the door so she couldn't tell who it was. Except that it wasn't Calum. Or Jake Slater. Or Bart, the foreman.

She hurried around the opening and eased the heavy trap door down until it clicked into position. Then she went to the door and stood looking through the window.

As if sensing her gaze, the man turned around. The light from the laundry room spilled out, bathing his hard-angled face in diffused light and soft shadows. He had short dark hair in a crew cut and wore a black leather bomber jacket with the collar turned up and a black sweater underneath. His dark eyes gazed back at her but she couldn't make out any emotion behind them. He was maybe forty, forty-five.

She didn't know him, but something about him looked familiar. Maybe she'd seen him around town.

He flicked a hand to indicate the doorknob, then stuck it back in his coat pocket. He wanted her to open the door.

She really didn't want to. She didn't know him. He could be hired by Calum, for whatever reason. Her phone was in her back pocket. If she opened the door and he pushed his way in, she would never have time to pull it out and call 9-1-1. Out of the corner of her eye, she could see the baseball bat leaning against the wall.

His eyebrows rose expectantly. Impulsively, she smiled and he looked surprised. She opened the door to the cold, at the same time turning on the outside light to bathe him with exposure. Hopefully Bea would see from her kitchen window.

"Yes?" she said politely.

"Ash Gantry?" said the man. Now that there was nothing between them, he studied her as if she wasn't what he'd expected.

"Yes." What did he want? Who was he?

As if hearing her question, he nodded. "My name is Frank Boudreaux." He waited, watching her face.

Ash blinked in astonishment. Frank Boudreaux was at her house. His house. What did he want?

Before she could open her mouth to ask, he continued.

"Miss Gantry, if you didn't want me to work on the house, all you had to do was say so. There was no need to mess with my guys."

What?

"Pardon me?" He was clearly angry at her. "I just got home to find the trap door open and a mess in the cellar," she said. "If anyone was messing around, it was your men."

"Sure," he said. "And the light turned itself off." He nodded toward the wall inside the laundry room where the breaker panel was. "And the trap door slammed shut on them all by itself."

Ash stared up at him but she wasn't really seeing him. She hadn't realized that Odette could have an effect on the physical plane. She glanced over her shoulder but saw no sign of the ghost. This was too weird. Frank Boudreaux didn't ask to be let in, preferring to stand on her stoop in the cold. Maybe he knew she wouldn't let him in. Or maybe he didn't want to step foot in the house.

And suddenly she realized she had a prime opportunity here, if she had the courage to seize it.

"Mr. Boudreaux," she said as calmly as she could, "I'd like to speak with your wife. Where could I find her?"

His head jerked back as if he had been slapped, then all expression fled his face. He looked down at her, dark eyes hooded by the light above the door and she suddenly felt as if she was perched precariously on a too-slender branch.

"My wife is at home."

She smiled slightly, even though her heart was beating uncomfortably fast, and shook her head. "I mean Odette, Mr. Boudreaux. How can I get hold of her?"

Even in the glow of the light, she saw his skin pale, leaving behind cheeks made red by the wind.

"Odette left years ago, Miss Gantry. I've no idea where she is now. Why do you want to talk to her?"

Ash shrugged, suddenly feeling as if she needed to retreat before the branch broke beneath her. "I guess it's not important."

They stared at each other for a moment longer. He smiled suddenly, showing most of his teeth. Like a shark. Then he turned and walked down the porch steps. She watched him get into a silver car and reverse down her driveway.

The wind found her exposed neck then and a massive shiver coursed through her.

CHAPTER 24

Dan Montrose pulled his leather glove off his hand to unscrew the lid of the thermos. The rich coffee smell wafted up comfortingly and he poured two inches into the cup before screwing the lid back on.

He'd grown up in rural Ontario, near Kapuskasing. He'd spent his life tromping through the woods. They didn't scare him. Especially not these woods, on the edge of a subdivision. He'd be lucky to see a coyote. Maybe a fox. Nothing dangerous. No, it wasn't a wild animal that was going to get him.

He wore a black wool cap, his lined fall jacket that had a hood, long johns, wool socks, heavy boots, and lined leather gloves, and he still thought he might have hypothermia. He sure as hell couldn't feel his ass anymore. He quickly swallowed the coffee and shook the cup out before screwing it back onto the thermos.

He couldn't figure out why he was here. Even with his binoculars he couldn't see a damned thing in that backyard. Not only was there no moon, clouds had moved in, covering up whatever starlight had been available.

Genghis Khan and his army could be marching around in the woman's backyard and he wouldn't be able to see them.

And Oscar got to sit in the comfort of the unmarked car and

watch the front, the lucky bastard. Almost three hours before they were to be relieved. He didn't think he'd make it. Masterson would show up at six to relieve him and find him frozen at the foot of a pine tree.

Something flickered at the edge of his sight and he looked around. What was that? He studied the back of her house for a few seconds. Maybe she'd gotten up? Then a light flickered again, but lower than the deck. He strained to see, then remembered the bloody binoculars.

"Idiot," he muttered as he brought them up to his eyes. Nothing. It was probably a raccoon's eyes, catching whatever light was available. Still, he studied the deck and the lawn carefully.

The light flickered again and he zeroed in on it. It was coming from under the deck. He swept the binoculars around and almost missed it--an irregularity around the trellis enclosing the bottom of the deck.

Someone was *under* the deck.

Keeping the binoculars trained on the deck, he pulled his cell phone out and punched Oscar's number.

"Yeah?" said Oscar. "You gonna whine again about how cold you are?"

"Shut up," said Dan softly. "Someone's in the backyard."

The soft crying woke Ash up. She knew without looking that it was three forty-three. She'd been floating at the surface of sleep, too disturbed by the evening's events to sink deeper, despite her exhaustion. It bothered her that Frank Boudreaux had come to the house. It bothered her more that she didn't know why he had come to the house in the first place.

It wasn't because he thought she'd been messing with his "guys." If that were true, he would have let Maddie deal with it. She was managing the property for him, after all. Why did he feel the need to confront her at the house, the house where he had killed his wife?

It was as if he'd needed to see her for himself. But why?

As she listened to Odette's soft weeping, she wondered why the ghost hadn't shown up when Frank was there. She'd freaked the workers out, but when Frank showed up, she stayed away.

Did ghosts retain fear? Was Odette still afraid of her husband?

Ash sighed softly. Clearly, Frank's visit had disturbed Odette, too, to make her revert to her old patterns.

The room was cold. All she wanted to do was burrow deeper into the blankets and try to sleep some more. But she couldn't leave Odette like that.

She opened her mouth to say something comforting to the ghost when she heard a dull sound from somewhere deep in the house.

She sat up in bed, the blankets sliding off, and strained to listen. She'd heard something. Hadn't she?

Breathing fast, she slid her legs out from under the blankets and stood up. She tilted her head toward the door, as if that would help her hear better.

Nothing. She was freaking herself out for nothing. She was just about to slip back under the covers when the air around her suddenly stirred, sending her heart slamming against her ribs. She felt Odette's presence right next to her, and in that presence, fear.

All the small hairs on her arms rose and she forgot to breathe.

Then she heard the soft thud of a boot coming up the stairs.

Dear God in Heaven. Calum had found her.

Gasping suddenly, she started to breathe again, then tried to stop for fear he would hear her. He wouldn't know which room she was in. She had a minute. She reached a trembling hand for her cell phone on the bedside table. She briefly thought of calling Jake Slater, but knew 9-1-1 was her better bet. She punched in 9-1-1 and slid the cell phone under her pillow to muffle the operator's voice, then reached for the baseball bat on her bed, almost panicking when she didn't find it immediately. Then her fingers found the hard wood length of it and she grabbed it, pulling it against her chest.

Where was he? Had he reached the top of the stairs yet? Her door was at the far end of the hallway. If he turned right at the top of the hallway, he would have his back to her. She would rush him, strike him with the baseball bat.

Then she'd run.

Just then she remembered that she had closed all the other bedroom doors. Hers was the only one that was open.

He would come straight for her.

Her hands were so cold she could barely hold the bat.

How had he gotten in? All the doors and windows were locked. All the doors had chairs wedged against them. Even if he had a key, he couldn't get in. There were two policemen watching the place—how had they missed someone breaking into her house?

She glanced around the dark bedroom, picking out the shape of the chair in the corner, the dresser by the closet. The bedroom window overlooked the back of the house. She squeezed her eyes shut. She'd kill herself jumping to the deck. But maybe she could scream for help. Surely the watcher in the woods would come running?

All she had to do was attract attention. Calum wouldn't dare hurt her if there were witnesses around.

Just as she moved toward the window, a cold brush of air on her face stopped her. Her hand tightened on the baseball bat and she opened her mouth to breathe soundlessly.

Someone was on the other side of the half-open door. She could hear his quiet breathing, as if he had paused just like her, to listen. If he moved slightly, he would see her. If she moved, he would hear her.

They stayed like that, poised, for long seconds.

Then the door slowly began to ease open.

Without thinking, Ash took a step back, keeping the door between her and Calum.

Suddenly, the door slammed back, knocking her into the wall. She dropped the baseball bat and it thumped to the rug next to her bed, out of her reach. She slid half senseless to the floor. The bat. She lunged for it but a dark figure reached down for her, grabbed her by her loose hair and yanked her to her feet.

She expected a punch to the gut, or hard hands around her throat. Instead, he began to haul her out of the bedroom by her hair.

"Stop it!" she yelled. "Help!" Years of conditioning fell away as she suddenly realized she could scream—*should* scream if she wanted to get out of this alive. Otherwise he would kill her.

He stopped suddenly, turning toward her, and she bumped into his solid length.

It's not Calum.

The realization washed over her just as she realized Odette was crying again, and that was the reason he had stopped.

"What the hell—?" he muttered and only then did Ash recognize Frank Boudreaux.

Fresh terror galvanized her into action. She jabbed her bare heel onto his booted instep. All it did was return his attention to her.

"You fucking little busybody," he said calmly. Ash braced herself for the blow, but it didn't come, though she could feel his desire to hit her.

He doesn't want to leave any marks.

His body smelled rank. Stress. Fear? He'd heard Odette...

"Murderer," she yelled, struggling to get out of his hold. He yanked hard on her hair and she yelped in pain.

"Yell as much as you want," he said. "No one heard Odette's screams either." He pulled her past the threshold of the door and she grabbed onto the door jamb to keep from going through. Where was he taking her?

"You could have minded your own business," he continued, pulling harder. "Now you can keep her company."

Then she heard Paul Coventry's voice in her head. Use his momentum against him.

She let go of the door jamb and propelled herself at him. She wasn't heavy enough to knock him off his feet, but she startled him enough that he let go of her to regain his balance. She slipped past him and ran for the stairs.

Just as she reached the top of the stairs, he caught up to her and hauled her back against him with her hair. She twisted in his grasp, ignoring the sharp pain as hair pulled out of her scalp, and scratched his face.

If they found her body, they might be able to identify her murderer with the skin and blood under her nails.

"You little bitch!" He snatched her hands away from him and turned her to face the stairs.

Then came the terrible sound of someone falling down the stairs, just feet away, and Frank Boudreaux let go of her as if she had burst into flames. Half turned away from her, he stared down the darkened staircase and the smell of his sweat suddenly filled her nostrils.

Small sounds came from the bottom of the staircase, like gasps of pain.

"Odette?" whispered Frank, still staring into the darkness. Fear laced his words.

With cold implacability, Ash took a step away from him, then, putting all her weight behind the effort, she shoved him.

He tried to catch his balance, scrabbled to catch her arm, but she stepped back and watched his dark shape tumble down the stairs. He landed with a cry of pain and Ash calmly turned on the lights and made her way down the stairs.

Frank lay sprawled out at the foot of the stairs, his right leg at an unnatural angle. He moaned, his eyes squeezed shut. Ash paused halfway down the steps when Odette materialized next to him. The ghost squatted next to Frank and studied him, head tilted to one side. Frank groaned in pain and opened his eyes. He turned his head and looked directly at Odette.

Ash became aware of a noise coming from the kitchen just as

a banging started up on her front door. As she reached the bottom step, a light flicked on in the kitchen and Officer Montrose emerged, holding a handgun out in front of him with both hands.

His face was covered in dirt and cobwebs. He took in her state with one up-and-down glance, then stared at Frank Boudreaux. Finally, he lowered his weapon.

"Could you let my partner in?" he asked Ash politely.

Ash nodded and silently stepped over the broken man. Odette looked up at her and smiled before disappearing.

Two cups of coffee later, Jake sat back in the chair and stared out of the French doors of Ash Gantry's dining room. It was almost seven in the morning. It was still dark out, but the sky was lightening and a rosy glow was creeping in from the east.

He had examined the outside of the house and could understand why Montrose hadn't seen Boudreaux until it was almost too late. The bastard had a hidden access to the house, under the bloody deck. A coal chute, left over from the early days. It was hidden behind shelves in the cellar. He'd been in that cellar several times and had never seen it.

Ash puttered in the kitchen, making fresh coffee. The girl looked like hell, with dark circles under her bloodshot eyes. Her hair was disheveled but he could understand why she was reluctant to comb it. The paramedic had disinfected the raw patch in her scalp but she had refused a bandage.

She was in surprisingly good shape for a woman who'd almost gotten killed.

Frank Boudreaux. Holy crap.

Ash returned to the table and eased herself down next to Officer Slater. Her hip was killing her. She'd twisted it at some point during Frank's attack and now she felt as if a hot ball of metal had replaced the joint.

Jake Slater had been very kind, but his questions had felt more like an interrogation. She wanted him to go. She wanted them all to go, but it looked like that wasn't about to happen.

There were people in the cellar, studying the coal chute opening. People in her bedroom taking pictures and measurements. People in the hallway, dusting for fingerprints. The house was cold from doors being left open by people tromping through. Their combined voices were like a low, irritating drone.

She wrapped her hands around the mug of coffee she'd left on the table, more to have something to do with her hands than because she wanted more coffee. Beatrice Stratford had called a few minutes ago to make sure Ash was all right. She had seen the ambulance and the flashing lights of the police cars. Ash was touched by her neighbor's concern and assured her that she was all right. She promised to call Bea later that day, when things weren't so crazy.

"What's going to happen now?" she asked.

Jake shrugged. "An investigation, of course. Frank will be charged with breaking and entering, at the very least. Attempted murder, maybe. Kidnapping, maybe."

Ash narrowed her eyes at him. "You and I both know he was planning to kill me."

Jake looked at her, then nodded. "Yes, we do. It's proving it that's the bitch."

"He said I was going to join Odette."

"That could be interpreted to mean that he was planning to take you to Odette."

Frustration welled up in Ash. Why was it so hard to get justice?

"He killed Odette," she said sharply. The voices in the hallway went silent. "He tried to kill me," she added in a lower voice.

Jake sighed. "I know," he said. He rubbed his eyes, trying to get the sand out of them. "It would be easier to charge him with murder and attempted murder if we could find Odette."

Ash looked out the French doors to the deck and the dark woods beyond. "I thought he must have buried her in the woods," she said. Jake nodded but without conviction. She continued, "but then I found out that she disappeared in winter. The ground would have been frozen. He would have left tracks."

Jake's attention sharpened. What was she on about? The woods? He followed her gaze out the French doors and stood up to get a better vantage point. He'd never actually thought about what Frank would have done with Odette's body, because he'd never wanted to think it was possible that Frank had murdered her.

But he did murder her. Jake knew that now as clearly as he knew Frank had tried to kill the woman next to him. He walked around the table and stood in front of the doors. But she was right. Odette went missing in the winter. No way a man as canny as Frank Boudreaux would have left a trail from his house to the woods. Too easy to follow. And digging through frozen ground was a non-starter.

"So what the hell did he do with her body?"

Ash limped over to stand next to him, her arms crossed in front of her, her hands tucked under her armpits for added warmth. She'd changed into jeans and heavy wool socks and wore two layers under her sweater and she was still cold. She wished they would keep the damned door closed.

"I think you know where she is," she said, startling him. He hadn't realized he'd spoken out loud.

A cool insubstantial hand caressed his cheek and he turned to look at Ash. She was staring to one side of him.

"She's still here," he said. He took a deep breath. "Holy shit. She's still here."

They had to borrow the ground-penetrating radar equipment from the Mounties in Toronto, and it took a day to get it. During that time Ash Gantry resisted their efforts to put holes in the walls to see if Odette's body was there.

Jake didn't press. He didn't think Odette was there, either. He thought she was down in the cellar. That was why Boudreaux was so anxious to pour concrete over the floor after all these years. He'd heard that Ash was asking around about Odette and worried that she might snoop in the cellar and discover his secret.

Jake stood behind the floodlight and watched the technician— also borrowed from the Mounties—operate the big machine. It was on rubber wheels and looked a bit like the contraption he used to spread lawn seed. The cellar was musty and all the shelves had been moved away from the walls. The coal chute was open to let in fresh air and to keep the cellar from feeling too claustrophobic.

It wasn't a big cellar, but the technician was being thorough. It was almost two hours before she finally made it to the space under the steps. A moment later, she looked around at Jake and nodded.

They had found Odette.

CHAPTER 25

Liesel Wirth was thinner than her pictures in the newspapers had indicated. Her gray hair was in a French braid, however, just like in the pictures, and there was intelligence in her blue eyes.

Along with a lot of pain.

Ash stared at her for long seconds. She had called Liesel Wirth yesterday afternoon and they had wept over the phone together. Now Odette's aunt was here and Ash had no idea what to say to the woman.

One of the day's specials had been chicken stew with dumplings and the smell lingered in the restaurant. The midafternoon sun filled the little restaurant with weak light. Outside, pedestrians passed in front of the big picture window, their chins tucked against the wind that was blowing colorful leaves around in the gutters.

Ash had just finished sweeping the place and had been about to leave for home. Knowing it was her favorite, Max had reserved a bowl of the stew for her to take home and now her stomach grumbled in anticipation.

Charlotte came out from the kitchen at the sound of the bells jangling over the door and took in the sight of Ash and the stranger staring at each other.

"I'm sorry," she said to the older woman. "We're closed."

The woman glanced at her, then turned her attention back to Ash.

"Charlotte," said Ash calmly, not taking her gaze off the other woman, "this is Liesel Wirth, Odette's aunt."

Ah. Charlotte nodded and removed her apron. Tossing it on the counter, she came around the open end and approached the woman.

"Ms. Wirth," she said, sticking her hand out. "I'm Charlotte Strelzow."

The woman shook Charlotte's hand. "How do you do?" she said automatically.

Charlotte released her hand and led her toward one of the tables by the window. Ash limped ahead of them and removed the chairs from the top of the table.

"Sit," said Charlotte firmly, indicating a chair. "I'll make tea." With that, she left them alone.

Ash smiled at Liesel Wirth and nodded to the chair. "Please," she said.

Liesel sat down and clasped her hands together on the table. Her eyes were bloodshot. Maybe from traveling overnight. Maybe from crying.

Maybe both.

"Where is she?" asked Liesel.

"In Ottawa," said Ash gently. "With the coroner." Jake Slater had warned her that they might never be able to conclusively prove cause of death. It didn't matter. Frank had buried her in his cellar and denied any knowledge of her whereabouts for years, telling everyone she had run off. Ash's own testimony that he had tried to kill her would be enough to send him away for a long time.

"When will I get her back?" asked Liesel.

Ash had suggested she should stay in Edmonton until there was more information, but she wasn't surprised to see the woman arrive at Soup 'n Such.

"I don't know," said Ash. "You can talk to Officer Jake Slater of the Albans Police Department." She hesitated. "He knew Odette in school."

Liesel nodded. "Yes. I remember him." There was no warmth in her voice and Ash remembered that Liesel Wirth had been very angry at the police for not helping when Odette was alive. She sighed.

"Would you like to see where she was?" she asked gently.

Liesel's head reared up in horror. "God, no!"

Charlotte arrived with a miniature Brown Betty and two mugs, then left them alone again.

"I'm sorry," said Liesel when they were alone. "I don't ever want to go back to that house."

Ash poured the tea in silence, measuring her words. Finally, she looked up at the older woman. "You may have a problem, then," she said. "As Odette's only living relative, the house may belong to you."

Liesel brought the mug up to her mouth but didn't drink. She blinked at Ash, her face wreathed in fragrant steam.

"What about Frank?" she asked, putting the mug down without drinking. She wrapped her hands around the mug as if to warm them.

Ash shrugged. "I'm no lawyer, but I don't think he can benefit from his crime. And the house would be considered a benefit, since it was Odette's, too." At least, that was what Officer Slater had said.

"If it's mine, then I'll burn it down," said Liesel fiercely, her eyes filling with tears.

Ash reached across the table and covered the woman's hand with hers over the mug.

"It's a good house," she said gently. "It has a good history. Odette wouldn't want the house to pay for what was done to her." Even as she said it, she wondered what she meant. After a moment, she realized that it was true. Generations had lived in that house, from the time Alistair McTavish had built it in 1890. It was unfair to let Frank Boudreaux's actions define the house.

Just as it was unfair to define Ash by Calum's actions.

CHAPTER 26

Ash slept in. It was Saturday, after all. She lazed in bed for a few minutes, considering the day ahead of her. She wanted to go to the gym and run a few errands, mostly to buy groceries—and maybe get a haircut—but otherwise the day was hers. Maddie had suggested a drive in the countryside to see the colors, but Ash had reluctantly turned her down—she wasn't about to stress the officers watching her any more than they already were.

But it would have been so nice to go for a drive.

As she got up and made her bed, she went back over the events of the past few days. It seemed she couldn't stop thinking about them. Processing, said Charlotte.

Liesel Wirth had refused Ash's invitation to stay with her, as Ash had known she would, instead deciding to stay with old friends who still lived in Albans. She was moving on to Ottawa this morning to talk to someone in the coroner's office.

It surprised Ash how little the rest of the story mattered to her. She felt as if an enormous weight had been lifted from her shoulders. Odette was now free. Frank stood accused of her murder and Ash's attempted murder, and would likely spend the rest of his days in jail.

What happened to Odette's mortal remains mattered very little to Ash. It was enough that the truth was known and Odette could pass on. Or whatever it was ghosts did. Ash hadn't seen Odette since the night Frank fell down the stairs. She was gone.

Ash wondered suddenly about Frank Boudreaux's new wife. Common-law wife. How was she dealing with these developments? Was she brokenhearted? Relieved?

She shook her head, like a dog shaking off water. This wasn't her problem anymore.

She'd had dinner with Beatrice the night before and filled her in on the most recent developments. She didn't tell her neighbors about the watchers, as Jake Slater had made her promise not to, but Bea quietly informed her that the whole street was aware of the watchers, and why they were watching. Then she told Ash that everyone was keeping an eye out for strangers.

Tears had come to Ash's eyes then and it was a long time before she could talk again.

In spite of everything, her situation hadn't changed. Calum was still out there, somewhere. Officer Slater was clearly frustrated at his inability to locate her husband but Ash found it hard to work up any worry. She was still too full of euphoria, as if Frank Boudreaux had been a stand-in for Calum.

And she had defeated Frank, hadn't she? Well, she and Odette had.

Every once in a while, just before she fell asleep, she thought she heard gentle humming. But it must have been her imagination because Odette was gone.

She hadn't been back to the gym since Monday. Her hip still ached but she had to see Barney and Paul and tell them what had happened. She knew Max had filled them in on Wednesday, but she wanted to tell them how their training had been instrumental in defeating Frank.

She wouldn't work out—Barney wouldn't let her—but she could do some stretching to work out the soreness in her hip.

As she drove around, she was aware of the dark SUV following her, and wondered which one of the officers was on duty. It bothered her that all those people were being put out because of her, but it also reassured her.

The gym parking lot was full and she had to park on the side street, which meant a longer walk to the back door. She practiced walking normally, reminding her hip muscles how they were supposed to move, but it was hard and she was sweating a little by the time she opened the back door.

The noise and activity that greeted her when she pushed open the inner door stopped her in her tracks. There were people everywhere—in the ring, at the punching bags, at the weights station, on the exercise mats. And they all seemed to be talking, or grunting, or calling out numbers. All she could smell was sweat and chalk.

She blinked in astonishment and let the door close behind her. She was glad she usually came early if it was this busy later in the day. Holding her gym bag and backpack in one hand, she leaned on the wall with the other and used her toes to work off her outside shoes, then she kicked them toward the pile of shoes by the door.

She turned to find Barney standing in front of her. His basset hound face was screwed up in an expression of relief. Without a word, he took her in his arms and hugged her.

In the end, she only had a few minutes to stretch. Barney had called Paul and, when her instructor showed up, the three of them retreated to Barney's office and she filled them in on what had happened. It took a while to answer all their questions, and by the time they finally fell silent, her stomach was rumbling. The breakfast smoothie was long gone.

"So that's it," she said. "Frank Boudreaux is going away for a long time." And good riddance to him. "I wanted to thank you both. If it wasn't for the training you both gave me, I might not be here today." She meant it. Without Paul's voice in her ear, she might never have freed herself from Frank. And without Barney pushing her to get stronger, she might not have had the strength to do it.

"Yeah," said Barney somberly, "but there's still your husband."

Both men sat looking at her while the noise from the gym filled the small office, even through the closed door.

Finally, she shrugged and smiled.

"Yes, there's still Calum." She took a deep breath and stood up, using the back of the chair to support herself. "I've decided to start divorce procedures."

Paul stood up, too. He stared down at her, his brown eyes worried. His black eye was fading. "Won't that make things worse?" he asked. "I'm no expert on abusive husbands, but if he isn't already after you, won't this make him come, for sure?"

Barney stood up, too. "I think that's the point," he said softly, staring at Ash.

She smiled at her two friends. "Don't worry," she said. "The police are looking out for me." But they couldn't keep watch over her forever. The moment she served divorce papers on him, Calum would go ballistic and come for her. He always said he'd never let her go.

She used to think it was romantic.

◊ ◊ ◊

"What if it's not him?" asked Jake calmly over the phone. He wanted to yell, but that would get him nowhere. Chief Kapinski expected his officers to have self-control.

"It's his car, Jake," said Kapinski patiently. "I would have thought it would be a relief to learn that Gantry's husband is all the way in British Columbia."

Jake stared out his windshield at the cars speeding by. He'd been on his way to Canadian Tire when the chief called and had pulled over so he could concentrate on what the man was saying.

Chief Kapinski had pulled Ash Gantry's security detail.

It was midmorning on a Saturday—not the best time to go to Canadian Tire, but his rake had broken and he needed a new one. Sunlight glanced off the cars' roofs as they sped past him, little shards of brightness stabbing through his eyes. He looked the other way, towards the woods lining the road, just as a gust of wind sent a volley of yellow birch leaves spiraling to the ground.

"I'd be more comfortable if we had confirmation that he's actually driving his car."

Kapinski remained silent for a moment. "We have no probable cause," he said finally.

But. There were always "reasons" to pull someone over. A taillight out. Going over the speed limit. A resemblance to another vehicle they were searching for.

Before Slater could point out the obvious, Kapinski said, "All right, all right. I'll ask the Mounties to do a verification."

Jake nodded with relief. All right. "And will you put surveillance back on?"

"Let's wait and see what the Mounties say, all right?"

Jake sighed softly. Damn it. He'd have to be out there watching her until they knew for sure that Stevenson was in British Columbia.

"Does she know?" he asked finally.

Kapinski cleared his throat. "She didn't answer her phone, so I left a message. I sent a uniform over an hour ago and her car was gone."

Jake's mouth went dry. Ash was probably shopping, or visiting someone. She was probably fine. But he had to be sure.

When she got to the mini-mall where the hairdressing shop was, Ash parked and pulled her backpack toward her. She'd meant what she said to Barney and Paul, even though it had only occurred to her moments before she said it.

She was going to divorce Calum. Just the thought of it released the tension around her chest. She was going to divorce him and be free, legally. She rummaged around the backpack, looking for her cell phone. First thing to do was call Mr. Caldwell, her lawyer. As her hand searched the bottom of the back, she watched people going into the small grocery store, Cox Foods. There was a deli next to the grocery store, then the hairdresser's, a shoe store, a

Coles bookstore, and the Shopper's Drugmart anchoring the other end. Most of the stores had their own front doors, but there was also a central door that gave access to the whole mall, including the stores on the other side.

After a moment with no success, she upended the pack onto the passenger seat. A pen, a small notepad, the Ziploc bag with her passport, birth certificate, name change certificate and marriage certificate, a pack of tissues, a small flashlight. She patted the front pockets. Wallet. No phone.

And then she remembered she had left the cell phone charging on the kitchen counter. Oh, well. She would call Mr. Caldwell when she got home.

She gathered her belongings and dumped them back into the backpack, then turned the engine off and climbed out.

The wind was nippy but the sun shining out of a cloudless sky felt warm on her face. The wind caught at her braid and she smiled. An hour from now, she would no longer have a braid. A handle, as Paul called it.

She threaded her way through the parking lot and went inside Clarabelle's Hair Salon. Bells jingled as she walked in and a hairdresser looked up from a client whose hair she was foiling.

"Be with you in a minute, hon," she said. She looked to be maybe in her forties, with bleached hair piled up in a loose bun at the top of her head. She wore a pair of yoga pants and a tight, long-sleeved top that was less than flattering.

Two more hairdressers worked on clients in the other two chairs, but neither one looked up when Ash came in. The older woman was the owner, then. Ash sat down at one of the three empty seats by the door and picked up a magazine.

Ten minutes later, the older woman came up to Ash.

"You must be Ashley," she said with a wide grin. "I'm Clarabelle. What did you want done today?" Her gaze studied Ash's face, lingering with a frown on the fading bruise.

When Ash told her what she wanted, Clarabelle tried to dissuade her. Then Ash took her hair out of the braid and spread it around her shoulders. Clarabelle studied it carefully, then nodded.

"You're right," she said. "It all needs to go. Fresh start."

It was only when Clarabelle was adjusting the water temperature prior to washing Ash's hair that she remembered the damage to her scalp.

"Watch the back of the head, okay?" she asked. "There's a scab."

Without a word, Clarabelle parted Ash's hair until she found the healing injury from when Frank Boudreaux pulled her hair out.

"Jesus, hon," muttered Clarabelle. "You've been through the wars."

Ash smiled. "It's been a rough week."

Fifteen minutes later, she sat in a chair in front of the mirror and watched as foot-long swaths of her dark, wet hair fell to the floor. Then Clarabelle began shaping the hair expertly, being careful around Ash's injury.

It felt odd to suddenly be in someone else's hands. The last time this had happened was when Mr. Caldwell's man, Sam, had rescued her from the hospital in Vancouver. Once she was healed, she left the apartment and never looked back.

Then she realized that she'd been in Grandma's and Mr. Caldwell's hands all along.

"There now," said Clarabelle, stepping back. "What do you think?"

Ash focused on the present again, and looked in the mirror. The young woman who looked back at her had short dark hair in soft spikes all over her head, with a ragged fringe on her forehead. Her green eyes looked huge and her mouth fuller. Only the faint scar on her forehead from where Calum had last struck her and the ugly bruise marred the image.

"Wow," breathed Ash, still staring.

"Honey, you look gorgeous," said Clarabelle with satisfaction. "Damn, I'm good."

Ash grinned up at her in the mirror. Before she could say anything, a bell began to clang loudly throughout the shop. Ash flinched and everyone jumped.

Clarabelle and the other two hairdressers looked at each other in dismay, then Clarabelle said, "Crap." She immediately moved toward the cash register, while yelling over her shoulder. "Fire alarm—everybody out! Grab your purses!"

Fire alarm. Ash slid off the chair and reached under Clarabelle's station for her backpack. There was no smoke that she could tell but she obediently followed the others to the door, only to stop when the others didn't go out. The alarm seemed to be coming from right above their heads, painfully loud.

"What's the holdup?" yelled Clarabelle from the cash register. She was busy stuffing money and receipts into a blue bank deposit bag.

"It's stuck," yelled one of the hairdressers, a young woman with tattoos crawling up her neck.

"The other way, then," yelled Clarabelle and they obediently turned around and headed toward the back of the shop and the inside mall entrance. Ash glanced over her shoulder at the glass door through which she had entered the shop. People were streaming out of the stores and into the parking lot, which was jammed with cars trying to leave. If the fire trucks were on their way, she couldn't hear the sirens over the raucous blaring of the fire alarm. Then she glanced down.

Someone had wedged a length of two-by-four under the door handle to prevent anyone inside from pushing it open.

The blood drained from her hands and feet, leaving them icy, and the room began to sway lazily around her.

Calum.

◊◊◊

Ash wasn't home. Jake walked around the house, checking the doors and windows. All were locked. He even went under the deck to make sure the coal chute had been blocked off. The board covering the hole was still intact and there was no sign that anyone had tried to remove it.

He finally made his way back to his Escape, punching her number into his cell phone as he walked. Kids were playing shinny just a ways down the road, their yells and laughter drifting up to him at the top of Ash's driveway. He stood next to the car, absently watching the kids at play, while the phone rang and rang.

Protected from the cool wind by the side of the house and with the sun beating down on his head, he was growing uncomfortably warm in his heavy jacket. Finally, he slipped the phone back in the inside pocket of his jacket. Maybe she'd forgotten her cell phone at home.

Or maybe it was with her but she couldn't answer it.

The phone rumbled against his chest and he fished it out again, glancing down at the screen. It was the station.

"Slater."

"Sarge, it's Montrose. Did you know that the chief recalled surveillance on the Gantry woman?"

In spite of his own worry, Jake's eyebrow rose at the implied criticism in the man's voice.

"Yes, Corporal," he said shortly.

"Well, one of her neighbors just called in a suspicious vehicle following her. And it wasn't one of ours."

Ash turned toward the back of the salon. Everyone had left already. She didn't want to follow them. That was what Calum wanted. That was why he had blocked the front exit. She shook the door, hoping to dislodge the two-by-four, but it didn't budge. She waved her arms at people running past, but no one was looking inside. They were all focused on getting away from the mall.

Think!

Whatever she did now, it had to be guided by reason, not fear. Fear was what Calum counted on. What he had always counted on.

Screaming for help was pointless, as was pounding on the

door—nobody could hear her from the outside, not over the sound of the alarm.

She looked around, trying to keep panic at bay. She had to break the window in the door but nothing in the hairdresser's shop would work. Maybe one of the waiting area chairs. She grabbed one but even as she slammed it against the door, she knew it wouldn't work. The chair was too light, the door too thick.

Maybe the plate glass display window?

She hurried to the window and swung the chair as hard as she could. She couldn't even hear the sound it made over the sound of the alarm, but it jarred her hands painfully as it hit. The chair bounced back, almost hitting her. She tried again, and again, her panic growing with every try.

She had to get out of there. Calum would come looking for her when she didn't come out the back door.

Galvanized by fear, she dropped the chair and looked around the salon wildly. The phone by the register caught her eye and she ran to it. She would call 9-1-1, tell them about Calum, tell them to warn Jake. She plucked the hand set from its docking station, but nothing happened when she turned it on. There was no light on the docking station, either.

Calum had cut the electricity.

Her whole body began to shake as the extent of her predicament slammed into her. No one knew where she was except for six panicked women who had run out of the shop without making sure she was with them. Calum was out there, probably inside the mall, waiting for her to come out. She couldn't call for help.

Think!

The hair dressing station. Those chairs were much bigger and heavier than the waiting room chairs. If she could lift one, it might have more effect.

She ran to the nearest station and tried to pick up the chair. It was incredibly heavy. In desperation, she grabbed it by the back and dragged to the front of the shop.

When she was close, she squatted and, ignoring the sharp pain in her hip, tried to pick up the chair by its base. The chair rose slowly and she turned, trying to give it some momentum before it struck the window. The padded seat hit the window without leaving a mark and the chair fell away, knocking a few plants off the shelf below the window.

Ash straightened the chair with an effort. She saw what she had done wrong. She had to pick it up by the armrests and swing the heavy metal base against the window. That would work.

Bending her knees, she hugged the back of the chair, grabbed the armrests and with as much strength as she could muster, hauled the chair up and around. The base hit the window with a clanging sound that she could hear over the alarm. Then the chair pulled out of her numb hands and fell back, almost landing on her feet. She scrambled out of the way.

There was a huge crack in the window. It was working!

Flashing red lights caught her eye and she looked beyond the crack to the parking lot beyond. The firefighters had arrived. She breathed a sigh of relief. They would go store by store, making sure no one was inside. They would free her the moment they saw the two-by-four trapping her. She could tape a piece of paper on the door, telling them she was trapped inside.

And then it hit her. The back door. Calum was expecting her to come out the back door. When she didn't, he would come looking for her.

She had to lock it.

Abandoning the chair, she turned toward the back of the shop only to stop cold as Calum emerged from the shadows. He said something she couldn't hear and started moving toward her.

A fatalistic calm descended on her. She had always known that Calum would come for her.

That didn't mean she had to make it easy for him.

◊◊◊

Jake made it to the mall in less than ten minutes and pulled up next to the uniform waving him down by Cox Foods. He rolled down his window.

The uniform was an older woman he'd worked with before—Adrienne Desharnais. He'd liked her calm efficiency then and he appreciated it now as she removed her cover and leaned in to talk to him.

"Her car is in the parking lot," said Desharnais. Her eyes were bloodshot and he wondered briefly if she'd been on night shift and been awakened to take part in the search for Ash Gantry.

"She was getting her hair cut," continued Desharnais, nodding toward Clarabelle's Hair Salon. Yellow crime scene tape crisscrossed the front door and the display window. The window had a huge crack through it. "When the alarm went off, Clarabelle, two hairdressers, and three customers ran out the back of the shop. Clarabelle says she thought Gantry was right behind them. It was only when they were allowed back inside that she realized something had happened. The place is a mess. It looks like there was a hell of a fight in there. Clarabelle found Gantry's backpack behind the counter. It contains a wallet, birth certificate, passport and a marriage certificate to one Calum Stevenson."

Jake listened carefully, fighting for calm. The firefighters were still here, but there was no fire. Someone had pulled the fire alarm.

He considered everything Desharnais had told him, then looked at her again.

"Why did they go out the back door?" They didn't know where the fire was—for all they knew, they could have been trapped inside the mall. They would have gotten outside to safety much faster if they had used the front door.

Desharnais smiled at him as if he were her star pupil.

"Someone jammed a two-by-four against the handle, just before the alarm went off."

Dismay slammed into Jake's gut. Not again. Jesus. Not again.

CHAPTER 27

Ash woke up to choking darkness and a throbbing headache.

She blinked, just to make sure her eyes were open, but the darkness didn't change. Twisting her head, she tried to make out the outline of her bedroom window but there was no light seeping through the edges of the curtain.

It was cold—so cold. She tried to pull up her blankets only to realize that her hands were trapped behind her. She was tied up.

It all came flooding back—Clarabelle's, the fire alarm, the jammed door... Calum.

She moaned, and only then did she feel the gag in her mouth, held in place by some kind of cloth.

She shuddered at the remembered shock of seeing him again. He had shaved his blond hair off and there was a few days' worth of beard on his face. He looked older. Harder. Meaner.

Oh, God. He was going to kill her.

Where was she? The last thing she remembered was throwing any object she could lay her hands on at him. One jar full of blue liquid with combs and brushes soaking in it had broken against his head, drenching him in cleaning fluid and cutting his scalp.

He had roared his rage then, and her courage had failed. She had tried to run past him, but Calum grabbed her sweater, spinning her around to face him. All her self-defense training deserted her at the sight of his bloody, contorted face less than a foot from hers. His eyes were narrowed in rage and his lips pulled away from his teeth. For a wild moment, she thought he was going to bite her. Then his fist came crashing down on the side of her head and she blacked out.

Despair welled up. Where had that bastard taken her? She tried to stretch out her feet but they were tethered to her hands. She had no feeling left in her hands, either from them being tied so tightly or from the awkward position she was in, half on her side, half on her back.

Wherever she was, it smelled of rubber and oil. And her cheek rested against a rough fabric, like carpeting.

She was in the trunk of a car. A parked car.

Her breathing grew more rapid and shallow as she fought panic. If she didn't gain control over herself soon, she would hyperventilate and faint.

She forced herself to take a deep breath, then exhale. And another one. She desperately wanted to spit the gag out of her mouth but it was held tightly in place by whatever he had wrapped around her head. Her tongue kept working at it and she fought the gag reflex that was threatening to undermine her efforts at calm.

Think about something else. Think about killing Calum.

The thought appeared in her mind, crystal clear and sharp, almost as if someone had spoken.

She blinked against the darkness as calm filled her. She'd always known, deep down, that it would come to this. That was why she had run—because she was afraid Calum would kill her, yes, but also because she was afraid she might have to kill him.

Where was she? Why had he left her in a car? Was he planning to come back for her? It was completely silent in the trunk. She strained to hear other cars, or people talking, anything...

but it was deathly quiet. Even if she could spit the gag out and scream, no one would hear her.

Breathe.

She began working at the ropes binding her hands together. At least, she thought they were ropes. Her hands were completely numb and she couldn't really tell, but she couldn't imagine what else he could have used that would connect with her feet, too.

A loud "click" sounded right by her ear and she started violently, spurring her headache to throb insistently.

She bit down on another moan as the trunk lid opened and a dark shape loomed over her, backlit by the faint light of a starry night. Cold air rushed into the trunk and she breathed in the smell of the river, laced with wood smoke. They were close to the St. George, then.

Unless he had taken her completely away from Albans. Where he could kill her and abandon her body.

A pencil thin light suddenly stabbed into her eyes only to shut off again.

"Good," said Calum calmly. "You're awake."

He grabbed her by the armpits and hauled her out of the trunk in one swift move, catching the back of her head on the trunk lid. Pain blazed through her and she would have screamed if not for the gag.

"Sorry about that," said Calum, letting her drop to the ground. Her sore hip hit first, followed by her shoulder and then her head. She groaned deep in her throat.

After a moment, she realized she wasn't on soil or grass. She was on pavement. And she could definitely hear the sound of water rushing close by. She lay on her side, trying to push the pain away so she could think. Something wet trickled down the side of her head.

Blood. From the reopened scab.

Bastard.

Suddenly her hands were jerked up behind her back as he

hauled on the rope linking her feet to her hands. Her shoulders yanked back in their sockets and a sob of pain caught in her throat. Just as suddenly, he let go and she slumped forward, the pain easing. Her feet were no longer bound.

Was he going to kill her now?

Once again, his hard hands grabbed her under the armpits and he hauled her to her feet, holding her steady as she stumbled on the blocks of wood that had taken the place of her feet. She used the moment to look around and get her bearings.

The wind ruffled her short hair and chilled her cheeks, ears, and forehead. She began to shiver uncontrollably. She was still only wearing the sweater. Her coat and gloves were probably still at Clarabelle's.

"Come on, sweetheart," said Calum, pushing her forward. She stumbled and fell on her knees. Unable to break her fall, she pitched forward and barely twisted in time to avoid breaking her nose on the pavement, landing instead on the point of her shoulder. Shards of agony stabbed through the shoulder and she squeezed her eyes shut against the pain. But Calum grabbed her upper arm and pulled her unceremoniously to her feet.

She struggled against his hold, but he shook her until her head threatened to fall off and nausea swamped her. When he finally stopped, she hung loosely against him, only his hands keeping her upright.

"There's a good girl," he whispered in her ear. One hand released her and she swayed precariously. She felt him reach away from her, then there was a loud thunk as the trunk was closed.

When he started pulling her through the woods, she finally understood that the pavement had not been a road—it was the path along the river.

Where the hell was he taking her?

He pushed her up the slope, away from the river and into the trees, making no effort to protect her from branches that threatened to gouge her eyes out. His hand tightened on her arm whenever she stumbled on a rock or an exposed root. It would leave a bruise, if she lived.

Nothing else moved in the woods, as if all the small creatures hid beneath rocks or roots before the wrath of Calum. She felt totally helpless, unable even to catch herself if she fell.

She couldn't understand why she was still alive. Surely he didn't plan to take her back to Vancouver? No. Even he wasn't crazy enough to try that. He had come for her, not because he wanted her back, but because she had defied him.

And Calum couldn't stand that.

Suddenly he pulled her to a stop and she looked up from watching the ground. There, barely hidden by a screen of poplars and fir trees, was her house.

He had taken her back home! Hope sprang up in her heart, lending her strength. Her watchers knew that Calum had her. Of course they did. Sure, the false fire alarm might have thrown them off, but they would have quickly realized that she had disappeared and reason that Calum had her. They'd be coming after her. After Calum.

But... would Jake Slater have left someone watching the house if he believed Calum had taken her? Or would he focus his efforts on the roads out of town?

Calum had taken her through the trees. They had passed right by the spot where officer Montrose had been hidden, keeping an eye on the back of the house. There'd been plenty of opportunity to stop Calum. And nobody had.

Because nobody was out there.

Tears pricked her eyes and her nose threatened to clog up. She concentrated on controlling her emotions because she knew beyond a doubt that Calum would watch her suffocate rather than remove the gag.

The house loomed against the night sky, the chimney jutting from the roofline, the dormered windows dark.

She glanced to either side but only the roof to Beatrice's

house was visible from this angle. Ash could only see the house if she was on her back deck.

Why had he brought her here? How was he planning to get inside? She tried to remember if the house key was on her or if she had slipped it inside the backpack, which was God knew where by now.

After a minute of standing quietly and watching, he pulled her out of the trees and onto her back lawn, their steps releasing the ghost of freshly mown grass. She twisted in his grip as they approached the deck, trying to see if there were any lights on in Bea's house. Despair closed in as he pulled her up the steps. It was late. Everyone was asleep.

There'd be no help from her neighbors.

Calum kept a hand on her upper arm and tried the handle of the French door. It was locked, of course. He turned back to her and patted both her front pockets, clearly looking for keys. Then he peered through the glass and finally noticed the chair wedged under the handle.

"Scared of the big bad wolf, sweetie pie?" he whispered next to her ear. His breath smelled of coffee. His lips would taste of it, she knew.

Ash kept her gaze fixed on the glass. Maybe Bea would wake up.

And maybe lightning would strike Calum dead.

Calum pulled her away from the door and forced her to sit on the wooden deck. She automatically tried to cross her legs tailor fashion to keep her balance but stopped when her hip warned her.

"Be good," he said softly, then turned and ran down the steps to the lawn, moving out of her sight.

She immediately struggled to her knees, then to her feet, swaying slightly as dizziness threatened her balance. Where was he? Had he left her?

She edged closer to the railing and saw his dark figure prowling the edge of the lawn by the woods. She had no idea what he was doing, but this was her opportunity. Crouching and moving as silently as she could, she headed for the stairs and went down sideways, one step at a time, keeping an eye on Calum. As soon as she was on the grass, she immediately headed for Bea's house. She would kick at the older woman's door until Bea opened the door or called the police.

Her nostrils flared in an effort to get more oxygen into her starving lungs. As she turned the corner of her house, the wind caught her, penetrating her sweater to the flesh beneath and she shivered violently. A few more feet and she would climb down to Bea's driveway.

Something hard and heavy slammed into her. Unable to break her fall, she crashed to the ground and slammed her head against the pavement.

Her ears rang and a sharp pain announced a broken rib. Through the agony in her chest, she was dimly aware of being dragged by the armpits, her running shoes pulling off, then her socks, and her bare heels smearing the driveway with her blood.

Then, mercifully, she blacked out.

Bea Stratford opened a sleep-gummed eye and focused on the clock on her bedside table. Three oh eight. In the friggin' morning. She groaned and pushed the blankets off to sit up. Every night it was the same story. No matter how tired she was, she woke up in the middle of the night. Usually she got up and had a pee. Not because she particularly had to go, but since she was already awake, she went.

If she woke up before three, she stood a good chance of falling back to sleep for a few hours. After three, it was a crap shoot.

Apparently, there was no end to the indignities of aging.

She stood up and shuffled bleary-eyed to the bathroom. After she finished, she stood at the sink for a moment, letting the water run so it would warm up. If she washed her hands in cold water, she might as well go downstairs and make herself some coffee because there'd be no going back to sleep. Same thing if she turned the lights on. Besides, she knew where everything was.

Finally, the water warmed up and she washed her hands. As she dried them on the small towel, she wandered over to the window to check out the sky. The stars twinkled down at her out of a cloudless sky. No moon. She shivered a little. It was probably very cold out there.

As she turned away, something caught her eye and she turned back. Her bathroom window faced Ash Gantry's driveway and side door. Because Ash's house was on a knoll, Bea was always looking up at it, except from this window. From this window, she was slightly above the driveway and main floor of Ash's house.

She studied the house for a moment, wondering what had caught her eye. Ash's car wasn't in the driveway, which was unusual. While Ash was a young woman and it was Saturday night—technically Sunday morning—Ash was always home by nine.

Bea could understand why. She frowned as her gaze roved up and down the driveway. The towel was clutched to her chest and she finally shook her head. She was being ridiculous. She should go back to bed and try to get some more sleep.

Then her gaze fell on a dark line on the driveway below her. It could be just a shadow, of course. Or maybe an oil stain from Ash's old Volvo. But as she peered, she realized there were actually two lines, side by side, one fainter than the other. She hadn't noticed them before. And then she saw the shoes off to the side of the driveway, as if they'd been tossed there.

A faint light glimmered suddenly through the window of Ash's side door, but before Bea could turn to look at it full on, it disappeared. Then it flickered and disappeared again.

Almost as if someone was using a flashlight inside the house.

◊◊◊

Ash came to her senses lying on the dining room floor, propped against the wall. Through the roaring in her ears and her labored breathing, she could hear Calum in the laundry room. She kept her eyes closed as his footsteps grew nearer, then stopped in the kitchen. She opened her eye a slit and saw him shining a flashlight around the kitchen. In the spillover, she caught sight of his face and tee-shirt, and would have gasped if she wasn't still gagged.

He looked like something out of a horror movie.

She quickly closed her eyes as he turned back toward the dining room. The blood—it must have come from the cut to his scalp when she threw the glass jar at him in the hairdressing salon. No wonder he didn't dare risk driving out of town with her in the trunk. One look at him in this condition, and people would call the police.

That's why he had come to her house... to clean up. Maybe find a change of clothes. Good luck with that. The only clothes here were hers and they would never fit him.

He had come unerringly to the house. His private detective had told him where to find her, clearly.

Was that the point of the fire alarm? To shake her watchers? No one would think to watch her house if she had gone missing from the mall.

His footsteps came close to her and stopped and she forced herself to breathe steadily. After a moment, he moved on into the hallway. She heard him in the living room, then in the study. Finally, she heard him going up the stairs.

He wasn't worried about anyone else being in the house. From where she lay, she could see the broken glass in the French door by the dining room table, and the chair that had been shoved away from the door. He wouldn't have made all that noise if he'd believed someone else was here.

Better move, she warned herself. He won't be up there forever.

She used her legs and the wall to force herself into a sitting position, then took precious seconds to fight against wave after wave of pain that threatened to drag her down again. The rib was definitely cracked, but it wasn't snapped. She could work through the pain.

The concussion was the real problem. She felt as if her brain was pressing against the inside of her skull.

Stop feeling sorry for yourself and move!

Obeying her survival instinct, she began to work her way to her knees and then her feet. She couldn't feel her hands anymore, but she still had her feet. If she had to, she would kick out the window in the side door.

Her feet left damp imprints on the floor. She didn't need to look down to know those imprints were made in blood. Deep inside, the rage she had banked for years began to break through her careful barriers.

The bastard. If she could just get her hands free, she would find a way to kill him.

She heard a board squeak above her head. He was in her bedroom.

As she passed the kitchen counter, she suddenly remembered her cell phone. It was still plugged in, half hidden behind the bananas. Calum hadn't seen it. She stared at it for precious seconds, trying to figure out how she could contort herself to drag it off the counter and punch in 911, with her hands tied behind her back. The gag caught her sob of frustration and she turned away from the counter. It wouldn't work.

She looked around the kitchen, her gaze stopping on the butcher block. But even if she could reach it, she couldn't hold a knife, let alone wield one. She thought about the recycling in her laundry room and the jagged edges of the cans' lids. Same problem. She couldn't feel her hands, let alone know where to start sawing.

Her only chance was the side door in the laundry room. The back of her heels felt cold and raw as they seeped blood onto the floor. She would not be able to hide from him.

Whatever she did, she had to do it soon, before he came back downstairs.

She entered the laundry room and saw the side of Bea's house through the window in the door. So close.

She had never felt so alone. Even Odette had abandoned her.

She crossed over to the door, turned her back to it and tried to feel for the handle with her bound hands. Overhead, Calum's measured steps moved back down the hallway toward the staircase. She had seconds left.

She bent over to give her hands better access but her deadened hands were like blocks of wood. Was this what it had been like for Odette? Had she struggled to save herself, all for nothing?

Even as she thought it, her gaze landed on the faint outline of the trap door. Her frantic fumbling slowed, then stopped and she straightened. If she could somehow manage to open the trap door...

The handle was a metal ring. Big enough for her hand to grasp and lift, but hers were trapped behind her back. Useless.

But her feet were free. She sidled by the washing machine, aiming for a good angle, then stepped onto the door. She slid the toes of her right foot under the ring, then lifted it free of its casing. Snugging her foot more securely under the ring, she sidled her left foot off the trap door and raised her right leg. The door shifted an inch then whumped back down. Ash paused, listening, but Calum was still upstairs.

She tried again, but it was difficult to find leverage when her legs were spread awkwardly. Just as she heard Calum start down the stairs, she found a spurt of strength and pulled up. The two-by-four frame of the door cleared the floor just enough to allow her to shimmy her free foot under.

Her breath coming fast, she hurriedly freed her right foot from the ring and slipped it under the trap door alongside the other foot.

The weight of the damned door was crushing her feet, but Calum was coming down the hallway toward the kitchen.

OhGodohGodohGod...

With an energy born of fear, she jerked the trap door up with one foot, then leaned in with her other leg so that the door rested on her knee. Then she pushed the door up, balanced precariously on the edge of the dark opening, walking it up until she could lean her body against the side of the trap door and with one leg on either side, gently rest it against the washing machine.

"Oh, Lizzie..." Calum sing-songed tauntingly from the dining room as a splash of light spilled from the dining room into the kitchen. She saw the splotches of blood her feet had left on the linoleum tiles and panic spurred her to the door. Without giving herself a chance to think, she raised a foot and kicked at the window.

But she had spent all her strength on raising the trap door and all she accomplished now was to jar her bad hip and leave a smear of blood on the double-paned window before losing her balance and falling to the floor. As she fought against the panic, she suddenly realized that breaking the window wouldn't help. It wasn't as if she could crawl out of it. She had to get that door open.

The flashlight beam played over her and Calum laughed softly.

"Look at you," he said contemptuously. "What were you thinking, running from me? You know better."

She looked at him, at the man she had fallen in love with, the man who had given her a baby only to take it away, the man who had turned her life into a nightmare.

She slowly rose to her feet, breathing through the pain in her chest, the exhaustion.

In the distance, faintly, she thought she heard a siren, but that could have been wishful thinking.

"What's this?" asked Calum, finally noticing the hole in the floor. Then his face contorted with rage. "You stupid little bit—"

He stopped suddenly and his hands went up to his face in alarm.

Ash blinked at the ghostly hands that covered Calum's eyes in an otherworldly game of peekaboo.

"What the hell?" cried Calum, forgetting to be quiet. He whirled, and as he did, Ash caught sight of Odette standing before Calum. In the beam of his flashlight, she could clearly see the kitchen through Odette's ghostly form.

Without giving herself a chance to think, Ash took one running step, then two and three, and propelled herself at her husband. At the last minute, ignoring her screeching rib, her protesting hip, her throbbing head, she launched herself into the air and with her weight behind it, kicked Calum in the chest. She had been aiming for his solar plexus, fully intending to kill him, but caught him mid-turn and mid-crouch.

Still, she had the satisfaction of seeing him reel back, lose his balance, and fall to the kitchen floor. She barely managed to keep to her own feet. Without waiting to see what he would do, she ran back to the laundry room, leaping over the gaping maw of the cellar only to stop in front of the door. The door opened inward, not outward. Crashing into it would do no good.

Refusing to look over her shoulder, she rubbed her face against the trim next to the door. The cloth holding the gag in place slid just enough to free her top teeth. Without hesitating, she crouched and used her teeth to turn the bolt locking her door.

Only then did she turn around.

Calum was on his feet again, but his attention was on Odette, though it was clear by the wild flailing of his flashlight that he couldn't see her. He could only feel her pokes and jabs.

"Who's there?" he cried, a note of fear in his voice.

How do you like being at the receiving end, Calum?

Her fumbling hands finally found the handle, which, thank God, was straight, rather than a knob. She pushed down and the door swung open. Relief flooded through her, threatening to rob her of whatever strength she had left. She pulled it open all the way, letting the cold air revive her as she stepped backward onto the small wooden porch.

Now what? Run? Only to have him catch up to her?

No. It was time to finish it.

"Jesus!" said Calum, still in the kitchen but stumbling back, trying to get some distance from Odette. But she kept herding him inexorably toward the laundry room.

Ash turned and used her injured shoulder to press against the doorbell. The sound pealed through the small room, startling Calum into turning toward her. His body tensed as he realized that she was escaping.

He reached for her, even though he was too far, and the beam of his flashlight revealed a face contorted with hate, marred with blood, almost feral. Then Odette wrapped her arms around him and he freaked, trying to push her away only to have his hands go right through her.

In his panic, he stumbled into the laundry room, turning this way and that, brushing at himself. Mad to get out of the house and away from whatever was attacking him.

Then he took one step too many and fell through the cellar opening. His back slammed against the edge and he screamed in pain before sliding through, his hands scrabbling futilely at the opening.

Ash stumbled to the opening to look down. She couldn't see a thing, nor could she hear him. Wedging a knee between the washing machine and the trap door, she pushed the door over until it slammed shut.

EPILOGUE

On a bright Saturday in late September, Jake Slater pulled up to the house on the knoll to find Ash Gantry and Maddie Bowen fiddling with something by the front door. He turned to his passenger.

"Hang on a minute. I'll be right back."

She nodded silently and he slipped out of the car, leaving the engine running. It might be clear and sunny, but it was also cold.

He strode up the walk, dressed in jeans and a heavy windbreaker over his sweater. On the porch, the two women turned to watch him approach.

He found himself smiling at them.

Maddie had displayed a stubbornness and a strength of character he hadn't suspected in his old friend until this whole affair started. She had taken on the provincial justice system, with the help of Ash's Vancouver lawyer, to make sure Ash ended up buying Frank Boudreaux's house. Liesel Wirth had given up any interest in the house and it finally went to auction six weeks ago. Unsurprisingly, there was very little interest in a house where a woman was murdered and two men were arrested. Not to mention the rumor that it was haunted.

Ash got it for a song.

Ash had decided to keep her hair short and it suited her, although right now, in the wind, it looked a little porcupine-y. She had recovered well from last year's ordeal. Physically, no one would never know what had happened to her, unless they saw her scars.

At least Calum Stevenson would never hurt anyone again.

Jake glanced up at the upstairs windows and wasn't surprised to see a pale figure looking down at him. He smiled slightly.

Maddie waited patiently for Jake to say something. He was always this way, whenever he came to the house. A little skittish. A little thoughtful.

A little weird.

"What are you two up to?" he asked as he reached the steps.

Maddie and Ash separated and when he saw the discreet brass plaque, tears came to his eyes.

"ODETTE'S HOUSE"

He nodded, unable to speak for the moment.

Ash grinned at him. "You're nothing but an old softie, Jake Slater," she said. The plaque was the finishing touch on the get-together she had planned for later. A potluck, with Charlotte and Max, Maddie and her family, Bea, Barney, Paul and his family, Jake and his, and a few of the neighbors who had befriended her over the past year.

She wanted to thank them all for their support and friendship, for helping her through the worst time in her life.

And while she couldn't formally invite Odette, Ash knew she would be there.

She had seen Calum during the court case, and had been shocked at the change in him. He was no longer the vibrant, handsome man in the prime of his life—but then, ending up as a paraplegic had knocked the vibrancy out of him. And the fact that he would spend the next few decades in jail hadn't helped.

It surprised her that she felt sorry for him.

Between the two court cases—Frank Boudreaux's and Calum's—and her legal efforts to buy Odette's house, the last year had been too busy for her to start university. But she was registering for the spring semester, now that her life was finally hers again.

"So, it's not that I don't appreciate seeing you," she continued, "but you're a little early."

"Who's that in your car?" asked Maddie, peering down past Jake.

Jake sighed. "She's the reason I'm here," he said softly. "I know this is bad timing, what with the party and all, but I was wondering if she could stay with you for a few days." He glanced over his shoulder at the young woman. From this distance and angle, you couldn't see the black eye. "She needs a safe place to stay until I can get her away permanently."

Ash's eyebrows rose, in spite of herself. She glanced at the car, but whoever was in the passenger seat had turned her face away.

"Bad relationship?" she asked.

Jake nodded silently.

Ash glanced at the window in the front door and wasn't surprised to see Odette standing there, waiting.

"Sure," she said, turning back to Jake with a smile. "We'll keep her safe for as long as she needs."

Over her shoulder, Odette Boudreaux smiled.

THE END

ABOUT THE AUTHOR

Marcelle Dubé writes mystery and speculative fiction novels and short stories. Her short fiction has appeared in award-winning anthologies and magazines. Her work has been short-listed for the Derringer Award and the Crime Writers of Canada Award of Excellence, which she won in 2021.

To find out more about her, visit:
www.marcellemdube.com

BOOKS BY THE AUTHOR

Mendenhall Mysteries series:
The Shoeless Kid
The Tuxedoed Man
The Weeping Woman
The Untethered Woman
The Forsaken Man
The Wronged Woman

A'lle Chronicles series:
The A'lle Murders
The A'lle Mutation

Standalone books:
A Little Strangeness (collection)
Ghosts of Morocco
Identity Withheld
Jilimar
Kirwan's Son
Obeah
On Her Trail
Shelter